Counterbalance

Kelly Moran

*To Lori —
Best Always,
Kelly Moran
XO*

This is a work of fiction. Names, characters, places, and incidents either are the product of the author's imagination or are used fictitiously, and any resemblance to actual persons living or dead, business establishments, events, or locales, is entirely coincidental.

© COPYRIGHT 2017 by Kelly Moran
All rights reserved. No part of this book may be used or reproduced in any manner whatsoever without written permission of the author except in the case of brief quotations embodied in critical articles or reviews.

Content Warning: Not intended for persons under the age of 18.

ISBN-13: 978-1541038677
ISBN-10: 1541038673
Cover Art by: Kelly Moran
Photo Credit: Adobe Photo
Createspace Print Edition

Published in the United States of America

Praise for Kelly Moran's Books:

"Breathes life into an appealing story."
Publishers Weekly

"Readers will fall in love."
Romantic Times

"Great escape reading."
Library Journal

"Touching & gratifying."
Kirkus Reviews

"Sexy, heart-tugging fun."
USA Today HEA

"Emotional & totally engaging."
Carla Neggers

"A gem of a writer."
Sharon Sala

"I read in one sitting."
Carly Phillips

"Compelling characters."
Roxanne St. Claire

"A sexy, emotional romance."
Kim Karr

Chapter One

"Your last appointment is here, Mr. Gaines."

Xavier glanced from his computer monitor to where his secretary's tinny voice emitted from his desk phone and hit speaker. "Wait five minutes and send her in. Thank you."

"Yes, sir."

Five minutes, and he'd finally have the meeting he'd been waiting weeks for since securing. Longer, if he accounted the past year when he'd last seen her at a charity function. He'd had to hold out for a break in her schedule to even get her to come in, and it had taken a lot of coaxing from his staff to accomplish that much.

Anxious, he shoved from his desk and stood to face the wall of windows in his top floor high rise office in San Francisco's Financial District. Gaines Industries was among many Fortune 500 companies that occupied the clean, angular skyscrapers in the triangular area east of Kearny Street. Dusk was descending, turning the Bay in the distance pink and purple through a haze of fog. Unlike many metropolises where the fiscal wards went quiet after hours, his city's historic financial borough stayed alive with restaurants, bars, cafes, and bakeries. It's what he loved most about living here. Business met pleasure. It had...personality.

The view didn't help to settle his nerves. Tension knotted his gut and, since he was alone, he rubbed the ache. Most would never know that under his thousand dollar suits, he was just a computer geek, struggling to fit in the world. His employees called him "deep freeze" and the media pegged him as a "calculating enigma." Though his company was secure and made millions, it was not the well-oiled machine he'd envisioned and his stock had gone down five percent last quarter. The end of his brief relationship with up-and-coming model, Pamela Squire, hadn't helped his image, either. Nor did the things she'd said about him. Very publicly. That's what he got for marginally trusting someone—phrases like *a cold-hearted suit* and *emotionally stinted*.

Business he could do. Being social, not so much. Unfortunately, public relations went hand-in-hand with industry.

Which was exactly why he needed Peyton Smoke. It was paramount he get her onboard and in a position to help him, especially with the new government contracts in the works for next month. He couldn't risk his numbers dropping any more, plus his ulcers had ulcers just thinking about the press the deal would generate.

"Miss Smoke to see you, Mr. Gaines."

He turned from the windows to face his secretary, but skimmed right past Fern to...*her*.

Peyton Smoke had only grown lovelier over time. Aside from a blip of a glance at a benefit last year, he hadn't seen her since high school. Long, champagne blonde hair fell past her shoulders, and she wore a powder blue suit over her slender frame that screamed sexy siren and take no prisoners in one breath. If memory served, and it did, she had cerulean blue eyes behind the black-framed glasses perched on her nose. And her skin was still like that of warm buttermilk with just a hint of peach in her cheeks. She offered a polite smile from her red-as-sin lips, and he snapped his gaze to Fern when his pulse hammered in response.

In her fifties, his secretary's wild brown curls were pinned in messy chaos at the back of her head. Her plain gray pants and blouse ensemble had slipped past his notice all day. The fact he paid attention now, if only to compare her to Peyton's polish, irritated him.

He cleared his throat. "That'll be all, Fern, thank you. Tell the staff they may call it a day."

"Yes, sir." Her gaze ducked to the floor as she stepped out and closed the door.

Most of his employees had a difficult time looking him in the eye. He hardly cared, but it didn't escape Peyton's notice, judging by the lift in her brows when she faced him again.

"Miss Smoke, thank you for coming. Have a seat." He moved to his chair and clasped his hands on his desk in an effort not to fidget. Something he'd worked massively hard at the past few years.

She took a glance around his office before sitting primly in a chair across from him.

He wondered what her first impression was and quickly took in the space trying to look at it from her point of view. He'd hired a decorator a couple years ago, but had given them no direction. Thus, his furniture on the far wall in the sitting area was black leather, the tables wrought iron and glass topped, the carpet a cool gray, and his desk a black walnut. His wall prints were abstract paint splotches of nondescript origin. It probably seemed as frigid and impersonal as the media portrayed him to be.

"It's great to see you again. You've changed a lot." She tapped her temple. "You lost your glasses and I got a pair. You're all grown up now."

Well, a growth spurt in college, followed by hours in the gym and contact lenses, had a way of altering a guy from the scrawny kid who'd been bullied to someone who could hold his own. It hadn't happened overnight but, to her, the differences wouldn't be subtle.

He nodded and focused on her necklace. A tiny key charm hung on a thin gold chain just below the dip of her collarbone. "I wasn't sure you'd remember me." The Xavier Gaines at sixteen hadn't exactly been a boy people noticed unless using him as an outlet to feel more superior.

"Of course, I remember. You got me through calculus, geometry, and algebra unscathed." Her tone was inviting and smooth as the silk white blouse under her jacket. Back then, she had a way of getting people to do whatever she wanted just by wielding her voice.

And, of course, she'd remember math classes. Him, however? He recalled how she'd been the only one to stand up for him or offer him a seat in the cafeteria. Her gumption should've made her a pariah. Instead, she'd been adored. People had a hard time not getting sucked into her orbit.

He clasped his fingers tighter to remind himself not to squirm under her direct gaze. "I'm pretty sure you would've done all right without my help."

The grin she offered stole the air from his lungs. "You don't give yourself enough credit, Mr. IQ off the charts. You sold a software app you developed in a dorm room for fifty million dollars, you're the youngest man to own a Fortune 500 at age twenty-eight, and I do believe you're listed as one of the most eligible bachelors on the west coast. I think it was *People Magazine*, correct? Said your incredible good looks and brains made up for lack of charm, but the right woman would 'defrost' you one day."

He bit his tongue in annoyance. "Someone did her research."

She tilted her head. "I read the alumni news." Her lips pursed. "And the *Wall Street Journal, New York Times*, yada." Blink, blink. "So, did you bring me here to catch up or is this a business meeting?"

He got the strangest urge to smile, which was odd because he was usually incredibly uncomfortable around people and he couldn't remember the last time he'd done it. "A little of both, actually." He needed her to say yes to his proposal, and he was getting the impression he wouldn't sway someone like her by having a desk between them. "Do you have plans for dinner?"

She pressed a hand to her breasts—which he tried and failed not to notice had developed since high school—and mock gasped. "Are you asking little ole me out, Mr. Gaines?"

One of the reasons he needed her so badly was this very thing—her ability to deem everyone around her more important. In his world, that could make or break a deal. "Call me Xavier, please, and yes. Why don't we discuss the topic over a meal?"

She studied him a careful beat. "That depends. Are we going somewhere fancy where I can't pronounce the menu or are we talking real food?"

Conceding, he allowed a ghost of a smile to faint his lips. The background check specified she spoke fluent German and French, and she could hold a conversation in Italian if the need arose. Language had never been her short side. In high school, she'd had a weakness for English, especially poetry. He'd caught her reading in the library more often than not.

He rose. "We can go wherever you like, Miss Smoke."

"If I'm using your first name, Xavier, you can do me the courtesy of calling me Peyton." Standing as well, she clutched her purse, which matched her strappy black heels and made his ankles ache just looking at them. How women moved in those torture devices was beyond him. "Lead the way."

Her assessing gaze took in the empty lobby as they made their way to the elevators, and he had a sinking suspicion she wasn't impressed by the efficient décor there, either.

Once the elevator doors enclosed them, he caught a trace of her perfume in the close confines. Light and airy, it held hints of berries, pear, and musk, and exuded subtle sensuality, not unlike her. Something floral about the fragrance lay quietly underneath, and curiosity got the better of his tongue.

"I like your perfume." Damn. Speaking before thinking was not usually his dynamic. Unnecessary conversation at all, really. He jabbed the lobby button and shoved his hands in his pockets.

"Thank you. It's *Mon Paris* by Yves Saint Laurent. It's made from an exotic white flower called datura. I found that fascinating."

Amused, he stared at the numbers overhead. "You picked a fragrance based on its ingredients?"

"Well, that and it smelled great." From his side, she glanced at him out of the corner of her eye. "And the bottle is pretty."

A surprise laugh huffed from his chest. He'd do well to stay alert in her presence.

"Ah, so he's not a glacier, after all." Her teasing tone matched the light in her eyes.

He grunted. "I see you read the Forbes article. I believe the exact words were, *as arctic as a glacier in Greenland.*"

"Don't feel bad. They also said you were *cryptically brilliant.*"

"You have a good memory." That article had been from two years ago when he'd first launched Gaines Industries after the sale of his software app.

"Photographic, actually." She shrugged. "When something interests me, I pay attention."

Unsure whether to be flattered she found the topic of him interesting or if he should be disturbed, he placed a hand low on her back to guide her from the elevator.

His bodyguard rose from his seat in the lower lobby and buttoned his black suit coat. "All set, Mr. Gaines?"

"Yes. Joseph Limerick, meet Peyton Smoke." Xavier turned to her. "Joseph is my personal security detail and ex-military. You'll be safe around him."

Xavier had hired Joseph one day after opening Gaines Industries' doors, and hadn't regretted the decision. The physically fit former army ranger was thirty-three years old, observant as hell, and easy to be around. He also took orders well and knew how to blend into the background when necessary. According to Xavier's ex, Pamela, the man wasn't bad to look at, either. His shaved bald head seemed to work for his rangy face and his brown eyes were piercing. He filled a suit better than Xavier.

Eyebrows pinged to her hairline, Peyton took in his bodyguard in one fell swoop. "Do I need to be concerned for my safety in your presence, Xavier?"

"Not with Joseph around. Though I've had a few threats, he's more of a precaution."

She rolled her eyes and smiled as if amused.

Right. "You were joking." He fisted his hands in his pockets.

"I was, yes." She held out her hand to his guard. "A pleasure to meet you. Thank you for your service."

Joseph shook her hand and offered a slight bow. "The pleasure is mine. Where are you two headed?"

"To dinner." Xavier cleared his throat. "Do you have a car with you, Peyton?"

"No, I took a cab."

He nodded. "We'll take mine, then. I can drop you off at home afterward."

They walked to Xavier's awaiting town car at the curb, where his driver held the rear door open for them. The temperature was comfortably cool and humid for August as a salty wind came in off the Bay. Xavier gestured for her to enter first, but she faced the driver instead, the door between them.

She set a hand on his arm. "What's your name?"

The middle-aged man's dark cocoa skin turned ashen as he glanced down. Xavier's help wasn't used to his guests speaking directly to them. "Archie Shift, miss."

"Very nice to meet you." She patted his hand and slid in the seat.

Archie's grin was fleeting, but it was clear, after point three seconds, Xavier's driver was under her spell. A quick glance at Joseph's smirk said his bodyguard was, too.

Shaking his head, Xavier climbed in after her.

They wound up at a pizza joint, of all places, per her suggestion, and a quick survey of the brick walls and vinyl booths proved he was out of his element. The delicious scent of garlic and red sauce reminded him he'd skipped lunch. "I'm a little overdressed for this venue."

While inside the doorway, her gaze skimmed over him. Before he knew what she was up to, she'd stripped his coat, unknotted his tie, and had rolled the sleeves of his shirt to his elbows.

She nodded, handing him back the jacket. "There."

They claimed a booth and he let her order, then he glanced at her necklace once again. Having a focal point helped settle him, and he wondered where she'd gotten the charm. Perhaps from her deceased fiancé. He'd found out through the grapevine about Mark's suicide last year. Xavier had never met the man, but Mark had served with Peyton's brother, Brian, in Iraq. Mark's death had come just a few months after Brian was killed while serving. She'd been raised by her brother after their parents had passed away in a car accident their junior year, leaving her no family.

No one, especially a person as light and friendly as her, should be surrounded by so much darkness. And someone would never know it by looking at her.

His mouth got away from him again as his gaze met hers. Damn, but her eyes were still a blow to the solar plexus. "I was sorry to hear about Brian and Mark."

Her gaze jerked to the table. She nodded slowly. "Thank you. Work has helped keep me busy." She fingered the charm and smiled. "How are your parents?"

"Very well, thanks." Xavier had a good relationship with them, but didn't get to see them often. His mother may have been a trophy wife to a career-driven corporate attorney, but his father loved her to no end. "Dad's retiring next year."

"Lucky guy." She smiled. "Well," she said through a delicate sigh. "What business would you like to discuss?"

Yeah, that. Tension tightened the muscles in his neck. "I'd like to hire you."

Up went the brows again. "I have a job."

"I know." She'd been on Mayor Harrison's campaign since his election three years prior. "Are the Harrison rumors of his senate bid true?"

Her award-winning grin turned sly. "I can neither confirm nor deny."

Unable to help it, he smiled. "Will you stay with him if he goes through with it?"

"The position has been offered to me. Why? What's your counter?" She set her chin in her hand as if they were discussing nothing more serious than fluffy kittens. That was her gift. Hook, line, and sinker—all while making a person want to be caught.

Deciding to give her the background first, he took a sip of water in an effort to recall his pitch. "I'm not sure how much you've followed regarding Gaines Industries, but we've been mostly focused on apps, devices, and software tech in the private sector. We've been quietly venturing into another aspect, something for the military. Everything from tracking returning vets for better medical follow-up care to more weapons accuracy for less injury, etcetera. I have the opportunity to secure government contracts for the next ten years if negotiations go well."

"Wow." She straightened. "That would put you in a whole new ballpark."

"Agreed." He frowned. "But there's some internal issues on my end. Concerns have been raised about my motives. You've read how the media portrays me, and with something as spotlight-driven as government contracts, they're hesitant to get in bed with someone who doesn't have emotions, a personality, or can comfortably make public appearances. Gaines Industries would be the face of this particular project, all while we maintain our current fields." He paused. "And I'm...rigid."

Her lips pursed, and she strummed her fingers on the table in thought. "You need a better PR person."

"Which is where you come in. I have a firm on retainer who does press releases and such, but not on this kind of scale."

The waiter came by with their order and left. Peyton dished out a slice for each of them, and they ate in silence for a while. Her brain seemed to be clicking while she chewed, so he sat idle.

After she finished a slice and a half, she nudged her plate aside. "I have some ideas, but what specifically are you looking for?"

Relieved that wasn't an outright no, he set his napkin on the table. "What I understand about PR could fill a thimble. From a company standpoint, I need someone on the inside. Keep the staff happy, morale up, business potentials interested, that kind of thing. Outside, I have to find a way to seem...less cold, I guess. I'd leave the how up to you. Other than that, whatever arises regarding media, you'd be responsible for handling. Events, releases, appearances."

She adjusted her glasses and stared over his shoulder as if in thought.

Worry ate away at his gut. "I know it's a big undertaking and I'd require a lot of work—"

"It's not that." She waved her delicate hand, dismissing his comment. "What you're asking is no more or less than what I'm already doing for Harrison, just on a different scale."

He nodded. "What concerns you, then?"

Her mouth opened and closed twice before she spoke. "Admittedly, politics was not where I wanted to end up when I got my marketing degree. However, from the start, Harrison and I clicked. His wife, too."

And, hell. That was the problem. Xavier didn't "click" with anyone. If he couldn't get someone like Peyton comfortable around him, he was screwed. The very thought of hiring for the position elsewhere made him break out in a cold sweat. Desperately, he tried to think of a solution.

"Why me, if you don't mind me asking?"

He lifted his gaze to hers. Leave it to her to save him by giving him an opening. "You have a spotless record and no secrets. Your ability to make people relax is something target-specific I need. Fact is, you have experience in all the areas on my list." He let out a quiet exhale and clenched his fingers in an attempt to not rub his neck in frustration.

"You could get that from someone else, though, if you interviewed well enough." Quietly, her gaze scanned his face. "I—"

"There's no necessity to make a decision right now. Sleep on it and perhaps we could get together tomorrow. I could show you around the building, discuss specifics." He closed his eyes and unclenched his jaw before meeting her gaze once more. All or nothing. "The truth, Peyton? I trust you, and I can count on one hand the number of people I can say that about. You knew me before I made my millions, and you were nice to me when you didn't have to be. That's the kind of person I want in my corner."

There. Christ, it felt like he'd sliced through an artery.

A slow smile curved her lips as a wrinkle formed between her brows. "I'll see you tomorrow. Your office, four o'clock."

Chapter Two

Desperately needing a caffeine boost, Peyton stopped at a vendor to grab a coffee on her three-block walk to Xavier's office. Thinking about his job offer had kept her awake all night and she was dragging this afternoon.

She breathed in salty, damp air from the Bay and smiled as she passed others strolling by. The Financial District was alive with business people and tourists alike, and she enjoyed the buzz. Restaurants, shops, and skyscrapers blended together in a mishmash of unique. Sunshine filtered through a thin cloud cover, and she got a little more pep in her step. It was a gorgeous day and, despite leaving work early to meet with Xavier, she was free tonight. She had a date with Thor and her couch via Netflix. Maybe she'd make it a threesome by adding Ghirardelli.

Though she'd been shocked by Xavier's offer, it couldn't have come at a better time. With Harrison announcing his senate bid next week, it was now or never to get out. She'd loved working for him and his wife, plus the job security, but politics just wasn't her cup of tea. Gaines Industries' potential government contract was exactly the kind of thing she could get behind. Especially if it aided injured vets.

A flash of Brian's face swam to mind, and her gut clenched. She missed her older brother every single day. His death during his service had left her with no family, but he'd died doing what he'd loved. Mark's memory, however, made her throat close. Her deceased fiancé had served with Brian, but he'd finished two tours and retired. Severe depression, mixed with a mild case of PTSD, had led to his suicide. She'd been struggling with his decision the past year, and it was still difficult to get out of bed some mornings. Guilt clawed at her at the most inopportune and random times.

God, she should've done more, been more aware of his situation. But he'd shut her out, hadn't wanted help, and had slipped inside his mind. Then he'd put a bullet in his head while she'd been at a press conference.

She drew a deep breath and shoved the pain away. She couldn't change the past or bring him back. Thus, Xavier's plans were ideal. A project close to her heart and one she'd love to rally behind.

Xavier Gaines, as a man separate from his company, had warning knells banging her temples. Sure, she'd known him in high school, and a rare glimpse of what lay under his surface had poked out last night, but she just wasn't one-hundred percent positive working for him was a good idea. For her, she had to have a connection with someone. Private PR meant getting inside the client's head, spending oodles of time one-on-one, and all but sharing air with them.

She'd decided last night, after tossing and turning for hours, to get a read on him today and go from there. Feel him out during her tour of the company. After laying her ideas on the table, issuing a plan, she'd watch his reaction and let her gut make the choice. What he'd said last night about trusting her and being nice to him before he'd become rich had stuck with her. The vulnerability in his eyes had nailed her right in the breastbone.

Stopping outside her destination, she tossed her cup in the trash and glanced up at the white fortress. Gaines Industries was in bright blue block letters over the door and, she knew from looking out her office window, also spanned the roof on a grander scale for an aerial view. The building wasn't as huge as some of the others in the vicinity, but twenty floors was no peon.

Popping a mint in her mouth to erase coffee breath, she pulled the handle and stepped inside. She showed her credentials to security and signed a guest badge. As she walked to the bank of elevators, she was reminded how clinical the decor was throughout the public areas. A topic for later. She rode the elevator to the top floor and checked in at the desk.

"Mr. Gaines said you should go right back when you arrive. Do you remember the way?"

Peyton smiled. "I do. Thank you, Fern."

The secretary blinked several times as if surprised Peyton remembered her name. "You're welcome."

She walked down the hall and past a conference room. There was only one other office on this floor, which was across from Xavier's, and it appeared vacant. The low rumble of his voice caught her attention, and she moved to the doorway of his office. He leaned against the desk, facing the wall-to-wall windows, his back to her and phone against his ear.

Since he was occupied, she waited on the threshold and watched him at work. Lord, but did he grow up nice. Gone was the lanky boy she'd known who used to get picked on. Back then, she'd tried to befriend him outside of tutoring, but she couldn't be everywhere at once and suspected he'd been subject to kids' cruelty. If those bullies could see him now, they'd regret their actions.

At six feet, he towered over her five-seven frame, even with her wearing heels, and his shoulders were wide, filling out his suit. Trim waist, large hands, chestnut waves of thick hair that was somewhat longer on top and trimmed neatly on the sides. She could envision the slight ripples of muscle under his pressed white shirt, like a runner's build.

"I'll have accounting send you a report." He paused. "I'm actually working on that now. I have a meeting..." He glanced at his watch and, as if sensing her, turned to look over his shoulder. His gaze locked on hers, and he slowly straightened. "Right now. I'll give you an update by next week. Thank you." He set the phone in the cradle, gaze never leaving hers, and a muscle ticked in his jaw.

In high school, his glasses had masked the potency of his golden brown eyes. Without the barrier? Assessing and aloof in the same beat. She mentally fanned herself. He could be doing quantum physics in his head or undressing her in his mind—she'd never know the difference. He was that hard to read. But to be the focus of all his attention, no matter what he was thinking, was unnervingly sexy. Prickles of awareness crept up her spine.

"Peyton." It wasn't the first time he'd said her name like a rough caress, and it seemed each instance pulled a deeper tremor from her. His gaze traveled quickly over her fitted sea foam green dress to her white heels and back up, too fast to take it as a perusal. He cleared his throat. "Come in, please."

She smiled and walked to stand in front of his desk, forcing her arousal back into a box. With padlocks.

Again, he grabbed the phone and hit a button. "Please put in an order for..." He looked at Peyton. "Do you eat Chinese food?" After she nodded, he spoke into the receiver. "Chinese, an hour from now. When it's delivered, you can leave for the day." He suddenly closed his eyes. "No, I'm not ill. Yes, I'm certain. I'm giving Miss Smoke a tour—" He pinched the bridge of his nose. "By myself, yes. Hold all my calls."

Peyton rolled her lips over her teeth to avoid grinning. She very much doubted his little tick of frustration was something most were privy to see. He got bonus points for not getting snippy with Fern, and he always said *please* or *thank you*. "I take it Xavier Gaines showing potential employees around is out of the ordinary?"

He inhaled in what she figured was an attempt to collect himself and stared at the desk. "Very, but I prefer to do your tour personally. Unless...?"

"I would prefer that, as well." She offered a relaxed smile when he looked at her, a wrinkle between his brows. Not for the first time, she sensed his careful control was a mask for something else. In the barest of flashes, he didn't seem like the cold business mogul the media portrayed. "Shall we?"

They started on the first floor and worked their way up. Technicians, programmers, and engineers had several departments dedicated just to them. Accounting, legal, and human resources utilized a lot of the other floors. Xavier definitely made his employees uncomfortable, judging by the way conversation stopped when they drew near and the utter avoidance of eye contact. Still, he knew most of their names, even though he had to have upwards of four hundred staff, and the accommodations were first rate. He even had a cafeteria and daycare inside the building, plus a media room. His dictations were clear and concise, but there was pride in his voice when he paused to explain aspects of the company.

The top floor was quiet when they returned a couple of hours later, and takeout waited on the coffee table in his office.

He rifled through the bags and removed a couple cartons. "Let me run to the conference room and grab plates. What would you like to drink?"

"Water is fine, thank you."

He nodded and strode out, returning moments later. He passed her a bottle of water and a fork. "They only sent chopsticks."

"I'm okay with those."

Pausing a beat, he gave a barely perceptible shake of his head. "Of course, you are." He gestured to the couch and took a seat next to her. "I, however, am not as skilled as you." Dishing a small amount of everything, he handed her a plate, then loosened his tie, removed his coat, and rolled his sleeves to the elbows before serving himself.

She got caught up in the corded muscles of his forearms and light dusting of hair, then stared at her food. "Thank you for dinner." She'd anticipated a tour and swindling, not an informal sit-down.

"You're very welcome. It's the least I can do for keeping you late. I suspect we have a lot to discuss. Right off the bat, I'll double what you're making now, plus full health benefits, if you join Gaines Industries. Two weeks paid vacation a year. One of the job requirements might involve travel, fully on company expenses, but I want you to be aware." He reached for a fork, but she stopped him by covering his hand.

She'd expected him to lure her with money. Though the salary alone made her heart thump, wealth wasn't everything. First test? Xavier may be a genius, but a man willing to learn new things and adapt to change was someone she could work with.

She set her plate on the table and handed him a set of chopsticks. "Humor me and try these."

He studied her a careful beat and dipped his chin in a nod.

Demonstrating how to wield the utensils, she wrapped her fingers around his. He frowned, but it seemed more out of concentration than irritation. Together, they raised a spear of pork to his mouth and their gazes locked. His full lips parted and an uneven breath escaped. Down toppled a brick in his wall, and she swore attraction looked back at her through the intensity of his eyes. Bourbon and fire, his irises.

After a moment, he glanced at the food and bit into the pork, severing the heated exchange. He had some difficulty with the chopsticks, but he never reached for a fork. Okay, so he passed the first test.

She dragged oxygen into her lungs and focused on her own plate once again, ignoring the pang in her belly. They ate in silence, barring a few pleasant exchanges about the staff packets he let her look through. Wages were competitive and he was good about yearly raises.

She took a healthy drink of water and recapped the bottle while he cleaned up. "I have some questions that might seem unconventional. If I'm to consider your offer, I need to understand you."

His lips curved in that smile which wasn't really a smile, and sat facing her on the couch. "I was serious about hiring you, so lay it on me."

Making a point, she removed her shoes, crossed her legs, and clasped her hands. "I hope you don't have plans. We're going to be here awhile."

He huffed an uncommitted version of a laugh. "I'm all yours."

"Do you date?" When he just stared at her, she elaborated. "Aside from your recent breakup with that model, I don't recall photos of you with a woman splashing the society columns."

His gaze dipped to her necklace. "I don't know if date is the right word. I've had relationships, yes. Nothing serious."

"Is it because you're gay?"

His gaze flew to hers. "I'm not gay."

She shrugged. "It's okay if you are. I just need to know to prepare."

"I'm not."

"Nothing to be ashamed about, especially in this day and age, and in California, no less."

"Peyton." He closed his eyes and sighed. "If I were gay, I'd tell you. I wouldn't be ashamed because I don't see anything wrong with the lifestyle. In fact, I support equal marriage. But," he leaned forward, "I'm. Not. Gay."

Oh, yes. Now she was getting somewhere. He had no idea how much he just inadvertently revealed. Xavier Gaines was open-minded, unbiased, and his armor could be chinked.

She grinned. "Didn't think so. Just checking."

Eyes narrowed, he ran his tongue over his teeth, amusement in his direct gaze. "The two areas of my life where I excel are the boardroom and the bedroom."

Rawr. Blow her over with a feather, but he had an alpha side next to his brains. She'd be turned on if he weren't a potential boss. Never mind. She was turned on, anyway. "Noted."

Resting his elbow on the back of the couch, he rubbed his jaw. "I have difficulty straddling the personal and professional line. Trust is an issue, too. I tend to keep my sexual encounters brief and quiet."

She could only imagine. He had more money than she'd ever see in a lifetime, and women were bound to use whatever tactics they had in their arsenal to land him. His good looks were just a bonus. However, humanizing him in the media would be part of her job, so they'd have to figure something out.

Moving on... "Do you have any hobbies?"

His gaze drifted. "Not really. I like computer games, if only for the programming aspect. I get ideas from them."

"Play any sports? Or watch them?"

"Uh, no." Again, he glanced at her necklace and she wondered why. "I work out and run, but I'm not very athletic. On occasion, I'll watch baseball."

Running, huh? "What's your average distance?"

Confusion hit his eyes as if he had no clue what she was after. "I just do it for exercise. I run about five miles twice a week."

Nice. Which meant she could get him involved in charity marathons to boost his image. Between this conversation and witnessing him with his employees, not to mention glancing at his staff packets, she was leaning heavily toward an answer. Yet, she needed to know if he could bend.

"I'm going to be blunt." At his nod of encouragement, she skimmed through the list in her head. "First, you have a number of employee incentives and turnover is pretty low. However, there are a couple things I'd suggest to boost morale, such as a Christmas office party and a company-wide family picnic. Two events split through the year to show appreciation."

His brows lifted as if he'd not thought of such a thing. "I can do that."

Hm. Obviously, he was willing to put money into his staff, understanding happy workers meant productivity. Points for him. "Second, this is a corporation, but there's no trace of individuality in the building. The steady stream of visitors and business coming through the doors are met with nothing. I think adding subtle touches would make a world of difference—framing newspaper articles about Gaines Industries for the lobby, a splash of color here and there, prints of the city, photos of those you help. That kind of thing."

"Consider it done." No pause. No hesitation. Just swift agreement.

She pursed her lips. "That means the conference room and your office, as well." She glanced around. "Maybe a picture of you and your family on a shelf. A couple plants. Definitely a rug with some color."

A grin teased his mouth. "Have at it."

Interesting. "I recommend getting involved in one charity and backing it. Seeing as the government contract is in the works and taking into account your current programming, something with the military. Injured vets or families of fallen soldiers. You also need a stronger social media presence. Facebook and Twitter, probably."

"You've put a lot of thought into this, haven't you?" He seemed equally impressed and amused. Slowly, he was unwinding and exposing the guy behind the mask. And she liked him. "Done and done. Next?"

More than a little surprised, she considered how to approach the following subject. It might cross a line for him. "About your image. You're required to attend a lot of benefits. Previous restraint in bringing a date to avoid association is wise, but it pegs you as a loner. Seeing as we'd have a working partnership and my role is in public relations, we should attend functions together. It'll put someone at your side without throwing speculation. If you begin dating someone seriously, we can reevaluate."

He glanced away, mouth firm in thought. "It never crossed my mind. That's a good idea. I'm up for it."

Floored, she blinked. Flat out, she hadn't expected him to be this agreeable. "I'd schedule public spotlights. Interviews, community events, yada."

For that, he paused. His respirations increased. Finally, he cleared his throat. "I'm no good at that sort of thing. If you're willing to coach me, I'll be amendable."

Wow. She wasn't seeing a downside. Her Spidey sense wasn't tingling in warning anymore, either. "I'm going to be honest with you. If you hire me, I will be your shadow, Xavier. This will be all but a marriage without the benefits."

He offered her a droll look. "If that's the case, let's hop a plane to Vegas and we can have benefits, too."

Well, jeez. He had a sense of humor. And she should absolutely not find that sexy. "Ha. Funny. We need open communication foremost. You're not going to like all my ideas and I'm sure you'll grate on my nerves, too, but I expect compromise. Are you comfortable with that?"

"Yes." He sighed, studying her. "I have a couple stipulations of my own." He held up a finger. "One, a signed confidentiality agreement. You'll be privy to corporate dealings and it's not just me I need to protect." Up went another finger. "And two, honesty at all times. I'm not always the best judge of character. I'm more of a numbers guy and you have a gift for reading people. I don't care what the situation, but if something feels off, if someone rubs you the wrong way, or if there's an issue in any aspect, you will come to me first. Always."

She didn't know what to be more upset about—the fact he felt he had to say either of those things or that he obviously had been burned once before to necessitate making the stipulations. "Agree and agree." This was a done deal in her mind. Still, she hesitated and decided to go for broke. Call it curiosity. "Tell me something no one else knows about you."

Brows furrowed, he stared at her a long beat, his gaze unreadable. "I'm allergic to coconut. Wait, my doctor knows that." He rubbed the back of his neck, frustration and something close to panic in his expression, then looked at her necklace.

Okay, he'd done that several times last night, too. To give him a starting point, she asked him about the quirk.

Closing his eyes, he dug his fingers into his lids. His chest stopped rising and falling. Just when she thought he wouldn't respond, he slapped a hand to his thigh and tentatively met her gaze. "I have a self-diagnosed social anxiety disorder. I'm fine in meetings and typically in small crowds, but if I don't know the person or if the association doesn't involve business, I can freeze up. Having something to focus on helps, like your necklace, for instance."

Every cell in her body shut down as she watched him. Utterly still, she rewound what he'd said and connected his words to his actions that she'd witnessed the past two days. "Self-diagnosed. Meaning, you haven't been in therapy or—"

"No. Not one soul knows that about me. In fact, aside from my parents and my bodyguard, this is the most open conversation I've had in I don't know how long. I think you should be aware of the condition, considering the work you'd be doing for me if you say yes." His throat worked a swallow, and he dropped his chin as if humiliated.

And, there. *There* was the man under the suit, the heart behind the shield. He wasn't cold or insensitive. He wasn't a machine or a robot. He didn't lack personality or character. Quite simply, he was functioning in the only way he knew how.

Without a word, he rose and moved to the wall of windows. His spine stiff, he shoved his hands in his pockets and appeared to take in the view before him. Dusk had settled and stars winked in the distance, a backdrop to the lights from the buildings. He looked so lonely, so lost standing there, and she had to wonder how many times he'd done this. A powerful, uber rich, incredibly smart man...standing all by himself.

Sudden emotion tightened her throat. The professional part of her clicked off and left her just a woman, sympathizing with him, her heart exposed.

Cautiously, she stood and stepped behind him, halting with a couple feet of distance between them. The window reflected his image, and his torn, wide-open gaze met hers in the glass. She could only guess how his honesty had leveled his confidence. Emasculating, really. And he'd trusted her enough to tell her. That said so very much about him.

She adjusted her glasses and chose her words carefully. "You are a brilliant man. To accomplish what you have at your age is remarkable. Behind the money and under the prestige, you're just a guy who prefers gigabytes and algorithms over people. There's no shame in that, and your field of interest didn't allow for much social interaction. A little nervousness is to be expected."

Hands deep in his pockets, he slowly turned to face her, jaw ticking. Shock and relief warred in his expression. "Peyton..." He shook his head as if at a loss. His gaze dropped to her necklace.

An idea bloomed, and she held up a finger, telling him to hold on. She strode to her purse on the table, dug around until she found what she was searching for, and moved back in front of him. His eyes shifted from the floor to her necklace again.

"Look at me, please. Up here." She waved her hand, indicating her face, and he complied. "I want you to understand me and look in my eyes. Get used to it. They're your focal point now, your safety net. Here, you'll find no judgment or pressure. I'll be there for all your appearances. If you start to feel nervous or overwhelmed, just find me."

His lips parted in shock. "Does that mean...?"

"I accept your offer."

He let out an extinguishing breath and slammed his lids shut, his shoulders sagging. "Thank you."

She waited for his eyes to open and then reached for his hand, depositing an item in his palm. "That's a military challenge coin. Service members collect them."

He studied the gold metal roughly the size of a half-dollar, running his thumb across the four branches engraving the front. "I don't understand."

"That coin is one of many my brother had before he died. He used to carry one on him at all times and, when he felt scared, he'd tightly fist it. He said it grounded him." She closed Xavier's fingers around it and met his golden eyes. "This is for your pocket."

"Peyton, I can't take this."

"I'm giving it to you, and yes, you can. If I'm not around, just slip your hand inside your pocket when you need assurance. No one will ever know." She smiled as his gaze reclaimed hers. "I knew you were a smart cookie who'd catch on fast. You haven't looked at my necklace in five whole minutes."

With a rough, low laugh, he shook his head. "I think you need a raise. Already."

Jeez. A girl could melt with that grin aimed her way. It transformed his whole face from cool disinterest to warm fuzzies. "At least let me fill out new employee paperwork first."

Chapter Three

Two Years Later...

Finished with his late-morning meeting, Xavier strode across the hall and into Peyton's office, only to stop short. More than half the room was littered with balloons and flowers. Since her domain was a mirror to his and roughly five-hundred square feet, that was saying a lot. And, best he could tell, she wasn't here.

Just as he was about to search through the rubble to see if she was buried underneath, she walked in. The clack-clack of her black heels hit the floor and he followed the path up her toned legs, past her fitted red dress to her hair. At the office, she always had it pinned up in a severe knot, which made him long for another charity event to see the champagne waves trail down her back.

She glanced over the rim of her glasses at him. "Hey, favorite boss."

He ran his fingers through his hair, trying to ignore the naughty librarian fantasy she evoked. "I'm your only boss and what the actual hell is all this?" It looked like Valentine's Day had thrown up all over. Except it was September.

Taking a seat behind her desk, she put her intercom phone piece in her ear. "It's my birthday. What can I say? Your employees love me."

Who didn't love her? But that wasn't the point. "You're going to get high from the helium alone." Or allergies from the pollen.

"It'll make answering the phone hilarious." She shrugged, her gaze darting around. "This is really nice, though, don't you think?"

Since her tone had a rare melancholy note, he moved to one of the thousand floral arrangements and read the card as a distraction.

Hope our best gal has the best birthday. ~Geek Division, 4th Floor

He sighed. There wasn't a solitary staff member inside Gaines Industries who didn't adore her to death, him included. And this abundance of...happiness was quite nice of them. Peyton had no family and, aside from Xavier or a handful of her friends, her birthday might've gone unacknowledged.

Speaking of... "I came by to take you out to lunch for your birthday."

"Thank you, but I ate with the kids in the daycare downstairs. It was chicken nuggets day."

Chicken nuggets were not a meal. He shoved his hands in his pockets. "Why? Is there an issue?"

"Nope. They're fun and I wanted some cheer, is all. I go down there sometimes when I need a pick me up."

Studying her, he shifted to the chair across from her desk and sat. She turned thirty today and all outward appearances indicated she was full systems go, as usual. Her smile didn't seem as bright, though. While she scrolled through her tablet, his gut bottomed out. He hadn't been aware she liked to visit the daycare. They never talked about it, but did she want children of her own?

"Do you plan on having kids?" He could picture her sitting on the floor with a few rugrats, playing dolls or cars or whatever today's youth did. Between her soft heart, her creativity, and her innate organizational skills, she'd make a great mom.

Her gaze drifted to the festive plethora of cheer exploding in the room. "I don't know. I mean, Mark and I talked about it before he died, but..." She shrugged and refocused on her tablet. "Last I checked, I'd need a man to accomplish pregnancy. At this rate, I might dry up first." She tilted her head. "There's always insemination."

And there was another thing. How was it possible some guy hadn't stolen her heart yet? She held every characteristic a man sought and, still, she was single.

Not liking her overall mood, he rubbed the ache in his gut. If he didn't know her so well, he might've missed the dimness in her baby blues or the slight shift in her voice. "Have I been working you too hard?"

She met his gaze and frowned. "No. You're the most undemanding person I know."

Resting his forearms on his thighs, he leaned forward. "There's not an aspect of the company or my life you don't have your fingers in, aside from my wardrobe or diet. You're being pulled in five different directions at once, so yeah, it can be demanding. You're irreplaceable."

"Technically, I picked out that suit." She grinned.

He rubbed his eyes. Curse her adorable charm. "Honesty, Peyton. You promised. Always. Tell me why you're off today." The whole week, really. Minute little things that added to bigger ones.

"Just birthday blues. Not a biggie. I'm fine, X."

She only called him X when they were alone. One of those personal, just for them things that made his heartbeat stupidly flutter. "You must miss Brian." Her brother had been her world. She'd talked about him often enough. Holidays and birthdays had to be the toughest without him.

"Something fierce." She chewed her lip. "He used to buy me a gigantic cupcake from our favorite bakery and stick a candle in it." Her smile grew wistfully sad. "He was deployed one year and paid them to deliver the cupcake to me. It was so nice of him, and just like Brian to do something like that."

What Xavier wouldn't give to bring her brother back to her. "Which bakery?"

"Sweetums over on Washington Str—" She frowned. "Hold that thought, and don't move. I have to talk to you about something." Before he could respond, she tapped her earpiece to take a call. "What's up, Fern?" She listened, rolled her eyes. "Gah, he's relentless. All right, patch him through. Thanks."

While Xavier waited, she rose. "Marty, it's Peyton Smoke. How's my favorite reporter?" She started collecting balloon strings and gathered them to create a cluster large enough to raise the roof. "I'd love to help you out, but you have a history of going off the rails in interviews." With the balloons tied together and in a corner, she grabbed two vases of flowers and walked out of the room.

Xavier followed her to the lobby. She set both arrangements on Fern's desk and mouthed, *for you*, to his secretary, who beamed at her.

Peyton winked at Fern, then made her way back to her office, only to grab two potted plants and stride into Xavier's office. "I tell you what, Marty. Because I like you, I'll think about allowing you to see Mr. Gaines if you send me a list of questions for pre-approval." She set one plant on his shelf by a family portrait and the other by the Giants baseball gear she'd bought him two years ago. "Okay, shoot. Let's hear 'em."

Running his tongue over his teeth, Xavier followed her, yet again, out of his office, into hers, and then to the lobby with two more vases. She was like a cyclone. One arrangement went onto a side table and...he bit back a groan. Bent over, her perfect round ass was all his gaze could lock onto as she placed the second arrangement. Damn, that dress was like a glove.

And back into her office they went.

"Nice try. I'll be in the interview. You'll get nothing past me." She swiped the screen on her tablet. "I can get you in for fifteen minutes at three-thirty." Her laugh was light and musical. "Fine. I'll pencil you in for next spring—" A roll of her eyes. "That's what I thought."

Since it looked like she'd finally sit down, Xavier walked closer. Except she turned abruptly, running right into him. And didn't move away. With her hand on his chest right over his pounding heart, every single subtle curve of her was plastered to him. The sultry scent of her perfume—which he hadn't been able to eradicate from his memory for seven-hundred and thirty days straight—swirled around them.

Frozen, he closed his eyes and tried to breathe, but that only served to bring his chest in closer proximity to her breasts. He threw his hands in the air, afraid he'd touch her somewhere besides her shoulders.

"Are you flirting with me?"

Shit. Was he? It was a little difficult to form logical thought right now.

He cleared his throat. "No." A) He didn't know how to flirt. Women usually sought him out or he went with the direct route and asked them on a date. No pretenses. And B) Peyton was irrevocably, permanently, absolutely, off limits. Period. No, make that an exclamation point.

She tilted her head up and looked at him, their faces close. She blinked.

Mercy, her eyes. Sapphire and blue fog with a cerulean ring around the edges. He'd gazed into those beauties countless times over the past couple years and it always felt like the first shocking blow each instance.

Not you, she mouthed as if his response had been ridiculous, and then—finally, blessedly—she sat behind her desk.

He reeled, did a trigonometry equation to restore a regular heart rhythm, and took a seat, too.

"I'm flattered, Marty, but I have a rule against accepting dinner offers that come up in the same conversation as requests for interviews." She scrolled a few notes on her tablet while Xavier ground his molars. "Perfect. How's your mom, by the way? I heard she was sick." She nodded. "Glad to hear it. See you at three-thirty. Bye-bye."

With a tap of her earpiece and a sound of exasperation, she dropped her forehead to her desk. "I need a bleach shower after that one. Smarmy, that guy."

Xavier strummed his fingers on his thigh. "How did you know his mother was ill?" He didn't even recognize the man's name.

Without lifting her head, she held out her tablet. A Facebook page for one Marty Ferguson of the Bay Gazette was on the screen.

Clever. "Does that happen a lot? Getting asked out on the cusp of a business transaction?"

Straightening in her seat, she sighed. "Ninety percent of date requests are really ploys to get to you through me. The other ten percent just want in my pants."

He opened and closed his mouth, unsure how to respond. Pissed didn't begin to cover the simmering heat bubbling under his skin.

"Anyway, two things. Are you coming to Hallucinogen with us tonight? Kate needs a head count to reserve the table."

Hallucinogen was a bar Peyton went to on occasion and Kate was her best friend. Normally, he'd decline the offer, but it was Peyton's birthday and he'd feel like crap for bailing. Yet, he'd rather do a press conference naked without her than hang out with Kate. "What time?"

"Seven." Her smile relayed she knew what he was thinking. "Kate promised to be nice. It's my present from her."

He'd bet his bank account that wouldn't happen. For whatever reason, Kate hadn't liked him from the moment they'd met. To paraphrase, she'd called him an *uptight, pretentious ass.* "I'll be there. Do you want me to pick you up?" That way she could drink to her heart's content and not have to drive home.

"Nope. Joseph said he'd be the designated driver."

What? He frowned. "My bodyguard's coming?"

Her grin widened. "Unofficial capacity. He promised to dance with me."

Hating the visual of her dancing with anyone, specifically Joseph, Xavier abruptly looked away. Joseph was the closest thing to a friend Xavier had, was one of the few people he could talk to with ease, even if the man did work for him. He knew Peyton and Joseph hung out on occasion when he was off duty, but...were they secretly dating? Sleeping together?

Xavier shouldn't care. It was none of his business. "You said there was something else you needed to talk about?" Christ, his stomach was a ball of tangled knots.

"Yeah." She leaned forward, her voice tentative. "For starters, let me say that the only reason I'm showing you this is because of the honesty pact, otherwise I'd ignore it for the nonsense it truly is, okay? Don't flip out. I have it handled."

"Congratulations. Now I'm freaked out."

She swiped her tablet screen. "This is an email that arrived in my box this morning." Chewing her lip, she passed him the device. "I get stupid emails all the time, but that was sent internally, which is why I'm showing you."

He glanced at the screen. And stopped breathing.

A picture of them at a charity event from this past summer was in the body of the message. Save the dolphins or dust bunnies or whatever, he couldn't remember. But Peyton's face was scratched out and a big red X placed over her. Below the picture was text that read: *I'm going to kill you, bitch.* The subject line said: *Die, bitch, die.*

The violent implication alone put his pulse near cardiac arrest, but the fact the email had come from their server made his heart relocate ribs. Blood whooshed against his eardrums.

"I have Carson from IT looking into it. What we know so far is, the email was created within our system, sent, then the account was deleted."

He gnashed his molars to dust. "You're getting a protection detail as of today."

She moaned. "I knew you were going to say that. It's just a harmless whack job, X. Do you know how many emails hit my spam threatening me to stay away from you?" She opened a drawer and pulled out a two-inch thick manila folder, dropping it on the desk with a thud. "I keep them all, just in case. Yet, here I am, limbs intact, no gaping wounds. This is part of the territory. You're rich, single, good-looking, and that brings out the crazies. Nothing's going to happen."

"Damn right, it's not. Because I'm putting a bodyguard on you right now." Hell. He got up and paced. Guilt coagulated with sickening worry in his gut. He'd had a few low-level threats before, which was why he'd hired Joseph. Xavier only used a bodyguard when away from home or out of the office. He didn't have one on him at all times.

But her getting threats was another story. And, son of a bitch, from within his own company. "I'll keep Joseph on you tonight. Tomorrow, we'll get you your own detail. You will not drive home, go to the bar, or so much as brush your teeth without him beside you."

"Happy birthday to me." She banged her forehead on the desk and rested her cheek there. "Tonight's his night off, you know."

"Not anymore."

"What if I want to get laid?"

Xavier kept his mouth firmly shut on that one.

"You're being unreasonable." She straightened, her pretty eyes pleading. "I'll be with you and Kate, plus other friends besides Joseph."

"And your apartment complex doesn't have security." He shoved his hand in his pocket and vigorously rubbed his thumb over the engraving on the coin she'd given him. Two years had felt more like two decades, they'd grown that close. It would kill him if she were hurt because of his quasi-celeb status. "You're in danger outside of this building."

"X—"

"No. I'm pulling the boss card. We talked about this on day one. I don't screw around with safety." Christ, especially hers. He pinched the bridge of his nose. "Working this closely with me puts you at risk. I'm shocked it's taken this long for something to happen." He moved to her desk and picked up her phone, then waited for Fern to answer. "Get Joseph up here now."

"Yes, sir."

Hanging up, he leaned against her desk in front of her and crossed his arms, their legs just inches apart. Her dejected, sullen expression didn't help the crappy sensation swirling in his chest. "I'm sorry."

She rested the back of her head against the chair. "I know you are. It's not your fault. And you're right, but I don't have to like it."

Peyton had no one, damn it. Besides Kate, he was it. She may be his employee, but he also considered her a sort of friend. Not that she wasn't capable, but who would look after her if he didn't? Plus, she'd have this risk no matter where she wound up. While she'd worked for Harrison all those years ago, she'd had her own security at events. This wasn't new territory for her.

"Would you stop looking at me with your wounded puppy eyes if I give you your present now instead of later?"

And...*yes*. A smile. "Maybe."

A knock sounded at her door, and he glanced over his shoulder at Joseph.

"You asked for me, Mr. Gaines?"

Xavier rubbed his jaw. "We're alone. You can be informal."

Peyton tilted her head to look around Xavier. "I showed Captain Paranoia the email."

Joseph ducked his chin in a nod, the fluorescent lights reflecting off his bald head. "I have an overnight bag packed and in the car. Roomie."

Xavier narrowed his eyes at the two of them. "You told him before me?"

"You were in a meeting, and what was the first thing you did, anyway?" She waved her hand. "You called for him. I saved time. One of the many reasons why you hired me." She looked pointedly at Joseph. "I draw the line at you watching me shower, though. Hard limit."

Joseph laughed. "Okay, Peyton. I'll meet you downstairs after work. Don't leave the building without me."

She offered him a sarcastic salute and shifted her eyes to Xavier when the bodyguard left. "Feel better?"

"Yes." He cleared his throat and reached into the breast pocket of his suit coat, removing her gift. He passed her the small box wrapped in silver paper and a gold bow. "Happy birthday."

Blinking rapidly, she studied the present. "It's not a car, is it?"

"I'm pretty sure that wouldn't fit inside."

Brows pinged, she pursed her lips. "You gave me a car last year. With the key in a box. I think this is the same wrapping paper."

"It's not, and I didn't buy you another car."

"There was nothing wrong with my old one. You spend too much money on me."

He ran his tongue over his teeth. "That thing was a deathtrap, and it's my money. I'll spend it how I see fit. I bought Joseph an SUV for Christmas, if you remember."

Her nose wrinkled. "It was a Ford, not a deathtrap. It was three years old and had forty-thousand miles."

"With no side impact airbags. Stop being argumentative. I have to show my appreciation somehow. Please understand, I couldn't do all this without you."

A swallow worked her throat and the smile fleeted. "My salary is more than enough, X. Flowers would've been adequate."

He glanced around the room. "Yes, because that's original."

She breathed a laugh. "Well, no one can accuse you of being unoriginal." With a smile, she fingered the bow. "Thank you."

"You haven't opened it yet. Thank me afterward if you like it."

"I know I'll like it." Regardless, she peeled away the paper and set it aside. She lifted the lid, gasped, and clasped her hand over her mouth.

"I remember how much it upset you when you lost the original." He jerked his chin at the key pendant necklace and matching bracelet. Her brother had given her the piece, and she'd misplaced it somewhere. She'd cried for three days. "Consider the necklace from Brian and the bracelet from me."

"Oh God, X." Tears welled in her eyes, and she removed her glasses, fisting them in her delicate hand.

"Don't cry. You know how it upsets my equilibrium and the world's natural balance."

She laughed as tears streamed down her cheeks. "Sorry."

He sighed and squatted beside her chair. Taking the necklace from the box, he clasped the thin gold chain around her slender neck, then attached the bracelet to her wrist, all while trying to ignore the softness of her skin and the heavenly scent of her.

Straightening, he rose, but she flew forward and wrapped her arms around him, thrusting his ass firmly against the edge of the desk with the momentum. He braced one hand behind him for balance and slid the other around her waist.

And closed his eyes. Because holding her was a rare thing. Her subtle curves fit way too well against the hard, angular lines of his body. It wasn't the first instance he'd thought such a thing and it wouldn't be the last. Not that they hugged often, but it gave him an arrhythmia every damn time. Like rattling hell's gate and falling from heaven's clouds.

"Thank you." She pressed a kiss to his cheek—he didn't need basic oxygen exchange, anyway—and rested her forehead to his temple. "That is the nicest thing anyone's ever done for me."

Damn, he hoped not. He kept his eyes shut another beat in order to clear a reaction from his expression as she eased away. "You're welcome."

Chapter Four

Peyton unlocked her apartment door and went to step inside, but Joseph put an arm in front of her.

"Hold up. Wait here." He strode into her tiny living room, set his large black duffel bag on the floor, and glanced around, then moved into the adjoining kitchen. Seemingly satisfied no one was lurking, he disappeared down the hall. "Clear. Come in. Lock the door."

Biting back a sigh, she did as he asked and dropped her purse on the small entry table. Heading to the kitchen, she checked her cell for calls.

A solid set of arms wrapped around her from behind and a hand clasped over her mouth. The phone fell from her numb fingers. Heart pounding, she wiggled to get free, but he had her trapped. Panic clutched her throat.

"Breathe, Peyton. Get out of the situation."

Right. Closing her eyes, she channeled what Joseph had taught her. With a feral cry, she jabbed her elbow into his ribs, stomped on his in-heel, and thrust her foot toward his ankle. Using the full weight of her body, she twisted and rammed into him, sending him to the hardwood floor by her coffee table with an *oomph*.

Flat on his back, arms sprawled, Joseph laughed through a groan. "Atta girl. You're learning, young grasshopper."

Chest heaving, she shook her head and picked up her phone. "You could've let me change clothes before sparring."

"And miss the element of surprise?" With limber grace, he rolled to his feet. "An attacker's not going to wait for you to slip out of your heels." He stripped his black suit coat from his shoulders and set it on her cream-colored couch. "Go put on something more comfortable. We'll get a few reps in before we head out to your party."

Her shoulders sagged. "But it's my birthday."

One corner of his mouth curled. "It's been a week since we had a lesson. Save the pout for someone who'll fall for it. I'm not Xavier."

"It doesn't work on him, either. You're here on your night off, aren't you?"

His laugh was dry. "Oh, it works on him. One bat of those lashes and he's putty. Except where your safety is concerned."

"Putty, my ass. Perhaps you missed the part where you'll be crashing on my couch." She glanced at the furniture, then Joseph. She didn't think he'd even fit. The guy was a wall of testosterone.

He dropped his hands on his hips. "He's worried, with good reason." His dark brown gaze swept over her, studied her face. "He cares about you a lot."

"I know." The feeling was mutual. One couldn't work that closely with someone for two years and not get attached. The Harrisons still invited her to holidays at their mansion. Her connection to Xavier seemed different, though. Perhaps because they'd gone to school together.

A flash of their office exchange today pinned her immobile and heated her cheeks. First with slamming into each other while she'd been on the phone, then again with the hug. As protective and sometimes distant as he appeared, Xavier Gaines was one damn attractive man who had a heart of gold.

Joseph rubbed a hand over his bald head. "He's a different guy since you joined the company." His direct gaze made her dislike the conversation. Even with Xavier's long time bodyguard and friend, Peyton didn't care to discuss her boss. Habit, she supposed. "He's less tense, smiles more. You've been good for him."

"Thank you." She adjusted her glasses. "I'm being a good sport, though I don't think having you as a shadow is necessary. We've had whack emails before."

"Let me put it this way. If something happened to you, Xavier isn't the only one who'd never forgive himself." He offered a stiff smile. "I care about you, too. You remind me of my kid sister."

"She must be awesome, then."

He barked a laugh. "True. You could avoid all this by moving into a more secure complex. It would lower his blood pressure and make him less defensive."

"It's not as if I'm living in a slum. This is a good neighborhood. There's a security camera in the parking lot and everyone needs a key to enter the building. I'm on the fifth floor, so someone's not going to climb in my window." She sighed. "Besides, Kate's right across the hall. I like it here."

"Preaching to the choir, Peyton." He nodded. "He does have a point, though. Now, go change. You've stalled long enough."

"Yeah, yeah." She turned and headed for her bedroom.

"Okay if I use your bathroom to change?"

"*Mi casa es tu casa*. Just don't leave your boxers on the floor."

Ten minutes later, they were on her rooftop between her neighbor's vegetable garden and a ventilation panel, and Peyton had an unloaded gun in her face.

"Take it away from me." Joseph waggled the fingers on his free hand. "Like I taught you."

She wiped the sweat from her brow with her forearm and squinted through the late-day sunlight. "God, you know I hate guns."

Recalling her training, she grabbed the barrel with one hand, shoving it hard to the right while using her other hand to knock his wrist left. The maneuver successfully unarmed him.

"Good. Now show me how to turn the safety on and off."

Barrel down, she pushed the switch. "Off." Back again. "On."

"Nice work." He pointed the glock at her head. "Again." As she went at him, he stepped back to make it more challenging for her. "What was he like in high school? Xavier, I mean."

Figuring this was a distraction, she stepped forward. "Shy. Quiet." She answered while disarming him. *Grunt.* "Brilliant." Gun once again in her possession, she rolled her head to loosen her neck and passed him the weapon.

"So, he's exactly the same." He tossed her a towel and shoved the glock in the waistband of his gray nylon shorts. Sweat dampened the collar of his tee. Muscles bulged as he wiped his face with his own towel.

"No." She patted the sweat from her neck and chest. "Well, he's still brilliant and quiet, I suppose. But he has confidence that wasn't present back then. He's more sure of himself." He'd always had those characteristics, but lacked the assurance to realize them. Instead, he'd hid behind a cold front as protection.

They chugged from bottles of water while walking inside and to the elevators. She thought about the other changes in Xavier, too. How he'd grown taller, built muscle along with an empire. Though sarcastic and dry, he had a great sense of humor. He was fiercely loyal to those that mattered to him. He still had a difficult time trusting people, but that was to be expected in his position.

She pressed the down arrow button on the panel. "Let me ask you something. Have you ever found yourself...attracted to him? You've been his bodyguard a long time. That's a lot of one-on-one." Joseph's door swung both ways, and he'd confessed to her once it had been a big factor in why he'd retired from the military.

"Sure, maybe once or twice. He's good-looking, but not really my type." They stepped into the elevator and he pushed the button for her floor. "I'm more attracted to women than men, with a few exceptions. Why?" He grinned. "Do you have the hots for our boss?"

"No." Perhaps a little. She was certainly aware of him sometimes. No doubt, it was a result of close working conditions and her lack of a love life since finally getting over Mark's death. "What *is* your type?"

A ding, and the panels opened.

"Sassy as hell redheads. Gets me every time." He guided her from the elevator and withdrew a key from his pocket.

She stopped and faced him. Interesting. "You don't say. Kate's coming out with us tonight."

"I know." He lifted his hand as if to block her response. "Don't get any ideas. There's an age gap there and I'm on the clock."

"Uh-huh." She tilted her head. "Seven years isn't a biggie. It's not like we're teenagers anymore. She's hot and single. You're hot and single..."

He unlocked her door and dipped his face close to hers. Amusement lit his eyes while he held the door with his foot. "Stay out of it, blondie."

"Fine." She totally wouldn't.

They walked inside, and Kate's voice immediately floated from the direction of the hallway near Peyton's bedroom. "There you are. Do you know there's a limo waiting—"

In a flash, Peyton was pinned to the door, two-hundred pounds of muscle caging her, and Joseph had his gun aimed right at Kate as she emerged into view.

Her best friend froze with her hands up, eyes wide. "What the hell?"

Joseph muttered a curse as his shoulders sagged. He tossed the gun on his duffel bag. "I could've shot you. How did you get in here?"

Peyton stepped around him, trying to reset her pulse. "She has a key." She looked at a confused Kate, dressed to the nines in a little black cocktail number, her red curls falling to her bare shoulders. "The gun wasn't loaded."

Kate, hands falling to her hips, tapped a foot. Now that her shock had faded, her expression was dialed to castrate. "First, what is Rambo doing here, waving a gun around? Second, you're not going out dressed like that. And third, why is there a limo out front waiting for us?"

Joseph crossed his arms and ignored her to face Peyton. "How many other people have a key?"

"Just you, Kate, and Xavier." Who else was there?

"Are you sure? No exes?"

She rolled her eyes. "Yes, I'm sure."

"Hello?" Kate waved her hand, her green eyes getting angrier by the second. "Remember me? You just tried to off me a second ago."

"You're a hard person to forget. And if I wanted you dead, you'd be dead." Joseph grabbed his bag and looked at Peyton. "I'm going to take a quick shower while you deal with Red. The door stays locked, and you don't leave."

Kate watched him disappear down the hall, then eyed Peyton. "I can never tell if he's hitting on me or insulting me."

"My bet is the former." She headed to the kitchen to toss out her empty water bottle. "Sorry for the scare. Joseph's on babysitting detail this weekend. I got a somewhat threatening email, so Xavier's playing it safe." She washed her hands in the sink. "Did he really send a limo?"

"Yep. I suppose it beats finding a designated driver, but can the guy do anything without throwing his money around?" Kate leaned against the counter, tapping her nails on the formica. "I guess this means he's coming tonight."

Peyton turned and mimicked her friend's pose. "He is and you promised to be nice."

"Only because it's your birthday." She grinned, her pretty face transforming from irritated to the knock-'em-dead heart-stopper that sucked in men. "Happy thirtieth, you hag."

"Thanks." Peyton laughed and shoved off the counter. "Come help me find something to wear while Joseph's occupied."

While riffling through Peyton's closet, Kate tilted her head. "So, what did moneybags get you this year? A yacht? A third-world country?"

Flopping on her bed, Peyton sighed. She had no clue why her friend hated Xavier so hard, but she suspected it had something to do with the fact he appeared uncomfortable or dismissive in Kate's presence. Which was only his anxiety rearing its head. Peyton couldn't say that, though. Thus, she'd tolerated the jabs for the past couple years. They'd both put her between a rock and a hard place. She'd known Kate since college and Xavier since...well, technically, high school.

She fingered the key pendant, emotion tightening her chest as she recalled what he'd said as she'd opened the gift. "He got me a replacement necklace for the one I lost."

Kate turned, a frown wrinkling her brow. She stepped closer to the bed and, when her gaze locked onto the charm, her features softened. "I'll be damned. How...thoughtful."

"He's a nice guy, Kate. I wish you'd give him a chance."

The three of them were rarely in the same room together, and it's not as if Peyton were in a relationship with him, but it would be more than a little fabulous if Kate laid off. Then again, her defensive stance on Xavier was just her mama bear response.

They agreed on skinny jeans, knee-high black boots, and a sparkly silver shirt with an exposed back. After a quick shower, Peyton opted for contacts instead of her glasses, letting Kate blow out her hair and apply smoky shadow to her eyes.

Hallucinogen was busy, but not packed, when they arrived. It was still early yet for a Friday. The trendy club had blue neon lights on the recessed ceiling and under the bar. Chrome and black woodwork throughout added a classically clean look. Three square hightop tables were pushed together for them along the back wall in full view of the semi-crowded dance floor. A pop beat thrummed from the speakers.

Peyton climbed on a stool at the end of their reserved tables and glanced around. A couple of her and Kate's friends—mostly Kate's from the law firm where she worked—were waiting on the far side, and she waved while they chatted with Kate. Simone and Reina weren't really here for Peyton, so she let them talk alone.

Joseph took a stool next to her and leaned closer. "Just do me a favor and give me a heads up if you plan to wander more than ten feet from the table."

"Aye-aye, captain."

While the other women took to the dance floor, she and Joseph sized up the fashionable patrons and heckled like Statler and Waldorf. Since there could be worse ways to spend her birthday than pretending to be the two old men in the Muppets, she grinned.

A half hour later, Xavier still hadn't arrived. Disappointment began to weigh heavy on her shoulders. She glanced at the door again which Joseph, of course, noticed.

"He'll be here, Peyton."

She wasn't so sure. Xavier hated crowds and he'd already given her a gift. Knowing him, he was holed up in his mansion watching CNN. She had no idea why it bugged her. Yeah, they were friendly and did things outside of work sometimes, but it wasn't as if he was more than her boss. Lord knew, she made him socialize enough because of Gaines Industries.

The rest of their group returned and ordered a round of drinks. She was too caught up in their discussion of the hottest bartender to notice Xavier stood beside her until she'd hopped off her stool and nearly plowed into him.

He was casual in jeans and a fitted black t-shirt that emphasized his lean, muscular build. A dark five o'clock shadow covered his wide jaw, giving him a seductive edge, and a strand of chestnut hair fell over his forehead, making her want to brush it aside.

A spark of...something—recognition, perhaps—flared in her belly. She shook her head.

"You came." She grinned and mentally bitch-slapped the giddy bubble his presence created. "You dress down real nice." Xavier Gaines in a suit was drool-worthy. Him in jeans was panty-melting.

Dang. What was up with her tonight?

"Thank you, I think." He held up a small pink dessert box. "Sorry I'm late. Had to stop somewhere on the way. This is for you."

Her breath stalled as she stared at the box. Sweetums was printed on the top and...shoot, her eyes watered at the thoughtful gesture. He'd remembered.

Slapping a hand to her chest, she quickly glanced at Kate, who closely watched their exchange. Besides Xavier, Kate was the only one who knew Brian's birthday tradition of getting her a cupcake from that particular bakery. Tenderness softened Kate's expression, and she winked.

When Peyton didn't move, Xavier set the box on the table, opened it, and removed a giant chocolate cupcake with pink frosting, placing it beside the box. Then, he dug in his pocket and stuck a candle in the top.

Her chest hitched, fighting a sob.

"Well done, moneybags." Kate smiled at him, and he offered her a baleful glance until he must've realized she was being genuine, then nodded.

God, he was just so thoughtful. Peyton had been missing her brother terribly this week. Xavier doing this was kind of like having Brian back, if only in spirit.

Joseph lit the candle and the group sang Happy Birthday. She pressed her lips into a thin line to prevent waterworks.

"Make a wish." Xavier, still pressed close to her side, raised his brows in expectation.

She got sucked into his golden eyes and long lashes for a moment before shaking her head. A wish? Thinking a beat, she smiled when the perfect one came to mind. She wished Xavier would find a woman to love who he could be comfortable around and who didn't have ulterior motives. He was such a great guy and he deserved happiness.

Nodding, she blew out the candle, and everyone cheered.

She wrapped her arms around Xavier's waist and smiled up at him. "I know you don't like public displays of affection, but deal with this one for a second. Thank you." She hugged him.

One solid arm came around her and his hand skimmed her spine. The warm touch against her bare skin caused an involuntary shiver. He inhaled sharply, apparently surprised her shirt was an open design in back. He quickly shifted his hand to her waist and cleared his throat.

"You're welcome."

Gah, his hoarse tone was delicious. Rigid, he didn't move, and the longer they stayed close, the more increased his respirations became. His fingers clenched her waist and his warm breath teased the hair at her temple.

"What did you wish for, Smoke?"

Jerking upright, she stepped away from Xavier's embrace and turned to Kate's friend, Simone. Wow. Hello, dizziness. "I can't tell you or it won't come true."

Kate snorted and pointed to Peyton with her glass. "Doesn't matter. She never wishes for anything for herself."

Joseph sent Peyton a confused eyebrow quirk. "Say what?"

Reclaiming her seat, she sighed. "It's something my mom used to say. A wish for someone else sends good karma out into the world." She shrugged. The group stared at her a long beat, Xavier's gaze feeling heaviest of all, so she reached for her glass. "What?"

Joseph shared a look she couldn't decipher with Xavier, then shook his head. "Just when I thought you couldn't get any more awesome, you shock the shit out of me." He clinked his glass with hers. "Rock on, blondie."

She swallowed the last of her martini, letting the liquid cool her raw throat, and stared at the empty glass while conversation started anew.

The table vibrated and glasses clinked. "Get over here, hot stuff."

She lifted her gaze to their waiter, setting down a tray full of cocktails, and squealed. "Justin. I didn't know you were working tonight."

Having met him a few years ago while still on Harrison's campaign, they'd been chummy ever since. The blond god looked like Adonis on a bad day and oozed seduction from his pores. They often exchanged harmless flirtation when they ran into each other. Since she was sandwiched between Joseph, Xavier, and the wall, she climbed under the table and emerged on the other side.

She gave Justin a one-armed embrace. "Xavier, Joseph, this is Justin." She blinked up him. "Joseph is the muscle tonight, so don't make him mad."

Justin laughed. "Got it. A little birdie told me it was your birthday. This round's on me. Bridgetown Breezes for one and all."

Xavier accepted his glass and stared at the pink liquid as if trying to gauge its contents.

Her heart leapt into her throat. "No!" She took it out of his hand and set it aside. "Don't drink that. It has Malibu in it." She faced Justin. "Can you get him a scotch on the rocks? Macallan if you have it. And a seltzer water with lime for Joseph. Make sure all this goes on my tab."

"Sure thing."

Kate cocked a hip and glared at Xavier. "You got something against rum?"

"He's..." Allergic to coconut, but Peyton didn't want to advertize the info. "Um, Malibu doesn't agree with him."

Xavier stared at the glass she'd confiscated, his jaw ticking and face pale. After a second, he lifted his gaze to hers, nodding a thank you. He looked at Kate. "I have an allergy to coconut."

"Oh." Kate pursed her lips. "Good catch, Peyton."

Absently, she nodded, shocked immobile that Xavier had shared something private with Kate. He was unerringly secretive about his life, and Peyton had always respected that. It was part of her job, in fact. But it seemed he was trying to offer her friend an olive branch, perhaps explain himself, so Kate would maybe change her view of him. Knowing Xavier, he could care less what she thought. Which meant he'd done it for Peyton.

Their gazes locked, and she let out an uneven breath at finding his wide open. Patience, gratitude, and fondness stared back at her.

Justin tapped her shoulder. "I'm on break in twenty minutes. Save me a dance?" When she agreed, he lifted the tray. "I'll be back in a sec with your order."

Xavier rose to let her return to her seat and then reclaimed his. She smiled at the conversation going on at the other end of the table, not following along in the slightest because she kept flicking quick glances at Xavier. He seemed more tense than usual all of a sudden.

When the ladies took off for the dance floor again, she leaned closer to him. "You okay?"

"Yes." His gaze slid to hers, roamed her face. "I'm always surprised by how different you look with your hair down and without your glasses. You're very lovely tonight."

"Thank you." Always with the compliments, her boss. Charity functions, press conferences, mandatory appearances—he never forgot to slip her a nice word. Her face heated, and she blamed it on the one cocktail she'd downed.

Justin returned thirty minutes later and took her hand. "You're all mine for the next set."

Xavier rose stiffly to let her out.

As Justin tugged Peyton from her seat, Kate eyed Joseph. "Want to dance?"

"Peyton, hold up." She paused. Joseph glanced at Xavier. "Is there a bodyguard on you outside?"

"No. I'm going from here to home. I'll be fine." He jerked his chin at Peyton. "Stay on her."

Rising, jaw set, Joseph's gaze searched the room while they waited. Eventually, he nodded. "Just stay at the table, then." He set his hand on Kate's back. "Come on, Red."

Peyton went with Justin, staying close to Joseph. Halfway to the dance floor, she glanced over her shoulder.

Xavier sat by himself, eyes cast on the table, and finger circling the rim of his scotch snifter.

Chapter Five

With Joseph assisting a very inebriated Kate off the elevator, Xavier hoisted a tipsy Peyton closer to his side and followed. She staggered and he nearly went down, but caught them both in time.

Outside the gals' respective apartments, Joseph glanced between the two doors as if torn. "Let me get her inside and I'll be right back."

"Take your time. I'll be with her." Xavier nudged his chin at Peyton.

Kate giggled and buried her face in Joseph's chest. "You're not staying?"

He glanced at the top of her auburn head. "Not while you're three sheets, Red. Another time, definitely."

Both women laughed and swayed. Peyton pointed at Joseph. "He's got a thing for redheads. He told me so."

Xavier ran his tongue over his teeth and glanced at his bodyguard. "At least they're happy drunks."

"Rodger that."

Somehow, Xavier managed to dig Peyton's keys from her purse and unlock the door, while Joseph did the same with Kate's.

Peyton halted over the threshold. "How did these get here?" Her head swiveled, gaze following the cluster of balloons and the million floral arrangements from her office now littering her living room.

"I brought them by on my way to the bar."

A dreamy sigh passed her lips. "You're so nice. You know that, X?"

"Yep." He was a real saint.

Cinching her closer to his side, he kicked the door shut and walked her toward her bedroom, flicking on a living room lamp along the way.

She stopped abruptly. "Wait. I have to take out my contacts first. I can't sleep in them. I got an eye infection last time."

"All right." Understanding completely, he pivoted and stepped with her into the bathroom, where she sat on the toilet lid. She'd only had two drinks and wasn't nearly as sloshed as Kate, but he questioned her ability to do something as elemental as walking, never mind a bedtime routine. She had zero tolerance, it seemed. "Can you take your lenses out by yourself?"

"Yes." She poked herself in the eye. "Ow."

That would be a no. Laughing—because, mercy, he'd never seen her tipsy—he rooted around in her mirrored cabinet to find her supplies. Now he knew why she only accepted one glass of champagne at work events. Finding what he needed, he poured solution into her case and glanced around.

Her bathroom was smaller than a postage stamp. Mint green walls, white cabinets, and a leaf-pattern shower curtain. Not a lot of room to maneuver. Since the toilet faced the bathtub and they were nearly on top of one another, he sat in front of her on the tub edge.

"Hold still. I've never taken anyone else's contacts out before."

She offered a serious nod, which only made him grin wider. Damn, but she was adorable.

Gently, he held her lower and upper lid open. "Blink." She complied, and the lens popped onto his fingertip. He did the same with the other eye and closed her case, setting it next to a candle on her vanity.

When he turned back, she was attempting to find the zipper on her boots. "I remember these being easier to get off than on."

Shaking his head, he reclaimed the spot in front of her and set her foot in his lap. Then, he got caught up in the way her skinny jeans molded to her toned legs and how the boots had screwed with his head half the night. Well, that and her open-back shirt. And her hair falling around her shoulders.

"Don't you like them?" She blinked. "You have that worry line of concentration—" she pressed a finger between his brows "—right here. That's the X is frustrated face." Her red lips mockingly pouted.

"I like them." He loved them, actually. So much, he got a whole slew of fantasies in mind that would send him straight to hell. Focusing on the task, he released the zipper and tugged off the boot. Underneath, she on had pink socks with little hearts on them.

"Oh, don't look at my socks. They don't match my outfit."

A laugh huffed from his chest. "Consider my eyes averted." He removed her other boot and set them aside. "Anything else?"

She tilted her head and looked at him through sleepy eyes. "Do I still have on makeup? Kate decided I needed to look like a hooker. I figured, it's my birthday, why not?" She paused. "Do I look like a hooker?"

"No to the hooker and yes to the makeup." She had on more cosmetics than her norm, and yes, she looked amazing. But slutty? Hell, she could make a burlap sack classy.

"There's remover pads in the vanity."

Whatever those were. Standing, he fished through the cabinet and found aspirin. He put two in his hand and filled a glass with water. "Here."

Blink. "Those aren't to remove makeup."

"Take them. You'll thank me in the morning."

A shrug, and she downed the medicine.

He rooted in her cabinet again, sifting through the contents. The intimacy wasn't lost on him. No matter how long a period he'd dated someone, he'd never done something so personal.

There. A small, round jar marked—imagine that—makeup remover pads. He handed her the container, but she stared blankly at it.

Right. Sitting in front of her, he unscrewed the lid and pried a wipe from the stack. Okay, this wasn't rocket science, but he assumed he just...what? Wiped her face with the thing? He read the directions on the jar.

"Uh, close your eyes." After she complied, he gently swiped the pad across her eyelid. Except it smeared, giving her raccoon shadows.

Perhaps this *was* too complicated. He kept at it until all the gray charcoal whatever was gone. Tossing the wipe, he grabbed another and did the other eye, then repeated the process with her lips.

And...man. If he thought digging through her vanity was intimate, doing this was akin to watching her undress. Slowly, the party Peyton disappeared and the natural her emerged. He'd only seen her without cosmetics a handful of times because she usually wore it for work. The few exceptions had been early in the morning while traveling for something company related. Seeing her in this moment felt different. Like he was privy to something private.

He set the container on the vanity. Her eyes opened, and she studied him, her expression unreadable.

He took in her pretty face, and his heartbeat picked up rhythm. For two years, he'd acknowledged her beauty, if only to himself, and accepted his attraction. The pull had never really been a factor while working closely with her. He'd kept it safely tucked away in a file labeled in-your-dreams.

But lately, it seemed like the magnetism had been amplified, and he had no clue why or what had changed. And she'd given off subtle vibes, as well. He'd swear to all that was holy, he was delusional and misreading her. Yet, even right now, those baby blues were staring at him with...

Christ, he couldn't go there. Not with her.

He dropped his focus to her necklace. Not helpful. Because he'd given her that particular piece and his mind kept shoving at him the memory of her teary eyes, her body pressed to his when she'd hugged him. Her scent. Her soft skin.

Damn it. What happened to all the air?

"What's wrong?" Her breathy voice grabbed him by the short hairs. "You haven't done that in a long time. Do I make you nervous?"

He cleared the sand from his throat. "Done what?" She was one of four people on planet Earth he was comfortable around. Thus, the sudden tension in his shoulders and the fact she noticed his nervousness, even while intoxicated, could not be a good omen.

"You're picking a focus point and staring." She fingered the charm, and his gaze flew to hers. "You only do that if I'm not in sight or if you're uncomfortable. I'm right here."

As if he didn't know that with every atom in his body. "I'm fine. Did you have a good birthday?"

Her features relaxed into a sweet smile. "The best." Then she knocked him straight into cardiac malfunction by cupping his cheeks and resting her forehead against his. Her breath smelled faintly of fruit and bathed his face. "I loved my present. That necklace and bracelet and..." She moaned. "No one's ever done anything so considerate for me before."

There wasn't a solitary soul he'd encountered who wasn't completely enamored by her charm or her wit or her infectious personality. Ergo, he very much doubted her claim. And if she didn't stop touching him, he was going to lose it. Just the sound of her breathing was killing him.

"Oh, X. That cupcake? I couldn't even bring myself to eat it. I..." Her eyes filled.

Save him. Not tears. Please.

Gently, he gripped her wrists and lowered her hands. Speaking of cupcakes... "What did you wish for when you blew out the candle?" Kate's comment about Peyton never asking for anything for herself had stayed with him. It was just like her, too. Who else, in this day and age, would do something so selfless as to—

"I made a wish for you." She squeezed his fingers and offered a sleepy smile. "Don't tell anyone or it won't come true."

"Okay." Except his brain misfired and his heart stuttered. Because hadn't she just said she'd... "You made a wish on my behalf?" What would possess her to do that? He had his health, a great family, a thriving company, and enough money to buy the state of Delaware.

She hummed—that sexy as hell sound which rendered breathing impossible—and pressed her cheek to his. "For love. You are noble and kind and smart. I wished for you to find a woman you could be yourself around and who doesn't play games or have an agenda."

Damn her to oblivion and back. He almost said she'd just described herself, but she turned her head and...have mercy, put their lips a breathy whisper apart.

His lungs emptied. "Peyton, honey. What are you doing?" He shook with restraint, trying everything in his arsenal not seal the millimeter of distance, and closed his eyes. Her sensual perfume wasn't helping an iota.

"You've never called me that before. Honey."

Yeah, well, the endearment described her with precision. Sweet as sin and able to cause a sticky situation if allowed in direct contact.

"I'm..." Hard as granite and aching something fierce. "Confused." Yeah, that, on top of a plethora of other things. He couldn't grab reality if he attempted the task with both hands.

"Sorry. I forgot you don't like to be touched." Yet, she brushed her nose with his and didn't pull away.

"That's..." Not true. "I do like to be touched." Specifically, by her. But she was tipsy on alcohol and he was drunk on her. She was the one woman off limits to him. He needed the strength to—

The front door closed, and he jerked away from her. He rose, grabbed the countertop as dots invaded his peripheral, and sucked oxygen like a man starved.

"Knock, knock." Joseph's footsteps padded in the hallway.

"In here." Xavier swiped a hand down his face. Shook from the inside out. Adjusted his erection.

"Everything kosher? Did she get sick?" Joseph leaned against the doorjamb.

"No, she's fine." But he wasn't. He cast a glance her way, and her eyes were closed as if sleeping upright. "Help her to bed, would you? I have to go." He eased around his bodyguard and down the hallway.

"Hold on. With no security, I should walk you out."

Xavier shook his head. "The limo's waiting out front. I'll ride back to the house. Just...stay with her. Please."

"Are you okay?" Joseph frowned. "You're pale."

"I'm fine."

After Joseph went into the bathroom, Xavier waited in the hallway a moment, listening to their muted voices, then he stopped in her living room on the way out. The urge to go battled with a need to stay.

Unsure what had come over him, he glanced around. It had been a few months since he'd been here. They didn't hang out at her place often. Usually, they wound up at his house or the hidden apartment attached to his office when not on company time.

Her salary at Gaines Industries was high. Beyond competitive. He'd made sure of that, along with other amenities. Yet, she lived in a one bedroom apartment roughly seven-hundred square feet. Her cream-colored missionary furniture was relatively new, as were the bare oak tables. Her walls were a pale yellow, and she had a multi-tone red and orange rug on the hardwood floor. A too-small twenty-inch plasma was perched on a corner cabinet. She had magazines and books on an abundance of available flat surfaces.

The decor matched her personality—warm and inviting. But why the hell she wouldn't buy a house or move to a larger place was beyond him. The utter lack of security had been a bone of contention for him for over two years.

Her kitchen—laughable, that—was separated from the living room by a half-wall. She probably had to hold her breath just to turn in the space. Two-burner stove, white countertops, honey maple cabinets. She'd added splashes of her personality, like a Swedish Chef cookie jar and magnets with crazy sayings.

With a sigh, his gaze landed on several floating wall shelves by the TV, and he stepped closer. There were quite a few pictures of her and Kate—one from many years ago when Peyton's hair had been short. He preferred it long, but it was cute either way. A full family photo from before her parents had died, and more of her and Brian, occupied a shelf. She and Joseph smiled at the camera in another shot. It looked like a selfie taken in her office.

There were two of Xavier and her together. One was from a benefit where she wore a long navy dress, him in a tux. In the other, they were posed near the vineyard at his folks' place in Napa.

Taking the latter picture off the shelf, he studied it. All of his professional images were unsmiling, and the ones from the media at charity events or press conferences had him in a polite grin. Thanks to her, he was more comfortable with crowds. Before she'd joined the company, he couldn't remember a single shot where he didn't look like he'd been blackmailed to attend.

But the photo in Napa? His parents had snapped it two years ago when Xavier and Peyton had visited for the weekend to discuss the Fallen Veterans benefit. Or, that's how the trip had begun. Very little planning for his charity had actually been conquered. It was the first time she'd met his folks and, swear to God, they'd adored her more than unicorns, rainbows, or raindrops on damn roses. Still did.

In jeans and a t-shirt, he stood next to her, head turned mid-laugh and hands in his back pockets. For the life of him, he couldn't remember what she'd spouted that had been so hilarious. She had her head tilted and a I-didn't-do-it grin on her face while the sun caught her white sundress. His family was his comfort zone, but he hated having his picture taken. Thus, it was rare to catch him off-guard and relaxed. Certainly not this...happy.

He flinched. When *was* the last time he could recall being happy?

Footsteps sounded behind him, and he turned.

Joseph studied the photo over Xavier's shoulder. "You don't smile like that very often."

He grunted and replaced the picture. "That's why I hired her. She finds the human factor the world can't see."

Moving to the sofa, Joseph sat and stretched his legs. "She asked me today if, after working so closely with you, I ever found myself attracted to you."

Xavier laughed and took a seat on the other end of the couch. "And you told her no. I'm not exactly anyone's type." Take rich and good-looking out of the equation, he wouldn't have a leg to stand on. None of his relationships worked out for that reason. It had taken him a year to let Joseph scratch under the surface to see the real him as a friend. Women were more complicated.

"No, I said you weren't *my* type." Joseph's brows arched. "I'm more interested in *why* she asked. Perhaps she's been battling some attraction herself?"

Dipping his chin, he narrowed his eyes. "Derail that thought train right now." Not only was the suggestion ludicrous, but... "Nothing can or will happen between us."

"Whatever you say." Joseph shrugged. "She danced with that guy Justin tonight and yet she kept looking at you."

Xavier doubted that. Very much.

He closed his eyes and pinched the bridge of his nose. He really didn't need a reminder of the shitty sensation he'd gotten in his gut watching her dance. With someone else. She may resemble a mythical angel, but she moved like an x-rated wet dream. And the waiter had been all over her.

Flirting and seduction of that sort were completely out of Xavier's realm. Naked and one-on-one? He had complete control and knew what he was doing. No orgasm unconquered or scream of pleasure unbidden. Out of the bedroom? Not so much.

Joseph shifted on the couch. "I've been with you going on five years, and she's the first person besides me you drop your guard around. Or who makes you grin like an idiot."

What she'd said in the bathroom about her birthday wish slapped him in the face—*for you to find a woman you could be yourself with...who doesn't play games or have an agenda.*

Mercy, he couldn't do this. Even entertaining the notion could blow his whole world out of the water. He shook his head and rose. "Did she get to bed all right?"

"Why don't you go find out?"

It took every ounce of restraint in his exhausted body not to glance in the direction of the hallway. Because, yeah, he wanted to do just what his bodyguard suggested.

"Relax." Joseph stood and made his way to the door, holding it open for Xavier. "She's fine. Nothing eight solid hours and a bottle of ibuprofen won't cure."

"Ibuprofen upsets her stomach," he mumbled, his usual filter unable to click into place.

"I'll make a note of that."

Xavier left before he'd need a full lobotomy to forget the night.

She didn't call the rest of the weekend, which wasn't unusual, and he left her alone. By the time Monday rolled around, he was jumping out of his skin to see how she behaved in his presence. That moment in her bathroom was on constant repeat in his mind, but he wondered if she'd even remember what had happened, considering her intoxication.

Chapter Six

Peyton typed notes on her device as the magazine rep chattered through her phone earpiece. She'd put in several calls to GQ early in her time at the company, but they'd blown her off. Apparently, a couple years and building Xavier's image had done wonders. Not only were they interested, but the promotion they were proposing could kick-start a whole new rash of donations for his charity.

She bit her lip. "When were you looking to do an interview?"

Daniel made a whining sound like he was thinking too hard. He had a loud voice, and though she'd never met him face-to-face, he had aw-shucks written all over him. "The sooner the better. I was looking to have this done for next month's issue. Initially, we were seeking January, but with the big veterans benefit weekend coming up in October, I shifted things around. How's next week?"

"Let me check." She paged through Xavier's appointment itinerary. "Tuesday looks good. How much time do you want and are you in need of photos?"

"We'd do our own shoot. After the interview, most likely. This is a five-page spread, so allot me at least a few hours to chat with him." Typing clicked in the background while her jaw dropped at the space they were talking. "I also want to sit down with you."

She straightened in her seat. "Why?"

"You're one of the closest people to him. We'd like some quotes to place throughout."

Sitting back in her chair, she strummed her fingers on her desk. "Let me discuss that with Mr. Gaines. Call it a maybe for now. We also reserve the right to refuse to answer any questions I'm uncomfortable with."

"I'm told you're present for all his interviews, so I was expecting as much." More typing. "Tuesday at ten? How's that? I'll come to you. We'll discuss the shoot's location at that time."

Xavier knocked on her door.

She waved him in and stood. "Bring your photographer along. We can find somewhere in the building. Mr. Gaines isn't fond of shoots."

"Works for me if the photographer is good with it." Daniel's voice dipped an octave. "I'm looking very forward to this, Miss Smoke."

She laughed. "I'll just bet you are. We are, as well. I'll see you Tuesday, Daniel."

Peyton tapped her earpiece to disconnect and looked at Xavier from across her desk. "You are never going to freakin' believe this. Guess who's getting a five page spread in GQ. And just in time to boost hype for the Fallen Veterans charity weekend."

His smile was stiff, as it had been all morning. "Good work." He set a long garment box on a chair and took a seat. "You look no worse for wear after your big birthday weekend."

Concern twisted her belly. Utter and sheer mortification heated her cheeks. She'd all but thrown herself at him in her bathroom, and he was obviously out of sorts about it. Other than a couple drinks, she had no idea what had come over her.

"I'm totally embarrassed."

His golden gaze cut to hers with a hardening of his jaw.

She could count on one hand the number of times she'd seen him angry. But he didn't seem just mad. Confusion and unease radiated in his eyes, too. And...shoot. She'd gone and upset their very well choreographed unit. Somehow, she had to put things right, no matter how turned on she'd been.

Peyton, honey...

She shook her head, and his low, coarse voice from memory. "I hope I didn't do anything too humiliating. I can't seem to remember anything after my second drink." She hated the white lie, but he needed to think balance had been restored. Hopefully, he'd chalk the whole thing up to drunken confusion.

His eyes widened for a fraction of a beat, then his shoulders sagged. A grin split his handsome face, and her girly parts wept. "You were as charming as always. Nothing to concern yourself about."

Just like that, they were normal again. She didn't know whether to be relieved or mourn.

"I brought your dress for Saturday. It just arrived." He pointed to the box beside him.

"Ooh. Let's have a look." She rounded her desk.

Since event apparel fell into the category of work expenses, and she shuddered at the designer price tags, he'd been picking out her evening wear for benefits the whole time she'd worked for Gaines Industries. And he never allowed her to wear the same one twice. She had a closet filled with thousands of dollars in garments going to waste. He had great freakin' taste. To date, there hadn't been one dress she'd disliked.

Lifting the lid to the black box, she gasped. "Oh, X. It's lovely." Pale pink silk. Saturday's charity was for breast cancer research and, thus, the color choice. Carefully, she removed it to check out the design. Strapless, it was an imperial cut and floor-length. "I don't know how you always get my size right, too."

"Call it a gift. Mathematical mind."

Laughing, she folded the dress back in the box and reset the lid. "I'm sure Gloria at the boutique is of some help."

The low rumble of his laugh skated across her skin. "Busted. For the record, I do choose the dress myself."

Reclaiming her seat, she sighed. "Quick question. GQ wants to interview me, as well. Said they want quotes to use."

He shrugged. "I trust you."

"A photo shoot is required, too."

"I heard that much." He frowned. "I'll deal. You'll be there?"

She nodded. "For all of it."

"Then, I'm good." He rubbed his jaw, gaze drifting like it did when lost in thought. "Do you want to get together Friday night? We can go over the press conference for next week."

If conferences regarding the government contracts were scheduled, she often prepped him thoroughly beforehand outside the office. It made him less nervous. "I can't. I have a date."

He reared. His gaze dipped to her necklace, his lips parting as if he was having trouble getting air.

Crap. What was wrong? "X?"

He shook his head. "Sorry. Two phrases I almost never hear you utter, and you just said both. I'm waiting for the sky to fall."

"Ha. It's Justin, so I doubt anything will come of it." Between drink one and two, he'd asked her out on her birthday. Though surprised, she hadn't seen the harm.

"The bartender?"

"Yeah. I'll come over on Sunday and prep you then." Her earpiece beeped once, indicating a call from the front desk. "Hold on." She tapped the headset. "What's up, Fern?"

"Mrs. Gaines is on the line."

"Does she want me or Mr. Gaines?"

"She asked for you."

Hm. "Patch her through. Thank you." She looked at Xavier. "Your mom is calling me."

Leaning back in the chair, he shrugged in a what-else-is-new.

"Hi, Elaine. It's Peyton. How are you?"

"I'm great, dear." Her smooth, affectionate tone always hit Peyton right in her breastbone. Both Xavier's parents had been utterly kind to her from the first time they'd met, and treated her like family instead of their son's employee. For a woman who had no relatives left, it meant a lot. "I was wondering if you both could come up for the weekend to discuss the details for the benefit?"

Fallen Veterans was technically Xavier's organization, but it was run by his parents ever since his father had retired. Peyton pulled up their schedule. "We can't this weekend, but the following is open. He's sitting right here. Let me ask." She relayed the plans to him and he nodded approval. "His majesty says okay."

Xavier narrowed his eyes playfully as Elaine's smooth laugh filled Peyton's ear. "Perfect. I can't wait to see you."

"Me, too. Can I ride the horses? Can I?" The Gaines' had three geldings on their vast estate, and Peyton, having never been around a horse before visiting Napa, was in love with them.

Xavier smothered a laugh with his hand.

"Of course, you can. Now, make my son leave your office. I have something secret to discuss."

Peyton grinned. "Oh, how James Bond of you. Xavier, go away now."

Obviously confused, he rose. She waved her hand to stop him and pointed to the chair. With a make-up-your-mind scowl, he sat back down.

"Okay, he's gone. What's the secret?" She grinned at Xavier's eye roll.

"Well, the first week of November is his birthday, and I'd like to throw him a surprise party. He turns thirty this year. I was thinking his house as the venue. He'd be comfortable there."

Oh. God. In. Heaven. He was going to kill her. Dead.

She hesitantly met Xavier's eyes. "A surprise birthday party at his house?"

He paled seven shades. Eyes bugging, he shook his head.

She winced. "What a lovely idea, but he's not real big on surprises. Or parties." Or people in general, really. He wasn't fond of acknowledging his birthday, either. He'd put up a stink when she'd gotten him gifts.

Undeterred, Elaine *pffed*. "I know, but just something small. Family and friends."

He was okay around family, but he didn't have many friends that weren't employed by him. "An intimate family and friends gathering?"

Xavier made a slashing motion and bared teeth, mouthing *no way in hell*.

"Why are you repeating everything I say?"

She rubbed her forehead. "Um, I'm just taking notes."

"Of course, you are. You're so efficient." Elaine gave a pleasant sigh. "I have to run, dear. We can finalize plans when you drive up. See you soon."

Peyton opened her mouth, but the line was dead. So was she if Xavier's expression was any indication. "Remember, manslaughter is a crime."

Jaw ticking, he glared at her.

She pouted. It was so, so very wrong she found him sexy as heck angry. All fierce and…rawr. "She came to me. It wasn't my idea. And I'll make sure she doesn't go overboard."

Not so much as an eye tick.

"Come on, X." She batted her lashes. "I'll get you a really awesome present. And we can work on your surprise face." She demonstrated with a shocked expression, waving her hands.

He closed his eyes and growled. "Cute won't save you." He leveled his gaze back on her. At her intensified pout, he groaned. "Stop with the puppy eyes."

She grinned because the vein in his forehead had finally stopped bulging.

Standing, he buttoned his suit coat. "This is unforgivable." His sullen expression relayed he was kidding, but she still felt bad.

"You know I can't say no to your mom."

He shoved his hands in his pockets. "You say no a hundred times a day to a hundred different people. Interview requests, invitations, donations, etcetera. And you make them think it was their privilege to be denied."

"But they're not *your mom*." She slapped the desk. "She's all nice and sneaky and...nice." Deflating, she dropped her chin in her hand. "Have I ever let you down? I promise, I'll keep her reined."

He grunted. One eyebrow quirked. "By what? Saying no?"

"Touché. At least you have people who love you enough to care about throwing you a party." He had no idea how lucky he was to have family, and a wonderful one, at that.

Once upon a time, she and Mark had wanted to start one. His relatives refused to talk to her after the funeral, either because they blamed her for his suicide or it was too difficult to be around her. What she wouldn't give to have someone besides Kate. Holidays sucked all by herself and it was rather pathetic. Nights. Weekends. Yada.

Loneliness clutched her chest.

Like a switch, all tension left Xavier's frame, and he sighed. "Shit, Peyton. You're right. I'm sorry." His brows slammed together and stark, raw emotion filled his eyes. "I..."

Great. Pity from him. "Forget I said anything. I'll find a way to slam the brakes on anyone but family for the party, okay?"

"Peyton..."

Her earpiece beeped twice, meaning an outside call not routed through reception. "Damn, I'm popular today." She tapped the headset. "Peyton Smoke."

"Hi, Miss Smoke. It's Carson from downstairs. I've got something on that email you queried about. Should I come up to you?"

She snapped her fingers to get Xavier's attention and stop him from leaving. "No, Mr. Gaines and I will meet you in your office. We'll be down in a few minutes." Disconnecting, she looked at him. "That was IT. They have info about the email." She chewed her lip.

"He called me direct instead of through the front desk. The staff never do that."

Mouth firm, he pulled his cell from his breast pocket and summoned Joseph to meet them downstairs. "Let's go."

Her stomach was a tangled jumble of nerves in the elevator. She'd thought the email was just another line in nonsense, but her gut said something else now. Awareness crept up her neck, making her hair stand on end.

Xavier set a reassuring hand low on her back to guide her to the floor. "It'll be all right."

She nodded and strode toward Carson's office deep in the tech department. Beeps and mouse clicks echoed in the room, and the faint scent of burnt coffee clung to the air as they passed many cubicles. Joseph and Carson waited for them just inside the entryway to his office.

Xavier shut the door behind them as they crammed into the small space littered with folders and computer gear. "What have you got?"

"So..." Carson ran his fingers through his longish brown hair, the motion stretching his polo shirt across his round belly. "We know the email came from our server. It had the distinct @ corporation address. The email pinged Miss Smoke's box at seven p.m. The account was created at six-thirty, then promptly deleted at seven-o-five."

He sat and faced the desk, his fingers flying over the keyboard. A black screen with white code popped onto the monitor. "It took me awhile of digging, but IP showed which desktop the email originated."

Xavier's hard gaze zipped over the screen as if he were reading a novel. "That can't be right."

"It is." Carson sighed. "This code hasn't been tampered with. The email came from Miss Smoke's office."

"What?" She stepped back and her knees wobbled. "I don't understand." The room spun, and she couldn't draw breath. Someone had been in her office? With all her files and personal things? Violated, she ran a hand over her stomach.

Xavier cupped her shoulder and squeezed in a silent show of support. "Our offices are locked at the end of the day. In fact, our whole floor is shut down. You need an elevator key to access it."

What about the obvious? "I didn't send that email."

Carson nodded. "I know. Which is why I went to security and looked at the digital feed." His fingers flew over the keys again. A grainy black and white video popped on the screen. "This is from the camera above the elevator." He pointed. "Note that it covers most of the reception lobby and the hallway to your offices. Watch. This is time stamped at six twenty-five."

The semi-dark room showed a figure at the bottom of the screen walk off the elevator and down the hall. They used a key to enter Peyton's office. Recognition dawned, and Peyton shook her head. No. It couldn't be.

"It's dark and hard to make out the person." Carson forwarded the video. "Now, this is at seven ten."

The same person walked out of her office, relocked the door, and headed toward the elevator. This time, clearly in view.

Carson paused the feed. "There's your culprit."

The air punched from her lungs. "Oh God." She looked at Xavier, whose gaze had hardened at the screen. "Fern? She wouldn't do something like that. She's worked for you as long as Joseph."

Xavier's gaze cut to Carson. "Get me copies of this."

"Already done, sir." Carson handed him a folder. "That has the codes, a copy of the email, the time stamps, and a disc of the security feed."

"Thank you. You did great work. Keep this quiet, please."

Carson nodded.

Xavier passed Joseph the evidence folder and guided Peyton out of the office, his movements stiff. Joseph followed them onto the elevator. On numb legs, she watched him insert a key into the lock and stall the car with them inside.

He glared at his bodyguard. "What the actual fuck?"

Joseph shook his head. "I don't know." Gaze dialed to holy-shit, he looked at Peyton. "Has Fern said or done anything to give you a reason for this?"

"No!" Tears brimmed her eyes, and she choked. "I went to her daughter's Christmas concert last year. She's always been nothing but sweet to me. I mean, she's a little weird, but I never felt threatened by her." She wiped her cheeks with a shaking hand. "Just this morning, she bought me a latte."

Even if this had been some sick prank, the betrayal sliced deep.

Xavier pressed his palms to his eyes. "This is going to be a nightmare." He slapped his hands to his thighs. "Never mind the inner office gossip, but if the press catches wind *my* personal secretary was escorted out of the building by police—"

"Police?" She eyed the two of them. "You're going to have her arrested?"

"Damn right. She threatened you." Xavier's enraged glare pinned her in place.

Knowing she'd never talk him out of it, she chewed her lip. "I'll deal with the media. I'll send out a statement. Human resources, too, for within the company."

"I don't want you giving the press a statement." His gaze slid to hers. "The email was sent to you. If there's a leak about the details, a Gaines Industries explanation will have more weight from me."

She blew out a shaky breath. "Okay. I'll prepare something—"

"I'll deal with it."

But…he never wrote his own statements.

Nodding, she glanced at the floor, her head swimming. Xavier was set to blow and a co-worker she considered a friend had sent her a heinously violent note. She couldn't form a tangible thought to save her life.

Rubbing his bald head, Joseph sighed. "In the mean time, Fern needs to be handled."

Chapter Seven

Hands on his hips, Xavier rode the elevator to his floor with two officers, two security guards, Joseph, and Peyton in tow.

What a clusterfuck. It was bad enough to learn she'd gotten a threatening email from within his company, but to learn that threat had come from his own secretary of four years was pure, unadulterated shit. No signs. No signals. Nothing to indicate the woman was a lunatic.

He thought of all the times Peyton and Fern had been alone in the office, all the opportunities she'd had to hurt Peyton. Nauseous, he closed his eyes for a beat.

Concern clenched his gut. The police would, no doubt, not be able to hold Fern on much. She had no criminal record and the email could be passed off as a joke. Which meant, if she really wanted to, Fern could have the freedom to go after Peyton. The fact she hadn't done anything so far but send an email was of little solace.

The elevator stopped and the doors swished open. At seeing the entourage, Fern rose to her feet from behind her desk and hung up the phone.

File in hand, he strode closer. "It's come to my attention that you sent this to Miss Smoke." He passed her the printed copy of the original email.

Fern, gaze wide, scanned the paper. After a moment, her jaw set and cool fury lit her eyes. Saying nothing, she handed the paper back.

Xavier nodded, barely leashing his rage. "Your employment is terminated. Security will escort you off the premises and the police have questions for you. Personal items will be delivered to your home address within twenty-four hours. Hand over your keys and badge."

Something akin to crazy twisted her face and her tinny voice rose. "You believe her over me?" Her sharp gaze darted over his shoulder.

"Don't look at her." Irrational panic narrowed his airway. He sucked oxygen through flared nostrils, his temples throbbing. "Yes, I believe Miss Smoke, and there's evidence to back up her claim even if I didn't. Badge and keys. Now." He was just irate enough to ring Fern's scrawny neck until her wild brown hair flew into more chaos. He wouldn't miss the dowdy wardrobe, either.

She shook her head as if in disbelief. "It's always about her, isn't it?"

Peyton's quiet gasp was like a shot in his ears, and he tensed to the point of pain.

Later. He'd take care of Peyton later. That was a goddamn promise. Knowing her, she was taking this personally and blaming herself.

Fern grabbed her purse from a drawer, plopping it unceremoniously on the desk. "Four years, and then that bitch comes along. *Miss Perfect* this and *Miss Perfect* that. All her annoying cheer. It's sickening. Did you ever stop to thank me for all I did? No. Ever think to promote me as your personal assistant? No."

He didn't bother correcting the nutcase that Peyton was media relations director, not a damn assistant. And three times as qualified for the position. Never mind the fact he'd given Fern a hefty Christmas bonus every year.

Fern smacked a white keycard in front of him, followed by a keyring.

Distracted by grabbing the items, he didn't realize her intention until it was too late. With a screech that rattled his ears, she palmed a stapler and threw it over his shoulder. Breath in his throat, he turned in time to watch it hit Peyton square in the temple.

His lungs collapsed.

She cried out in pain—a sound he'd never unhear, no matter how hard he tried—and pressed a hand to the spot. Wide, shocked eyes besought Fern's as if to ask why.

His bodyguard stepped in front of Peyton and pulled her to the side, blocking her from Xavier's view. The officers surrounded Fern. Handcuffs and Miranda rights followed. She wailed and spit and fought their hold. They hauled her to the elevator and waited.

Postal didn't cover it. Xavier's chest heaved and his vision grayed. Homicide charge? Hell, it would be worth it. "Joseph, get Miss Smoke out of here. Go to my office."

But he was already enroute, an arm over her head as they disappeared swiftly down the hallway. All Xavier could think about as he stared after them was whether she was okay. Did she need an ambulance? Alarm battled with wrath inside his head.

Fists clenched, he eyed the guards. "What's the status outside?"

Duane, the taller one, used a walkie-talkie to inquire. Seconds later, the thing crackled and a voice answered.

"We've got about ten reporters and a small group of pedestrians. Another San Francisco squad is standing by."

Damn police scanners. Media used them like beacons.

Xavier pinched the bridge of his nose. The sooner he dealt with that mess, the sooner he could check on Peyton. She was safe with Joseph, in good hands, but he wasn't Xavier. And this was all his fault.

They headed downstairs, through the main lobby and to the curb as a group. Xavier watched quietly as Fern was loaded into the back of a cruiser. Reporters migrated like geese until the squad disappeared around a corner, then they flocked to him.

With security guards on either side of him, he raised a hand for silence. "I'll make a brief statement and I'd appreciate no questions." He glanced at the faces in the crowd, at the buildings lining the street. He was too pissed off to be nervous, and he feared he'd never calm down.

He cleared his throat. "As you can see, we had a bit of an incident today. No one was hurt and everyone is safe. This was an internal matter that has been dealt with. That's all I'm going to say for now. Thank you."

Questions fired at him as he strode back inside. Cameras flashed, but he ignored them.

Out of public view, he faced the security guards in the hallway. "Keep an extra man down here the rest of the week. I also want someone posted on the top floor until further notice. I'll let HR know about overtime or adding more help." At their nod, he forced himself to look them in the eye like Peyton had taught him. It was still a struggle at times. "You did great work today. I appreciate it."

"Thank you, sir," they both said in unison.

He found the two lobby receptionists and offered a stiff smile, focusing on the one he recognized better. "Can you have all calls from the upstairs line forwarded down here?"

"Sure thing, Mr. Gaines. Miss Smoke already asked. It's been done." The blonde with the short hair nodded. Jackie, he thought was her name.

Wait. How had Peyton gotten on top of that already? He fisted the coin in his pocket. "Thank you." He sighed. "We're going to be getting a ton of calls. If the press inquires, just state no comment."

"Miss Smoke had us do that, too. We're on it, Mr. Gaines. No problem."

Again, with Peyton. He glanced at the ceiling and frowned as if he could see her through the floors. "Can you please also reschedule the afternoon appointments on her docket and mine?"

"Consider it done, Mr. Gaines."

"Thank you." He went to head toward the elevators and paused. "One more thing. Tomorrow morning, before you report here, come up to my office, would you?"

Jackie, if he remembered her name correctly, had been a smiling face as he entered the building every day for at least the past twelve months. Best he could recall, she was always neatly dressed and had a pleasant tone. She appeared to be efficient and might be an optimal replacement for Fern, plus he preferred someone orientated to the company.

The receptionist's smile faltered. "Sure, sir. Is nine okay?"

"You're not in trouble, and nine is perfect. Just come right up." He smiled, nodded, and found the elevator. Punching the up arrow, he checked his cell.

No calls from Joseph or Peyton. Concern had him gnashing his molars. Visions of that damn stapler flying through the air skyrocketed his pulse. Jesus, he hoped she was all right.

Back on his floor, he made haste toward his office, only to find Joseph standing outside, pacing.

"She hasn't stopped moving. Phone calls and talking a mile a minute. She wouldn't even let me look at her head, which is bleeding. I was giving you five more minutes and then I was going to tackle her."

Shit. Xavier ducked his head in the room. She had her headset on and stalked the length of his office and back, a wad of tissues pressed to her temple.

"Yes, that sounds good. Send the email out to every employee right away." She checked the tissues, winced, and replaced them.

All that red sank his gut to the vicinity of his ankles. He turned to Joseph. "Tell Archie he's relieved for the day." He wouldn't be needing his driver. "And you're free to go, too. Take the rest of today off."

"Are you sure? There's no guarantee they'll hold Fern—"

"Yes. We'll stay in the apartment here." If he had to restrain her, he would. No doubt, she had a concussion and couldn't be alone. He hoped she didn't need stitches.

Xavier walked Joseph to the elevators, saw him out, and locked down the floor. Shutting off the lights, he worked his way back to his office.

She was still pacing. "Correct. No, I already talked to the front desk. Just get interviews set up for the position."

Xavier took the headset from her and stuck it in his own ear. "Can I assume this is Lauren in HR?"

"Yes, Mr. Gaines. Hello."

Peyton huffed. "What are you doing?"

He ignored her. "An email went out to the employees explaining the situation?"

"Yes, sir."

"And you're lining up a replacement for Fern?"

"Yes, sir."

"I want Miss Smoke in on the interviews. There's a receptionist downstairs. Blonde, young, a little pudgy. Jackie, I think? I want her at the top of the list. If she works out, you can hire another downstairs. I have her coming up tomorrow morning at nine."

"Yes, sir."

He eyed a pissed off Peyton. "I approved an extra security personnel in the lobby for this week and a permanent post up here. Last thing. Send Carson in IT a bonus. Same for Duane and Frank at the security desk. Tell accounting I okayed it. I want it done before day's end."

"Yes, sir."

"Miss Smoke and I will be unavailable the rest of the afternoon." He disconnected before another *yes, sir* could form.

Peyton huffed. "I had that handled."

"I know." When wasn't she juggling eight balls at once? Jesus, being in her orbit again finally settled his heart rate, though. He tossed the headset on his desk.

"And what do you mean, we're unavailable?" One tiny hand fell on her slim waist. The other still held a wad of tissues to her head. Her fitted green dress stretched across her ample chest with the motion and he forced his gaze to remain on her face. "I have appointments all—"

"They're being rescheduled."

"What?" She adjusted her glasses. "Says who?"

"Me." Infuriating woman. She was entirely too irresistible all worked up. "You've been threatened, scared, shocked, and injured in the course of two hours. You're taking the rest of the day off, spending the night with me in the apartment where I can watch you for concussion side effects, and you're going to do it without argument. You live alone. What happens if you need something?"

"Damn it, X. I'm not a child and Kate is across the hall."

Unsatisfactory. "Boss card. I'm pulling it. You have two choices. A night here with me in a secure building where I can monitor you, or a trip to the ER and home with two bodyguards. Decide."

She growled, which might've been more effective if she hadn't paled right afterward. "Off-the-clock babysitting isn't job-related. You can't pull the boss card."

"I can and just did." Twice in a week, in fact. Exactly as many times as he'd used it over her two-year employment.

"Why is it necessary to—"

"Because you scared me to death!" Hell. He closed his eyes and drew a much-needed lungful of air.

An email threatening to kill her.
Stapler. Thrown. At. Her. Head.
Blood.

"The incident happened in my building, doled out by one of my staff." He shook his head and looked at her. He'd obviously dropped another bomb by yelling at her because her pretty red mouth hung agape and those gorgeous blue eyes were huge. "I hired her. I hired you. This is my fault. I should've seen the signs and protected you better." He scrubbed a hand down his face. "I think you know you're more to me than just an employee, Peyton. You and Joseph…"

Unable to continue, he dropped his arms in defeat. "I was scared for you."

A shaky exhale passed her lips as she lowered the tissues. "I'm okay," she whispered.

Perhaps, but it would take him longer to get to the same state. He strode over and cupped her shoulders. "Can I look at the cut? See if it needs stitches?"

"Sure," she breathed. Trembling, she blinked up at him. "You've never shouted at me before."

"That was uncalled for. My apologies." He inspected her temple. There was a good size egg and bruise forming. She also had a jagged gash that was about a half inch long, but didn't appear deep. It had stopped bleeding. "No stitches."

Gently, he brushed a loose strand from the area and let his touch linger. He had the strangest urge to press a kiss to her hairline as if that would offer her any comfort. Her scent swirled around him and warmth from her body seeped into his.

"You're more to me than just my boss, too." She peeked at him from over the rim of her glasses and bit her lip. "I don't know, X. I can't define us. Friends?" Her gaze roamed his face and settled on his mouth. The tiniest of wrinkles formed between her brows.

Damn, but there she went again with the vibes. Except this time, she was sober. And…his mouth detached from his brain. "Peyton, honey, we're whatever you say we are."

She hummed, part surprise, part moan. "You did it again. You called me honey."

Yeah, well, thought tended to obliterate when she was this close and… Wait. "Again? I thought you didn't remember."

Her nose scrunched. "I lied. I was out of line on Friday and it obviously disrupted The Force. You were nice enough to help me and I thanked you with unwanted advances."

He didn't know what was hotter, her Star Wars reference or the breathiness with which she spoke it. "Not unwanted." At her confused expression, he said to hell with it. "The advance wasn't unwanted."

"But..."

His brain wailed to abort, demanded common sense, but his body shredded the memo. He lowered his head and kissed her.

She panted against his lips as if she couldn't catch her breath, which only stole his. Cupping her neck, he offered more pressure and dipped into the wet cavern of her mouth to taste her. Just once. It was imperative he do so.

Except the instant her tongue stroked his and she moaned, the algorithms in his hard drive scrambled and his coding short-circuited. Like she'd downloaded a virus right into his system, he got feverishly hot. And hard. Made worse when she pressed against him and gripped the lapels of his suit, aligning their bodies as if they were designed to be merged.

He wrapped an arm around her back and hauled her halfway up his body until she was on tiptoe, and it wasn't close enough. She tasted like the sweet tea she was so fond of drinking. Her hands wove into his hair, teased his nape, and she swayed. Or he did. Honestly, he couldn't even tell if they were still upright.

The first time they'd nearly crossed the line, she'd been drunk. The second was on the backstroke of a head injury. What a stellar gentleman he turned out to be. Damn it.

He pulled away and stared at her, breaths soughing. Shit. "That just happened."

"Yes." Her eyes opened and cerulean irises were all but swallowed by her pupils. She blinked her heavy lids like she was trying to focus, and those long lashes created to drive him to the brink fluttered. "I'd say do it again, but I'm dizzy."

Chapter Eight

After that bone-melting kiss, Xavier walked her to the bookcase in his office, punched a code into the side panel, and a section of the wall opened inward to reveal his apartment. She stepped inside with him and the door closed behind them.

She knew he didn't use the apartment often, just for late nights at the office, and she'd been inside maybe a handful of times. That she was aware, only a few people knew it existed. It had its own private elevator that went straight to the parking garage and a back staircase for emergencies.

The space was an open floor plan, about fifteen hundred square feet, and clinically decorated. Bamboo hardwood, white walls, and gray leather furniture. Black tables accompanied the pieces. No art on the walls, but the living room had floor-to-ceiling windows that faced the Financial District.

He walked into the kitchen, which was separated from the living room by an island. White cabinets and gray tile. He had an array of expensive machines she wondered if he ever used. Cappuccino maker, another coffee pot, heavy mixer, a cocktail dispenser.

He glanced at her. "Pull up a seat. I have a first aid kit around here somewhere. Standby."

She climbed onto one of the high wrought iron stools at the counter while he rummaged in the cabinet closest to the fridge. Digging in her purse for her cell, she pulled it out and texted Kate, just in case her friend noticed she hadn't come home.

"If that's Kate, ask her to pack you a change of clothes for tomorrow. Joseph will stop by in the morning to grab them." He set a bottle of peroxide on the counter along with a white box.

She sent off another text and put the phone away. "I'm fine, you know."

He grunted. "Humor me." He poured peroxide onto a swab, then eyed her. "Can you take off your glasses?" After she'd done what he asked, he stepped close enough for her to climb inside him. "This might sting. And it's cold."

She stared at his white dress shirt just inches from her face. He'd shucked the coat and tie. He smelled so good. Like light aftershave, rain, and warm male. He shifted, raising his arms, and the shirt molded to the edges and dips of lean muscles. One of his hands held the uninjured side of her head, the other perched over her temple, sandwiching her between two solid biceps.

The first swipe burned. The second seared and nearly launched her off the stool. "Ow." Maybe the cut was worse than she'd thought.

"Sorry." The quiet rumble of his voice pulled a shiver from deep inside her. Then, he…God. He blew gently on her temple, and the sweetness of the gesture slammed her eyes shut. "It's pretty swollen. You'll have a nice bruise, too." His upper body eased away from her. "Are you okay? You're quiet."

"Yes." No. He'd kissed her right out of her high heels and was now taking care of her. It had been so long since she'd experienced either, she didn't know what to do. "Just a headache."

"I'll bet." He poured two aspirin into his hand and passed them over with a bottle of water. After he put the supplies away, he came back to stand in front of her with an icepack. She went to take it from him, but he shook his head. "Let me."

Again, he held her head, placing the icepack on one temple and stroking the other with his thumb. "Your pupils seem reactive. Are you dizzy? Nauseous?"

"No. Does stupid and helpless count as side effects?"

"If so, I have them, as well." When she glanced up at him, emotions she couldn't name swam in his golden eyes. He shook his head, his forehead wrinkling. "I'm very sorry this happened."

She shrugged. "It's not your fault. Or mine." She pouted. "Still feel stupid, though." She thought about the things Fern had said. "Am I really chipper and annoying? I don't act like I'm perfect, do I?"

He gave her a placid shake. "Don't you dare let her get to you. Our business correspondents, the staff, my parents…everyone adores you. She's a lunatic trying to justify her jealousy. Nothing more."

"Okay." Yet, the woman's feelings had to have originated somewhere.

His sigh ruffled her hair. "I was so worried about you that I did a press statement on the fly without getting nervous. Granted, I think I said three sentences, but that's progress, right?"

Closing her eyes, she laughed. His self-deprecating humor always made her smile. He didn't give himself enough credit. "I'm very proud. Soon, you won't need me anymore."

He went utterly still, and the thumb stroking her temple twitched.

She opened her eyes to find his gaze on her necklace. "I was only kidding. I'm not quitting. I may demand a stapler ban in the immediate future, but office supplies won't chase me away that easily."

"Peyton." His hands shook. Jaw ticking, he swept his gaze over her face. "I think I'm still unnerved. Forgive me."

"Adrenaline crash. It happens."

His lips parted like he wanted to argue, but he said nothing.

"Talk to me. You'll feel better."

He stared deadpan at her. "I don't think that's wise in this circumstance."

Because he suddenly looked lost, she set her hands on his waist. He sucked a harsh breath like her touch burned. Until now, she'd wondered if the blips of attraction she'd been experiencing were only on her end. But he had kissed her back in his office and she hadn't been the one to start it.

"Honesty, always," she reminded him.

A quiet exhale, and he set the icepack on the counter. His throat worked a swallow. "When you got that email, and again when we found out who it was, all that ran through my mind was insane, irrational fear. I keep thinking about what could've happened if we didn't learn the truth or all the ways she could've easily gotten to you."

Reaching up, he traced his finger across her forehead. "You bring out this protective side of me I don't know what to do with, and I worry it goes beyond a normal office relationship. Friends, maybe, but it's testing those limits, too."

He studied her a beat. "I'm very attracted to you, Peyton. You have to know that, had to have seen it through the years. You're too clever to have missed it. But out of nowhere, you started sending signals and I just..." His lips firmed into a thin line. "I can't keep things professional or friendly when there's no defense against you."

And...wow. No, she hadn't a clue he'd wanted her, and no, she didn't know what to do now that she was aware. "X, I..." Curses. She couldn't make her brain work when he said stuff like that and her body was aching to be against him again. "I didn't have any idea, actually."

He stared at her as if in total disbelief.

Slowly, she slid off the stool. He didn't step away, which brought them in complete alignment, and every nerve in her body fired. His chest rose and fell rapidly, and she went with instinct. Wrapping her arms around him, she buried her face in his chest. After a moment, his arms enveloped her and he rested his chin on top of her head.

"I can't run Gaines Industries without you." His chest rumbled as he spoke, his hands skimming her spine in a caress. "Technically, I can, but I don't want to. Everything that makes my professional life click is due to you. That's why I can't do anything to jeopardize what we have. Am I making sense?"

Perfect sense. To him, playing upon their attraction would splinter his world, crack his foundation. For now, she'd give him some space and let him sort it out. It would be a shame to waste their obvious chemistry, but she cared about him too much to disrupt his life. If they were meant to take a romantic course, she figured his will wouldn't be enough to erect even a speed bump, anyway.

"I'm not going anywhere." She offered a quick squeeze and stepped out of his embrace.

He nodded and checked her temple. "The swelling's down." He looked at her green dress and shoes, then frowned. "I think I've got something more comfortable for you to wear. How about a bath to relax? I can heat up some soup while you do that. Or run downstairs to the cafeteria?"

"Soup's fine. And a bath sounds great." She chewed her lip. "Are you sure you want me staying here? I can make Kate keep an eye on me."

As an answer, he narrowed his eyes, crossed the room, and went into the bedroom. She followed. He opened a dresser drawer and pulled out a tee, tossing it on the queen-size bed in the middle of the room.

"I think that'll be huge on you, but if you need jogging pants or something, just holler. There's an extra toothbrush in the bathroom cabinet. Help yourself to whatever." He rubbed a hand over the back of his neck, tension knotting his frame. His gaze pinged around the room, to the bed, on her, and back again like he was completely shocked to find her in his personal space.

"I repeat, I can go home and stay with Kate."

He ran his tongue over his teeth. "No."

"Then, breathe."

His gaze jerked to hers. The air all but crackled between them. That kiss had lit a match and there was no undoing it. They were going down, one way or the other. She could only hope she didn't ruin the career she loved or the friendship with him in the process. Truly, besides Kate, he was the closest thing to family she had.

"Breathe," she repeated, for herself and him. "Why don't you change, too? It'll make you more comfortable."

With a quick nod, he opened a couple drawers, pulled out a few items, and strode out of the room.

"You can have the bathroom first," she hollered at his back.

"I'm good."

Uh-huh. Grabbing the t-shirt, she walked into the adjoining bath and shut the door. This room, too, was white. Everything. Well, except the towels, which were navy blue and uber soft. And didn't it figure, her living room could fit inside his bathroom.

She checked out her injury in the mirror and winced. The whole temple and part of her forehead was an ugly shade of purple. A small, jagged cut bisected the discoloration.

"That's going to look so pretty tomorrow."

With a sigh, she started bathwater in his enormous, square tub and eyed all the dials. Jet settings, shower, hot water, cold…and one button she couldn't figure out. Curious, she pushed it and hard rock blared from an overhead speaker. Jumping, she squealed and smacked the button to shut it off.

"Of course, he has a stereo in his bathroom. Who doesn't?"

He knocked. "You okay?"

"Yes," she said slowly, embarrassment heating her cheeks. "Your stereo tried to give me a migraine to go with a concussion, but I killed it."

He paused. Laughed. "Soap's in the bottom cupboard. Don't drown." His footsteps padded away.

Funny guy.

She surveyed the selection of products, and they all smelled like him—a combination of rainwater and light cologne. Which was not going to help in eradicating arousal.

Regardless, she used the body wash, soaked in blessedly hot water for twenty minutes, and toweled dry. The t-shirt was dark blue, had the Fallen Veterans logo on the back, and fell to her knees. It covered more than the dress she'd had on, yet she felt naked. She contemplated the thick gray bathrobe hanging on the door, and snatched it on her way out.

Xavier was standing at the stove, stirring a small pot when she emerged. He wore a black pair of sweats that hung low on his hips and a white t-shirt. His dark chestnut hair was in disarray as if he'd run his fingers through it repeatedly. She got more than a little breathless watching the fluid motion of his lean muscles. His casual attire, combined with the domestic task, did something naughty to her girly parts. Her ovaries cried uncle.

Forcing herself to snap out of it, she walked to the counter and put her glasses back on she'd left there. "Thanks to your soap, I officially smell like you, and I stole your robe, so I look like you, too. Just call me Gaines."

A grin split his profile. "I doubt you—" His heated gaze swept her from head to foot. He cleared his throat. "Yeah, I never looked that good." Shaking his head, he returned to his task and poured soup into two bowls. "I'm afraid I have almost no food. I stay at the house more than here. Tomato soup's about the best I could do, though I can run out, if you want."

"I'm good with soup. I'm not that hungry."

He paled. "You're not nauseous, are you?"

"No, doc. I just don't eat a big dinner." When he still looked concerned, she sighed. "I'm fine. Sit, X. Eat something."

Setting the bowls down, he wove around the counter and took the stool next to her. His feet were bare, and for some reason, she got incredibly turned on.

He caught her staring and looked down. "What?"

She shrugged. "Never noticed how big your feet are. Bet you don't have to rent skis." She made a point to take a bite of soup.

A bark of laughter filled the room, and he shook his head. "I have no clue how to respond to that, so I'll keep mum."

They ate and bickered over sleeping arrangements. He insisted on her taking the bed and he the couch, and she finally conceded just to shut him up. He was usually pretty easygoing, so on the rare occasions when he became argumentative, she just caved.

He rose and rinsed their bowls in the sink. "You have your choice of a movie or cards. There's nothing else to do."

"I can kick your butt at poker."

Grinning, he shook his head and went to a living room shelf.

She walked to the windows and watched the pink and orange sunset behind the buildings. Stars were beginning to poke through the fading daylight and lights shone randomly in windows. To her left, part of the Bay could be spotted, shrouded in fog.

He came up next to her and crossed his arms, staring out quietly beside her. "I love this view. Second only to the balcony at my folks place in Napa."

"My guestroom faced the other direction. I'll take your word for it."

Rubbing his jaw, he sent her a side-glance. "You can have mine next weekend when we drive up. Or remind me to take you closer to the vineyard. There's a great hill to catch the sunset."

Since it sounded romantic, she kept quiet. And she loved this side of him. As comfortable as he'd grown with her, he still measured his words carefully most days. But like this? He didn't hesitate, just went with his gut, and she longed for more.

He shifted his feet. "I was in Paris once, the year after I graduated college." The low quality of his tone had a melancholy note she'd never heard before. "I started in Rome, moved on to London, then hit Paris last. What they say about rose-colored glasses is true. The light's different there. San Francisco's sunset is close, but not quite right."

She faced him and leaned a shoulder on the glass. "I've never been. Always wanted to travel abroad, but never got around to it."

Frowning, he turned and mirrored her pose. "Why? You speak, what, four different languages?"

She shrugged. "College was a struggle to make ends meet and, to be honest, I was scared to go anywhere while Brian was serving.

Mark's depression was too severe to take a trip after graduation. Well, then they both died and…I dove into work."

He stared at her like he had never seen her before. "I give you two weeks vacation a year. Do you need more?"

"No." She waved him off. "I only use one and don't travel alone. If Kate can go with me, sometimes we take a few days up the coast. Besides, you and I go on business trips often enough."

"That's work. Not pleasure. What do you do when Kate can't go?"

"Stay home. There's lots to do here." Which was an excuse. Truth was, the only thing sadder than vacationing alone was vacationing at home. Alone.

He rubbed his chest as if it hurt. "Why don't you travel by yourself? If you research, there's safe ways to do it."

Because if something happened to her, she had no one at home who'd know, who'd miss her. And why wouldn't he let up on this? *"Non ha senso nel vedere bei posti se nessuno è lì per vivere con voi."*

"I hate it when you do that." His eyes narrowed. "It's like you know I won't care for the answer, so you give it to me in another language. What was that? Italian?"

"Yes." She leaned her head against the glass and decided it didn't matter if she told him. She often got the impression she was just one of his many charities. "I said, there's no point in seeing beautiful places if no one's there to experience it with you." She straightened. "Wipe that look off your face. I didn't kick your puppy."

Wounded golden eyes stared back at her as his throat bobbed with a swallow. "I don't have a puppy, but I'm pretty sure you just kicked me in the gut."

She rolled her eyes and moved to the couch. Plopping on the cushion, she glanced back at him. He was still rubbing his chest. "Am I going to beat you at poker, or what?"

In silence, he made his way over and sat at the opposite end, setting a deck of cards between them.

It took him a round, but he snapped out of his Pity Peyton Party and they discussed other things. By eight-thirty, the day had caught up to her and she was less useful than a limp noodle. She called it a night.

Lying awake, she stared at the shapes on his ceiling and felt more lonely with him in the next room than she ever had at home. It took an hour to get to sleep because even the sheets smelled like him.

The next thing she knew, his quiet, rumbling voice called her name and a warm hand settled on her shoulder. She blinked up at him where he sat on the mattress by her hip. She glanced at the clock, noting it was almost midnight, then at the chair in the corner, which suspiciously had a blanket on it as if he'd been sleeping there.

"What's the French translation for you snore?"

"What?" She shifted onto her elbows. "I don't snore."

"You're right. You don't. This is just a concussion check." His endearing, half-awake grin came close to knocking out her irritation. Close, but no cigar.

"As soon as I get a cup of coffee in me tomorrow morning, I'm gonna kill you."

"I'll put it on the calendar. Go back to sleep now."

Huffing, she rolled over and shut her eyes. His footsteps padded on the floor behind her, but he didn't leave. After a moment, a *whoosh* sounded, followed by the scratching of material on material in the silent room. He *had* been sleeping in the chair. Was he really that concerned?

"X, you know what happened today wasn't your fault, right? And trust me when I say, I'm okay."

He didn't respond for the longest time, and when he did, it was nothing more than, "Goodnight."

The second time he woke her, he demanded to know who the president of the United States was, and he laughed at her irritated response of, "It doesn't matter. It should be Betty White. She has my vote."

The third time he woke her, he had one hand on either side of her shoulders and was leaning close enough she could count his eyelashes. He looked exhausted and his hair stood up at a hundred different angles.

"Hey, you were slower to rouse this time." His fingers skimmed her cheek, a barely there caress that bespoke of heartbreaking tenderness. "Do you know where you are?"

"Your bed."

He inhaled. Hard. His eyes snapped shut. Blowing out a measured breath, he looked at her for a beat. A battle waged in his expression until he leaned forward, kissed her forehead, and returned to the chair.

Chapter Nine

An hour before they were supposed to be at the breast cancer awareness fundraiser, Xavier glanced at the note taped to Peyton's apartment door and frowned. What the hell was she doing on the roof?

Turning for the stairs, he checked his phone. Nothing. Shouldn't she be getting ready?

They'd had a hellacious week, and even though his new receptionist was working out, orientating Jackie took time. And the press was still a nightmare. Plus, he and Peyton had been forced to fill out police reports and statements. He was still pissed she'd dropped the assault charge. She'd been convinced Fern would walk away and leave them alone. Xavier wasn't as confident. He kept a bodyguard on her when she went to and from work, but conceded to stopping overnights.

Reaching the door to the roof, he shoved through and halted at the female grunt that raked his ears. Panicked, he walked around a ventilation unit and found Peyton pinned to the ground, Joseph on top of her with a... Fuck him. A gun at her head.

"What in the hell are you doing?" He stormed forward, but Peyton shook her head.

"Stay back, X." A warrior cry, and she kicked her leg, wrapping it around Joseph's neck. One hand shoved the gun, the other Joseph's arm, and in three beats, she had him pinned under her and the gun on him. "Yeah. Suck it, bad guy."

While Xavier stood like an idiot wondering what was happening, Joseph let out a rip-roaring laugh and smacked... Her. Ass.

"Good work, blondie. Now get up. I need a shower."

It was then Xavier realized the two of them were in workout clothes. Hers were so skintight the spit in his mouth dried. "You're teaching her self defense?"

"Yep. For the past couple months. The gun's not loaded, by the way." Joseph rolled to his feet. "She learned quicker than you, too."

"Because I'm awesome." Her wide gaze scanned Xavier, his tuxedo. "Oh crap. What time is it?" She vaulted over to him, grabbed his wrist, and twisted it to read his watch. "Joseph, you jerkface. We have less than an hour to get ready. Now we really do need to shower together." She raced through the door.

What to the what? Xavier pinned Joseph with a look bordering on homicidal.

His bodyguard held up a hand. "Relax. She's kidding."

Swear to God, Xavier couldn't take any more shit this week. He just couldn't. It was bad enough he had to throw on a tux and play nice for the next however many hours, but to watch Joseph and Peyton flirt would be the gigabyte that broke the geek's back.

They followed Peyton inside and found her back on her floor, standing with Kate outside her door.

"You," Peyton pointed to Joseph, "shower at her place. You," she pointed to Xavier, "come in here. I'm going to do the fastest prep in the history of womankind."

He'd no sooner shut the door behind them in her apartment and she was gone. The shower ran. Curses were muttered. Cabinets slammed. Joseph returned in a suit as Peyton's hairdryer kicked on with a whir. Xavier stayed by the door, too frightened to step deeper into the unit with her on a tear.

"Someone come zip me," she shouted from what he assumed was the bedroom.

Joseph raised his hands in surrender. "Not it."

Xavier shook his head and made his way to her room, only to stop dead over the threshold. He absolutely needed to quit picking out evening dresses that put him in a constant state of asthma simply by looking at her.

Pale pink silk molded to her ample breasts and slim waist, the hem skimming her bare toes. She held the material across her chest with an arm to apparently keep it from slipping while she put in an earring. Her champagne hair fell around her shoulders and she was sans the glasses.

"Well, come on, X."

Right. He closed in behind her and fingered the tab, doing everything possible not to swallow his tongue while he pulled up the zipper. Jesus, her skin was pure buttermilk. And she was wearing that perfume that wrapped around his windpipe and squeezed.

She passed him a pair of silver heels. "Take these." And she was gone.

Back in the living room, she tossed a small case at Joseph. "Carry that. I'll have to do makeup in the car. Let's go." She snatched a purse off the end table that matched her shoes and rushed out. She tapped Kate's door with her palm as she breezed by. "Bye, Kate. Love you."

Apparently, the elevator was too slow. She pushed through the fire exit staircase.

"She should work for NASCAR," Joseph muttered as they trailed her down five—count that, five—flights of stairs and to the curb.

She cupped Archie's cheeks as his driver held the limousine door for them. "Drive it like it's stolen. We're running late."

A craggy laugh, and the old man's cocoa skin blushed. "Yes, ma'am."

On the road, she swiveled in the seat next to Xavier and put her feet in his lap. "You, shoe duty. Joseph, cosmetic bag."

Joseph tossed her the case he'd been ordered to bring and rolled his lips over his teeth to hide a grin.

Xavier gave him a thanks-no-thanks glare and eyed her shoes. They seemed simple enough. A little buckle or something. He fiddled with it while she opened a compact mirror thing and added charcoal or whatever to her eyes. She had both lids done before he'd gotten one shoe on her delicate foot. She applied lipstick and Xavier got the other shoe on as the limo rolled to a stop.

"Time?" she barked as Archie opened the door.

Xavier glanced at his watch. "Seven fifty-five."

"Yes. Five minutes to spare." She beamed a three-hundred megawatt smile at Xavier. "I'm ready."

He shared a holy-shit look with Joseph as his bodyguard stepped onto the curb, eyed the street in front of the art museum, and nodded an okay.

Xavier climbed out and held his hand for Peyton. She clasped it and exited the limo. Drawing a deep breath, she blew out what appeared to be any frazzled nerves from her system.

"The tickets?" He lifted a brow.

"As if the whole of society doesn't know you. It's not like they'd turn Xavier Gaines away." She reached into the breast pocket of his tuxedo and extracted two tickets.

"I don't want to know how those got there." They walked up the front steps, her hand in the crook of his arm, and a bellman held the door for them. "You look lovely, by the way."

That earned another grin. "Thank you." She turned to the bellman. "And thank you, kind sir."

Admiration inflated his chest. Not only did he get to attend these nerve-wracking events with her, but she made it a point to address everyone, no matter their status, as if they were royalty. Once they got inside, there wouldn't be a face she didn't know or some quirk of hers to make him comfortable. She was seriously one in a million.

Photographers snapped pictures and flashes filled the small entryway. Joseph jerked his chin, indicating he'd wait for them along the far wall in the lobby.

Hand low on her back, Xavier guided her to the left and into the showroom. Stark white walls and thick pillars were met with splashes of color via framed contemporary art. To the left was a bar, to the right, an orchestra. Several waiters milled about with trays of *hors d'oeuvres* and champagne. Pink bow ties and dresses socialized.

He looked at Peyton. "Do you want something to drink?"

"Not right now. I haven't eaten since breakfast." She brushed a strand of hair from her cheek.

"Why?" And she'd gone head-to-head with Joseph without sustenance? "Never mind." He stopped a passing waiter, loaded a few canapés and sushi rolls on a plate, and gave it to her.

"I'm not that hungry, actually." She eyed the food and nibbled.

She did seem rather pale, even for her fair complexion. He ushered her to a far corner. "Are you coming down with something? We can leave."

"No, it's just…" A wrinkle formed between her brows. "Don't go all Xavier on me, but I haven't been sleeping or eating much since what happened with Fern. I know she won't come after me, but I just can't get the guilt out of my stomach. Every time I close my eyes, I see the anger on her face or hear her voice—"

"Stay at the mansion with me tonight."

"No." She waved him off. "I'm just being silly." She bit into a sushi roll as if to make a point.

"You need a good night's sleep and you were coming over tomorrow to prep me for the press conference, anyway."

She didn't respond, other than to give him a polite smile.

Chest aching, he took in the slight shadows beneath her eyes and the remnants of bruising on her temple. He'd been so busy in the aftermath, he hadn't paid much attention to her. She'd been running herself ragged, too. The thought of her scared and alone at night tore a fissure through him.

He waited until she'd eaten what he'd given her and took the plate. "Wait here. I'll get you something with juice in it." Dropping a kiss to her hair, he stepped toward the bar and relieved himself of the dish. Returning to her with a pineapple, orange juice, and club soda combo, he passed it over. "Tell people it's a fuzzy navel or something."

Her laugh puffed like smoke. "Thank you." Her pretty blue gaze scanned the room. "We should mingle." She subtly tilted her head toward an elder couple. "The Van-Heusens, if you recall. He's in investment banking and she heads this fundraiser. Ask her how her daughter, Eloise, is doing since chemotherapy. She was diagnosed four years ago with stage three breast cancer. It came back six months ago. We sent flowers to the hospital room."

He didn't remember the couple, had no clue their daughter was ill, and he could do little more than stare in awe at Peyton's skill.

Without further ado, she led him toward the couple and made nice about Mrs. Van-Heusen's dress.

At a pause in conversation, Xavier cleared his throat. "How is Eloise doing since treatment?"

"Oh, very well, thank you." Mrs. Van-Heusen patted her chest. "Thank goodness she's done with chemo. And that arrangement you sent," she grabbed Peyton's forearm, "was just gorgeous. Everyone said so."

"I hope it brightened her day." Peyton smiled. "Mr. Gaines picked it out himself."

The little liar. He smiled and shook hands before they moved on. "Out of curiosity, what flowers did I pick out?"

"Gardenias, freesia, and lavender." She took a sip of her drink and glanced past him. "Shoot. Put your arm around me like we just climbed out of the sack. Michael Petri is headed our way. Producer and very handsy with women. He grabbed my ass at the Governor's Ball. Distract him by enquiring about his new action flick with Tom Cruise."

Before he could process what she'd said, she slipped a hand between his tux jacket and his shirt, sending his pulse into hyperactive.

"Michael, good to see you again." Her smile belied none of her discomfort, but Xavier didn't care for the tightness around her lips.

To her credit, the guy was staring right at her chest. Mid-forties, he had a paunch and a ring on every finger. Birds could've nested in his wiry salt and pepper hair. Or his eyebrows.

Irritation pounded his temples. Doing as she instructed, Xavier put his arm around her and his hand low on her hip, the position implying she was his. "How's filming going? I hear Cruise can be fun to work with."

"Actors. They're all divas." Michael sipped champagne, gaze sliding over Peyton's body like an unwanted touch. "Ravishing as always, Miss Smoke."

When Xavier stiffened, she rose on her toes and spoke quietly in his ear. "Breathe. Look to your left and pretend to see someone we must talk to."

He brought his lips to her ear. "You should've told me at the ball he'd touched you. He'd be minus a hand. And I do not care for the way he's undressing you with those beady eyes like he's planning to have you for dessert."

"Then walk away with me or show him you already ate me."

"Sweet Christ, Peyton." His fingers tightened on her hip and fire licked under his skin. Visuals, so many visuals, shoved to mind, he couldn't draw air.

She grinned as if to say, *good job for understanding.* "Michael, do forgive us. I spot someone we must see. Have a wonderful time."

Xavier pulled her to the center of the room and released her. Shoving his hands in his pockets, he glared at her as he attempted to undo the tendrils of lust she'd wound around him. In a crowded room at a benefit, no less.

Finally, he unhinged his jaw. "As my employee and my plus one, I expect to be told if someone does something inappropriate with you so it can be dealt with. I don't want to learn about it months after the fact."

Anger flared in her eyes, turning all that blue to ice. "Well, since I'm your insubordinate, you should be aware it happens quite often and I handle it all by my withering, incapable self. I simply run to the nearest strong, able male, bat my lashes, and fall upon their good graces to defend my honor."

Damn her. "That's not what I meant and you know it. You shouldn't be treated like some piece of tail and no one has the right to touch you."

She stepped closer and spoke through her teeth. "You can't have it both ways. For months during our first appearances, we dispelled the rumors about us being a couple. If you go all caveman every time a guy hits on me, it'll send the wrong message. I *am* a single woman, I *am* your employee, and I *am* nothing more than your plus one."

The hell she... He glanced away, grinding his molars.

Every atom in his body wanted to argue her point. But she was right. He'd stood in his apartment not five days ago and told her their attraction couldn't be acted upon. Yet, his damn protective beast couldn't be caged, not with her, and for months, he'd been rattling the chains of restraint, roaring to get free. He was this close to saying screw common sense.

She chewed her lip. "Mrs. Atherton is coming our way. Widow, chairman of the garden society, and just had her first grandchild. A girl. I'm going to run to the restroom. Ask her to see pictures of the baby. It'll keep her occupied while I'm gone." She went to step around him. "And remember to smile, Mr. Gaines."

Her barb at addressing him formally hit its mark. Napalm right to the chest. To avoid a nervous tick or fidget, he fisted the coin in his left pocket and rubbed his thumb over the engraving as a woman approached.

Shit. What was her name? He couldn't recall, but he held out his hand. "You're looking beautiful this evening. I hear congratulations are in order. Do you happen to have any pictures of your new addition?"

Two grueling hours later, Xavier dismissed Joseph once they were at the limousine and sent him home. Though she hadn't outright agreed, Peyton would be staying at Xavier's place tonight, and the mansion had more than enough security. As Archie wound the vehicle through the streets, her eyes grew heavier by the city block until, finally, she closed them altogether.

From the seat across from hers, he watched her sleep—the play of light and shadow on her face, her angelic features—and his throat pinched. He'd always admired her beautiful heart, her intellect, her damn adorable charm, and her ability to do her job above all else. But the sheer, utter longing inside him was beginning to consume.

He'd had no connection to previous lovers other than a physical interest. Hell, half of them he couldn't even spout a solitary personality trait. But, Peyton? He knew every expression, each mannerism and its meaning. She had upwards of thirty variations of her smile, and he could give a detailed account of all of them, could write a book of code describing them.

No woman had ever made him want like she did. Ache. To the point of agony.

The limo drove over the hills San Francisco was known for and eventually turned into his gated driveway. Maples lined the long path, interspersed with lampposts. Archie would've alerted the butler, Sam, that they were coming, and proved Xavier correct when they pulled up to his federal colonial style home and found the lights were glowing.

Xavier knelt in front of Peyton and brushed his knuckles over her arm. "Hey, we're here." She didn't stir. Not even a flutter of her lashes. He glanced at Archie, the open door between them. "Let Sam know we're headed inside."

With a nod, his driver turned and climbed the brick stairs to the wide double front doors.

Xavier tried once more to wake her and gave up. She was, no doubt, exhausted. He stripped out of his coat, loosened his tie, and set the items on the seat.

Carefully, he slid an arm around her back and under her legs, lifting her from the vehicle. Cinching her snug against his chest, he glanced down at her. Dark lashes fanned her cheeks and her red lips were slightly parted, her breathing deep and even. With her cheek on his bicep and her hair cascading everywhere, his knees nearly buckled.

"You sure know how to stop a man's heart, honey," he whispered.

The door opened at the top of the stairs and Sam stood next to Archie in blue striped sleepwear. Normally, Xavier didn't require Sam's services after eight and he felt terrible for summoning him. Archie and Sam were brothers, both with light cocoa skin and graying hair cropped close to their heads. And both gentlemen had worry lines creasing their foreheads as Xavier climbed the stairs, Peyton in his arms.

"You can go, Archie. Thank you."

"Yes, sir."

"Is Miss Peyton all right, sir?" Sam followed him inside and shut the door.

"She's fine. Just tired." Xavier glanced up the long, winding staircase and thought about asking if the guestroom was made up. "You can go back to sleep. I've got her."

Sam nodded and headed toward the kitchen, where the entrance to the staff quarters were located.

Climbing the stairs, Xavier tried not to jar her. At the top, he glanced left at the guest accommodations, then turned right. Unsure what the hell he was doing, he wove down the long corridor, past several other rooms, and entered his bedroom suite. He set her in a chair so he could turn down the bed, then froze, staring at her.

Have mercy, but she was in his bedroom, where no other woman had been, and she looked so damn...right. Perfect.

She didn't have her glasses on, which meant he'd have to wake her anyway so she could take out her contacts. He figured she wouldn't want to sleep in a gown, either. Crouching in front of her, he wondered if she was still pissed off at him. She had every right.

"Peyton." He took her hand and rubbed his thumb over her knuckles. "Peyton, honey. Wake up."

Chapter Ten

Peyton shoved the dregs of unconsciousness aside and opened her eyes. Panic and confusion followed as her heartbeat tripped. Aside from Xavier kneeling in front of her, she didn't recognize a thing. Last she remembered, they were in the limo after the benefit.

"Where am I?"

He rubbed his jaw as if suddenly nervous. "My house. I was going to let you sleep, but you have your contacts in and…" He gestured toward her dress. Rising, he moved to a dresser.

She glanced around. They weren't just at his house, but in his bedroom. Or a guestroom. Maroon and cream striped wallpaper. Four-poster king-size bed with an etched, inlaid design. Matching mahogany dressers. Thick beige carpet. Heavy burgundy drapes covered what looked to be a patio door. A stack of computer manuals and mysteries laid on the nightstand next to a lamp. The place was the size of her entire apartment.

"How did I get here?"

His spine stiffened in the process of rooting through a drawer. "I carried you."

"You…" Of course, he did. Because that was normal. And she'd slept through the whole thing.

He sighed and hung his head, back still to her. "Don't be mad. I'm sorry about what I said earlier and I only want you to get some rest."

She wasn't mad. Oddly touched, but not mad. She was beginning to grow entirely too dependent on him, though. Or, that's how it had felt lately. Perhaps she just enjoyed being taken care of for once, even if it was Xavier's awkward attempts.

When she said nothing, he turned and faced her, crossing his arms. Gone was the tie and jacket. The first couple buttons of his shirt were undone and he had the sleeves rolled to his elbows. God, he was such an attractive man. Thick chestnut hair, expressive bourbon eyes. A half-day of scruff had begun to darken his jaw.

"Is this your bedroom?"

He cleared his throat, gaze on the floor. "Yes." Suddenly, he turned and was back to digging in the dresser. Removing a t-shirt, he walked it over to her. "Bathroom's through there. Help yourself to whatever. When you're done, I'll get my stuff and sleep in the guestroom."

"But this is your room."

The look he sent her indicated he was all too aware of the fact and that she was here. Then, he refused to look her in the eye, but he jerked his chin toward an open connecting door. "You're tired. Go on."

With a sigh, she headed for the bathroom and shut him out.

She'd never been in his private quarters. Once, a year ago, she'd spent the night in one of his many guestrooms down the hall, and she'd been downstairs many times. His house was very different from the apartment. Instead of cold functionality, there were warm tones and rich, dark wood throughout. His private bathroom was no different. Sage tile, a corner shower, huge tub, earth tone accents, soft emerald towels.

So he didn't have to wait on her, she quickly opened cabinets and found contact solution and an extra case. Lenses out, she washed the makeup from her face and changed into the tee. Discovering an unopened toothbrush, she used it and cleaned up her mess. Unsure what to do with the dress, she hung it over the shower stall for now.

She stepped out, and his gaze immediately jerked to hers as if he'd had no choice. He stood in the middle of the room, hands on his hips, and a furrow between his brows. Slowly, he raked his eyes over her body, then closed them as if pained. Tension tightened his jaw.

Before she could respond, he grabbed something off the chair she'd vacated and stalked into the bathroom. The door promptly shut behind him.

Rendered immobile, she stood frozen and tried to get a grip.

She looked around and decided she couldn't do this. No way could she stay in his bedroom when he was clearly unnerved having her here. The lines of their relationship had been blurred enough as of late, and she wasn't going to force him out of his own sanctuary.

Seeing her purse on the dresser, she snatched her glasses from inside. Quietly, she stepped from the room and waited for her eyes to adjust to the dark hall. Remembering where the guestroom was located from her previous stay, she walked two doors down and peeked inside. It appeared ready to use, so she switched on a lamp and tugged back the covers, slipping inside.

Except, she wasn't tired anymore. Exhausted, sure. Aroused, confused, rattled—definitely. This room was in muted yellow tones and more feminine with floral drapes and a comforter. White furniture pieces. Sitting in bed, she chewed her lip and wondered if he'd care if she stormed the library downstairs for a book. A few pages to take the edge off...

Footsteps padded down the hall, and he ducked his head inside the room. With a sigh born of pure relief, he leaned against the jamb. Rocking a pair of plaid blue flannel pants and a white tee, he studied her. She'd forgotten how sexy he looked in glasses, too. Thin black rectangular frames gave him a geeky hotness.

"I told you I'd stay in here." He focused on her necklace, and her heart about broke at the raw torment in his eyes.

"Come here." She patted the mattress by her hip.

He paused a beat and shoved off the frame, taking a seat facing her at the edge. "Not to bring up a sore subject, but I wish you'd told me about that Michael person. I know full well you can handle yourself. Hell, you continually handle me, and I'm a huge undertaking. But, the point is, there are some things you shouldn't have to deal with, especially when I'm around."

A smile teased her lips, even as her eyes misted with emotion. "Gonna slay my dragons, X?"

"I'm no warrior."

She hummed her disagreement. "Now, there you're wrong."

His gaze skimmed her face. "Joseph's been teaching you how to fight. You two have been chummy since—"

"No. I'm not into him and he's into Kate." She swore, it was like he couldn't fathom why she'd be attracted to him above all others.

He huffed a laugh. "I'll pray for him." Gently, he held her chin and tilted her head to look at her bruise. His thumb grazed her temple, the touch ever tender. "Joseph was pretty distraught over this, as well. I'm not the only one."

"I told you, I don't have feelings for him. I love him, yeah, but not in that way. I'm attracted to a genius computer nerd turned billionaire who gives endlessly to charities, hates the spotlight, and doesn't think he's good enough."

"That's not what I meant. I only wanted to point out Joseph cares, too. You're not alone and…" He blinked as if just catching up to the latter part of her statement. "What?" His chest didn't seem to be moving with basic oxygen exchange.

"He also loves his family, treats his employees like gold, and tries very hard to hide the fact he's been taking care of me for a long time."

Closing his eyes, he let out an uneven breath. "Peyton, honey…" He pinched the bridge of his nose, nearly dislodging his glasses.

"He calls me honey when his defenses are down and he's close to his breaking point."

He let out a laugh that bordered on sarcastic and shared intimate space with frantic. "You got that right. What about the bartender? Didn't you have a date last night?"

"I went. I had fun. There won't be another." She shrugged. "No chemistry."

He seemed skeptical. Adjusting his glasses, he looked at her and took hers off, setting the frames on the bedside table. "Goodnight." Leaning forward, he pressed a kiss to her bruise and started to rise.

Forget rules. She grabbed his hand to stop him, cupped his face, and kissed him.

For a fractured beat, he paused, then he tilted his head and groaned. The vibrations wove from his lips to hers, sending a ripple of pure need straight to her core. Firm, sharp strokes of his tongue darted in her mouth, teased, and retreated. Increasing the pressure, she opened wider, seeking more, and he gripped the back of her neck like he'd thought she'd pull away.

Like the first time, he kissed with dominance and barely leashed control. A man who clearly knew what he wanted, sought his pleasure, and still managed to make the experience all about her needs. He explored as if learning and simultaneously recognizing her in the same breath. Utter annihilation. She trembled and moaned.

"I give up," he muttered against her lips, his breath hot and heavy. "Yes, I'll slay your dragons. I'll do anything you goddamn want." With a hand under each thigh, he lifted her from the mattress, dragged her across his body, and deposited her in his lap to straddle him. "I could wear a full body suit of Kevlar and you'd get through. I don't have the strength to fight you."

And wow, could the man say anything that didn't squeeze the beat from her heart? She could climax on his words alone. Her breasts grew heavy and her nipples hard at the direct contact with him. She traced her fingers over his jaw, the whiskers rough. The quiet rasp made her quiver. Such a beautiful mouth. Firm lips, the lower just a tad fuller than the top.

He stared into her eyes and swallowed. "I didn't bring you home for this. I want you to know that."

"I do." She smiled to soften his tension. Placing kisses across his cheek, she wove her fingers through his hair, earning a sharp intake. She nipped his earlobe, his chin.

"Peyton…" He groaned. "Holy Christ."

"Hmm?" She moved to his neck, licking and sucking his warm skin. Gah, he smelled so good, she could feast on him.

His respirations increased. Rough, deft fingers clenched her thighs and slid up to her waist, under her shirt, and stopped to splay over her ribs. The distinct thick, hard ridge of an erection pressed her mound, and she went from damp to drenched. Wanting more, she rocked her hips, and he set his forehead on her shoulder, emitting a full body shudder.

"Mercy, woman. Your mouth is torture enough. Don't throw your body into it, too."

Without warning, he lay back, taking her with him to sprawl across his chest, and looked up at her. Pushing her hair from her face, he drew a ragged breath. "I want you. Bad. Which is why we should stop. You need some rest. In the morning, let's discuss this. Ad nauseum."

Unable to help it, she grinned. "Talk, huh?"

"It's what we do best."

"Not for long."

His laugh was rough and ended in a groan. "Help a guy out here, honey."

"Okay, okay." She gave him a brief kiss and rolled off, shifting to her original position by the pillow. He didn't move, just pressed his palms to his eyes. She thought about the restless nights this week and desperately wanted to…be held. "Sleep with me?"

He turned his head with a look of carnal banality. His jaw ticked. After a moment, he must've read something in her expression because his gaze softened.

Sitting up, he climbed off the bed, wrapped his arms around her, and carried her into his room. "If I'm sleeping with you, we're doing it in my bed."

Dropping one knee on the mattress, he lowered her to the sheets, went back to shut the door, and switched off the lamp. He set his glasses on the nightstand. A moment later, his bathroom light came on. He partially closed the door as if leaving her a nightlight, and climbed in bed beside her.

On his side, he faced her, and she adjusted to do the same. Shadows played over his face, but she could make out his features through the muted darkness. Affection stared back at her.

One corner of his mouth curved and he reached up to brush the hair from her face. "Is it all right if I hold you?"

Her heart cracked right in two and her eyes filled. Just like that. "Yes."

Concern wrinkled his brow. "Don't do that. Please." He brushed his thumb across her cheek as if to check for wetness, then her lower lip. "You are exhausted, aren't you?"

She nodded, her chest aching. In all her years, no one but her brother Brian had ever been so unerringly protective, gentle, or charismatically honest with her. "I've never been carried to bed before." She grinned to free the lines of worry from his face. "That was pretty badass, X."

He grunted, but a smile followed, melting everything but contentment from his face. "Never done it before, either." With an arm around her back, he slid her across the sheets and flush against him. "Listen to me this time, would you? Go to sleep."

After a second, he tugged the blankets around them and resettled. Burying her face in his neck, she breathed him in and the last of her tension dissolved. He rubbed soothing circles over her back and rested his cheek on the top of her head.

She woke up nine hours later in exactly the same position, with Xavier wrapped around her like a shield and one thigh wedged between hers. And she really had to pee.

His deep, even breathing indicated he was still sleeping, so she eased away a fraction and gave herself a moment to watch him. It was surreal, being here with him. Part of her thought it was strange, cozied up to her boss in the most intimate of ways. She'd worked with him day in and day out for what felt like way longer than a couple years. Heck, it was weird just seeing him out of a suit. But another part of her connected to him. A silent cry she'd long ago ignored to find a tether to someone again. In truth, Xavier was a lot of the things she'd wanted in a partner.

He carried around so much tension at work, sometimes outside the office, but his features were adorably relaxed while asleep. Lips parted, he emitted almost no sound. His dark, thick lashes gave him a childlike appearance, until she dipped her gaze to the shadow of whiskers on his jaw. She followed the path to the corded tendons on his neck and wanted to suck that spot until he groaned like he'd done last night.

Her bladder couldn't wait, though.

Carefully, she extracted herself from his hold and slipped from bed. She tiptoed to the bathroom, relieved herself, brushed her teeth, and exited back into his bedroom. He was still zonked out, and she didn't have the heart to wake him.

A glance down at herself showed she was pretty well covered with his shirt if the staff were around, but she dug through a dresser until she found another set of pajama bottoms. They were several inches too long and she had to roll the waist to get them to stay up, but they'd do. She grabbed her purse and headed out.

Once downstairs, she glanced around, putting her purse on the entry table. If the staff was here, they were quiet. She checked her cell for messages and found none.

The base of the staircase opened into a foyer and an expansive living room teeming with mahogany ceiling beams and buttercream walls. He tended to favor oil paintings of the ocean or vineyards, and the art on the wall portrayed that. His furniture was red, classic-lined, and fuss-free. The floor-to-rafters fireplace was her favorite part of the house and was made from aged fieldstone with a decorative mantle.

She poked her head in the library and found no one. This room was small, but the shelves were stocked to the hilt. Leather chairs and a desk took up the remainder of the space. Also empty were the home gym and his mancave den, where he had a pool table and a TV large enough for an epic center. Video games and controllers littered the shelf underneath, and the furniture was much more lived in than elsewhere, proving he spent most of his time there.

God, the house was just too enormous for one person. She thought about him here in a big old empty house alone, and wondered if he got as lonely as she often did in her tiny apartment. He'd never discussed starting a family of his own, but he had to want marriage and kids, right? He adored his parents and she couldn't imagine him not wanting to carry on the name.

Needing coffee more than air, she made her way to the kitchen and found Xavier's butler, Sam, at the table doing a crossword. "Sam I Am, it's good to see you."

He smiled at her nickname, set the pen down, and rose. His gray suit was neatly pressed. "Miss Peyton, you're awake. I was beginning to worry."

She glanced at the clock and noted it was almost ten. "Wow. It is late. I was so tired." She gestured at her clothes. "And this isn't a walk of shame. I only slept here."

He chuckled, the lines around his dark eyes deepening. "It's not my business."

"Uh-huh. Can I grab coffee? I might turn into a harpy if you say no."

Another chuckle. "Of course, let me get it for you."

"No, no. You sit. I'll pour." She filled a cup for herself and topped off his at the table.

Xavier didn't have a cook on staff, so she rummaged in the massive pantry and the cupboards for breakfast fixings. She loved his kitchen. Open and airy, it had a huge window over the sink to his backyard. The long, rectangular space was split by an island. Granite countertops, chipped white cabinets, and sandstone tile.

"Please, Miss Peyton. Let me fix you something."

"No way. I love to cook and never get to do it at home." She shot a grin over her shoulder. "How's that grandbaby of yours? Is she walking yet?"

"Oh yes. A terror, that one. Like her mama." His chair scraped the floor as he sat.

She laughed as she chopped melon. "You'll have to show me a recent picture when I'm done here. I haven't seen one in months."

Cantaloupe cut, she moved onto mixing batter for muffins. She added fresh blueberries from the fridge, folded them in, and poured batter into baking cups. Once they were in the oven, she grabbed another refill of coffee and took a seat by Sam.

She cooed over a picture of his granddaughter, round brown cheeks and wild black hair, and a pang of longing hit her square in the womb. "She's so precious."

"That she is." He put the photo back in his wallet and returned to his crossword puzzle.

When the muffins were done, she transferred them to a cooling rack by the bowl of melon and helped Sam with his puzzle. They were just into the twentieth hint when Xavier walked in, hair standing on end and wearing PJs. He halted over the threshold and looked around as if royally confused.

Shoot. Had he expected her to leave? Her car wasn't here, but Archie would've driven her home. Except, they were supposed to go over the press conference notes.

Sam rose and handed him coffee. "Morning, sir."

Xavier absently took the cup. "Morning." He eyed the island, then Peyton, still not seemingly orientated. "Are those blueberry muffins? Those are my favorite." His deep, sleep-roughened voice had her clenching her thighs.

"Imagine that." She did place orders at the caterer for his business meetings. She knew a thing or two.

He glanced at her clothes and…frowned. "Sam, give us a minute, please."

"Of course, sir."

When the butler left, Xavier's gaze slid over her again. "I never sleep in."

Nerves pinged in her belly. She was getting the distinct impression he was uncomfortable with her here and wanted her gone. "We had a late night."

He stared at her, his expression unreadable. "You weren't in bed when I woke." He rubbed his neck. "I don't ever sleep with women. In my own bed, I mean."

Okay, she was out of here. Before things got even more epically uncomfortable and it affected work, she rose and put her cup in the sink. Gone was the gentle, sweet man from last night, and in his place was the cool front he used with strangers.

Disappointment clamped her throat, and she bit her tongue to stave off tears. Humiliated, she took a cleansing breath before turning around. "Please ask Archie if he can take me home. I just need to get my dress and shoes from upstairs."

"Wait." He grabbed her arm and set the coffee on a nearby counter. "Why are you leaving?"

Keeping her mouth shut, she stared at his chest, unable to meet his eyes. She'd been vulnerable with him last night, and shame mingled with devastation. She'd thought perhaps they were beginning something together. But no, that was just her, clinging to a bit of affection since it had been so long since she'd had any.

God. "I'll wash your clothes and bring them to the office tomorrow." Her voice broke and she could only pray he hadn't noticed. She might die if he made her change back into the dress before going.

Extracting her arm from his grasp, she quickly walked out and made haste through the living room. If Archie wasn't waiting with the car when she got back down, she'd hoof it home. It was, like, fifteen miles, but whatever.

Xavier shot in front of her before she could round the banister and halted her retreat at the base of the stairs. "Please, stop." He growled in frustration as she tried to move around him and put his hands on her shoulders. "Just…stop."

Hanging his head, he let go of her and ran his hands through his hair. "I really shouldn't speak until I'm fully caffeinated, but I obviously said something to upset you. Let's backtrack. I just woke up from the soundest sleep of my life, after six a.m., mind you, which has rarely happened. I never have overnight guests, certainly not ones who share my bed, yet the first thing I noticed was you weren't in it. I get downstairs to find my favorite muffins and you looking goddamn adorable in my clothes. Does that cover it?"

Too stunned to move or respond or dare breathe, she blinked at him. So…he didn't want her to leave?

Letting out a long-winded breath, he straightened. Scratched his jaw. Searched her gaze. "Shit. That doesn't cover it." Cupping the back of her neck, he hauled her against him and kissed her.

Chapter Eleven

By the time Friday rolled around, Xavier was jumping out of his skin. He and Peyton had discussed their...situation last Sunday, had sucked face like bandits to seal the deal, and then she'd gone home.

He hadn't kissed her since.

They'd agreed to keep the relationship from Gaines Industries and the public eye until they had a better grasp on what to do or in the event things became serious. Except, they were serious now because *he hadn't kissed her since*. Unsure of the boundaries or expectations, he didn't text or call her unless it was company related. The only time he'd seen her was at work.

And damn if fantasy after fantasy about her and his desk didn't pummel him at the most inopportune times. Like the conference call he'd just finished.

He shoved away from his computer and paced his office. They were set to head to Napa in two hours. His suitcase and hers were in his car in the parking garage because they'd be leaving right from work. And that was the other thing. Could they tell his parents about their relationship? He kept nothing from them and he was pretty damn certain they'd figure it out. Especially in close quarters for a whole weekend.

Out of his ever-loving mind, he strode to the door. "Miss Smoke, could you come in here a moment?"

"Be right there, Mr. Gaines." With a smile, she walked out of her office and into his.

He ducked his head into the hall to be sure Jackie was at her desk. Then, he shut his door, pinned Peyton against it, shoved her glasses on top of her head, and kissed the hell out of her. A mewl of surprise shot from her mouth into his, and he pressed closer, sinking deeper into the kiss, into her.

She grabbed the lapels of his suit and arched into him, sending his heartbeat thundering toward detonation. Mercy, how could he have missed this so much after only a week? She'd quickly become a drug and him a helpless junkie. Two years, and he'd managed not to cross the line, no matter how much he wanted her. One moment in his office had rendered all good, smart intentions to dust under her high heels.

Cupping the back of her neck, he inhaled and tilted his head the other way to go at her from another angle. Tongues stroked and teeth clashed and her soft curves ground against every square inch of him. Her fingers drifted, explored—across his chest, around his back, up to his shoulders, down to his ass.

He broke away and heaved air, face tilted toward the ceiling. And he'd thought kissing her would help? "Been wanting to do that for six damn days."

She nipped his chin. "And what took you so long?"

Carefully, he righted her glasses and stroked her jaw. Her dress matched her pretty cerulean eyes, and he stared helplessly into them for a moment. He couldn't count on all his fingers and toes the number of times he'd sought all that blue to ground him or ease his public anxiety. Since they'd kissed that first time, a whole new element had been added to the punch.

"I need some clarification." He swallowed. "About...us."

Was there an "us" in the equation? The math wasn't adding up for him. Not that he'd been in a lot of relationships, but this felt more like a torrid affair except fully clothed. Any other woman, and he'd know what to do. Sex was easy. Basic. He didn't want just a physical thing with Peyton, though. And all they'd hashed out was the agreement not to go public.

"What would you like to know?" Her tone was still husky from their closeness, but it held the soft note he'd grown to adore. It never failed to ease something inside him.

"Are we exclusive?" Foremost, he needed an answer to that one. He despised the idea of her being with someone else.

A hint of disappointment darkened her eyes. "You can see whomever you want. I know this won't pacify you for long."

His eyes narrowed. "What does that mean?"

"You don't date, X. Not one woman and not for an extended period."

Was that really what she thought? Though her statement was buried in truth, she, of all people, had to know why. Between his notoriety, his wealth, and his social anxiety, not to mention trust issues, relationships were not a simple leap for him. The last time he'd tried had ended in a very public disaster.

"I don't want to be with anyone else." Hell, he couldn't even think of any*thing* else.

She blinked as if surprised. "Okay. There's your answer. Nor will I date another while we're together. Any other questions?"

"Yes." He was starting to feel like an idiot teenager. "I need a definition of us or, at the very least, boundaries. A label, perhaps."

"Label." Her lips pursed as if mulling over the word. "I don't understand. If we're dating, we're just like any other couple, besides the not going public part."

Frustrating. She was so damn frustrating. As was the entire situation. One misstep and his world would crash. "We're not like everyone else, Peyton. Can I call you? Stop by? Take you out to dinner?" Obsess about getting her between his sheets nonstop...

"Oh." With a sigh, she softened. "I get it. Tell you what. When we're at the office, a work function, or attending an event, we'll just act like colleagues. Business as usual. Alone, off company time, we can explore the dating end of the relationship. Let things progress naturally. You can call me, take me out, or stop by as you see fit. Is that what you mean?"

"Yes." Christ, yes. Finally. There was still Hurricane Craptastic swirling inside his chest at the mere thought of screwing up their dynamic or losing her in any capacity, but at least he had guidelines in place in order not to fuck up at the starting gate. "I broke the rules kissing you in my office, then, didn't I?"

Her smile melted the last of his tension. "I think I can forgive you this one time. It was a great kiss."

Such a way with understatements, his Peyton. He straightened, giving her a little breathing room. "One last thing. Can we tell my folks?" And...there went her smile. At her nervous lip bite, his heart skipped rhythm. "I don't like keeping secrets from them."

Her gaze darted over his shoulder, a clear indication she was thinking of a way to be tactful. "I'll leave that up to you. But you should be prepared for them hating the idea."

"Of what? Us?" He frowned. "They love you."

"Sure, as your employee and the woman who keeps your life in order. Not as your girlfriend."

He tripped over the *girlfriend* part, decided he liked it, and moved onto the insanity she'd spouted after. "It won't change their feelings about you." His mother had been subtly hinting at the two of them lately. Little things, comments here and there. Enough for Xavier to get the message.

"Just...don't be disappointed or angry with them if I'm right."

Well, she was wrong—a rare occurrence, indeed—thus, it didn't matter.

A couple hours later, they were out of work clothes and on Highway 101 headed toward Napa. He wore jeans and a tee, a fact she seemed to find interesting, judging by her nod of approval and quick flicks to check him out. If that was all it took for her to give him a second glance and for desire to light her eyes, he'd wear denim daily. She had on navy blue leggings he wanted to peel off slowly and a long pink shirt that hid none of her subtle curves.

Since his black Charger was her favorite of his vehicles and it took bends like a dream, they drove it north over the winding roads. Late day sunlight filtered through a thin cloud cover and fog threatened to thicken the closer it got to dusk.

From behind the wheel, he glanced at her in the passenger seat. She'd been unusually quiet and seemed content to watch the scenery. He had the satellite radio programmed to a mix of his music and hers. Rock blended into pop and back again. Her sultry perfume filled the interior and he wanted to bury his face in her neck, breathe nothing but her for the next three days.

Now that he knew where her head was at, understood their specific limitations, he went with instinct and reached for her hand. Clasping it in his, he rested them on his thigh and peeked at her. Elbow on the window well, she stroked her fingers over a blooming smile while she kept her gaze on the passing hills. An adorable blush formed on her cheeks, and he zeroed in on the highway again.

Grinning, he checked the mileage sign. Napa Valley was only a two-ish hour drive, depending on traffic, and they were an hour out. "Are you hungry?"

"Not really. Your mom's making dinner, anyway."

"Is she?" News to him.

"She called me at the office to make sure I brought the list of people we sent the save-the-date reminders to for the Fallen Veterans benefit."

He earned another smile and a deeper blush when he kissed the back of her hand, resettling it in his lap. He'd bet his entire company she flushed like molten heat when she came. Focusing on the drive, he tried to get the visuals out of mind in order to keep the car between the dotted lines.

In no time, vineyards spanned the countryside with grape-lush vines in neat rows. The sun dipped its last descent west behind the vast hills as he wound through the valley. Though his parents lived in wine country and their property was surrounded by vineyards, they didn't grow the crop themselves.

He turned onto the private drive of their large ten-acre estate, past the security gate, and closer to the two-story Tuscan-style home. Olive and lemon trees spotted the northern grounds, where as the east side had lavender fields. His headlights gleamed off the steel barn on the south end, a decent hike from the four-car garage. Mountains shadowed the far distance.

Parking outside under a palm tree that sheltered the garage, he turned to her. She chewed her lip, staring at the carriage doors.

He squeezed her fingers. "This is a rare flip, you being the nervous one."

She offered him a withering side-glance. "I'm going to be heartbroken if they stop liking me."

Shit, she knew how to bring him straight to his knees. "Hey." He cupped her chin and turned her to look at him. Shadows played across her face. "I don't know where you're getting this idea, but let's go inside. I'll prove I'm right."

"Lead on, X." She waved her hand in dismissal and opened the door.

They crossed the inlaid Spanish tiles up the front walk, where he unlocked the house and gestured her inside. Stepping in after her, he closed the door and smiled. Home. He hadn't grown up in this house, but it had been in the family for fifteen years as a weekend getaway and was now his parents' permanent residence.

The wide open floor plan boasted a vaulted ceiling, venetian glaze plaster, and salvaged Wyoming wood accents. Wrought iron sconces and overhead chandeliers provided soft light on the butter cream walls. The scent of roasted chicken hung in the air and a fire crackled in the built-in hearth between the living room and the kitchen, even though the temperature outside was a mild sixty degrees.

His folks, however, were not in sight. He glanced up the curving staircase, but it seemed quiet up there. "Wonder where they are." He opened the front door again, this time slamming it shut for emphasis. Footsteps padded from the kitchen, around the divider wall, and toward them. "That's more like it."

"You're here." His mom, wearing khakis and a green blouse shades deeper than her eyes, opened her arms. And...hugged Peyton. Both were the same height and build, but somehow Mom managed to swallow Peyton as if she were half the size. "I made chicken soup and sandwiches since I know you like to eat light."

"It smells awesome."

Dad followed and, after eying the women, gave Xavier a brief embrace, complete with a back slap. "Good to see you."

"You, too." They switched, and Mom wrapped her arms around him, squeezing the breath from Xavier's lungs. "You're a python." He glanced at Peyton over his mother's shoulder, tucked to his father's side. "Note that she hugged you first."

She rolled her eyes in response and smiled up at his dad. "You're looking as handsome as ever."

"Flirt." The grin the old man shot her in return was not out of his courtroom handbook, but genuine and from the gut. "Keep going. I'm all ears."

Her laugh was the best damn sound Xavier had heard all day. "He got your build, eyes, and grin, that's for sure. And your sense of humor, when he uses it."

Mom snorted. "Inherited his poor eyesight from his father, too." She glanced at Xavier. "At least you got my hair, darling. There's that."

"Fascinating as I find Peyton hitting on Dad and Mom not caring, we have something to tell you." Xavier studied Peyton and grew angry when she slipped out from under his father's arm to stand by herself as if expecting a verbal assault.

Mom clapped. "Good news?" Her gaze darted expectantly between them.

"I think so, but we wanted you to know right off the bat. Peyton and I are seeing each other."

Dad frowned—part confusion, part irritation—and the concern lines on his forehead deepened. Mom's expression seemed more like Xavier had clocked her upside the head with a blunt object. She stood stock still, completely motionless.

"Uh, as in, we're dating," he hedged.

Not a sound. Not even a cricket.

Peyton, head down, exuded the quietest ragged exhale in existence. "I told you," she whispered, setting her wounded gaze on him. Pressing a delicate hand to her midsection, she closed her eyes for a beat.

His gut plummeted to his knees. "Peyton, honey—"

"I'm going to take a walk." She offered fake smile number four in her arsenal, the one that said she was trying to be polite and not cry in the process, then turned for the door. "Discuss amongst yourselves. I'll be back in a few minutes."

Unable to move, he watched her quietly walk out and stared at the wood like that would bring her back. After silence hung, he faced his parents again.

Mom tilted her head. "I'm confused. Weren't you two already...?" She propelled her hand like someone should finish her sentence.

Xavier reeled. "Already a couple? No. What gave you that idea?"

Her mouth opened and closed. "You're only ever seen with her at events and out in society. I mean, you're always yourself around her and you two do everything together. I've not seen you bring another date to charity functions or..." She shook her head. "I was hoping to have an engagement announcement by Christmas, but if you're telling us that you only now caught up to the obvious and just started a relationship, then I think I might need a drink."

Xavier glanced between the two of them. Confusion must be contagious because he was baffled. "Did it not occur to you that Peyton and I never held hands, kissed, *anything* romantic?"

Dad shrugged. "I assumed you were uncomfortable with public displays."

Extending his palm, Xavier shook his head. "Let me get this straight. You're not upset I'm dating her? You're upset I haven't been until recently?"

The bewilderment evaporated from his mom's eyes and was replaced with irritation. "What kind of question is that? Of course, we're not upset. I couldn't have picked a better woman for you if I climbed an X chromosome tree and plucked her off a branch myself." Hands on her hips, she huffed.

Christ, he had a headache. And Peyton had thought they'd hate the idea. She was probably near tears right this second, figuring she'd lost their good graces. Instead, his folks were trying to get them hitched.

He turned on his heel and strode toward the door. "I'll be right back."

"Dinner in ten minutes," Mom called after him.

He walked past the house, but couldn't find her in the lemon grove, nor the lavender field. Weaving around the backyard pool and garden fence, he headed for the barn, breathing a sigh of relief when he found the light on and the door ajar.

Six stalls lined the right side of the long space, equipment and shelves on the left. The scent of hay mingled with grass and earth as he zeroed in on her. She stood in profile by the farthest stall, petting Diablo over the half door. The other horses were quiet as she cooed and stroked the gelding's brown fur.

That particular horse had been a rescue and had taken awhile to acclimate to people. Not Peyton. On her first visit, he'd walked right up to her at the pasture fence and nudged her shoulder, like he was doing right now.

She laughed. "I told you, I didn't bring any treats. Tomorrow, before we ride. I promise."

Xavier leaned against the doorframe and crossed his arms. Moon rays filtered from the skylights, turning the champagne hair streaming down her back to more of a salted caramel. She'd shoved her glasses on top of her head, keeping the strands from her pretty face. A yellow glow from the stall cast her in a transient mix of fairy and starlight. A punch of desire collided with something deeper inside him, and he rubbed his chest.

From a career standpoint, he'd been scared to death of losing her if they crossed the line. But ever since he'd made the best mistake of kissing her, fear of screwing up on a personal front was just about all he could think about. He tried to imagine a life without her in it, and he got physically ill. She made him laugh as often as she made him ache. Witty, adorable, and addicting, Peyton was just about everything a man could want.

And he wanted. With ferocity.

He should be backing off, trying to salvage what they'd had before he'd scrambled their motherboard, but all that managed to do was reload a new program. One with a virus attached. Being with her could be the missing piece he'd hoped for all these years. A true partner. Someone to seal the gaps. Or it might fuck up his whole existence.

Her musical laugh floated toward him again, and he couldn't stop his stupid grin when she turned her head to look at him. Quickly, she glanced away, stroking Diablo's mane.

"Is dinner ready?" With a last pat for the horse, she walked toward Xavier, but he blocked her path leading outside.

"They thought we were already dating." He set her glasses back on her nose and tucked a strand of hair behind her ear.

She blinked in puzzlement. "What?"

"My parents. They assumed we were dating and were just keeping it under wraps. Ergo, their dumbfounded expressions when you left." He set his hand on her waist and urged her closer. "They're not upset we're together. I told you they wouldn't be. In fact, Mom was expecting an engagement."

Her head jerked, eyebrows pinged in surprise. "Are you serious?"

"Yes." He stroked his thumb over her ribs, studying her. She was at home here as much as she was in the office, her apartment, or his house. The realization wasn't lost on him, but she seemed to have some strange hang-up about their worlds colliding, which had unease rattling his cage. "Why did you think they wouldn't approve?"

She closed her eyes for a beat and, when she opened them, her focus landed on his chest. *"Nous venons de différentes classes sociales et—"*

He pressed his fingers to her lips and ran his tongue across his teeth. That sounded like French, which meant she was in a melancholy mood. Not good. "In English, please."

A hefty sigh, and she stared over his shoulder. "We come from different social classes and it wouldn't be in the realm of insane for people to think I was after your money. We're on opposite ends of the personality scale, plus I work for you."

Here he'd thought his head was messed up. "First, regardless of what others say, my parents would never assume you were after my bank account. And as for the rest, you're right. Those things might make or break us." He hauled her flush against him because it settled the crazy inside. "But the longer I sink into the idea of there being an us, the more I realize we're a perfect...counterbalance."

Slowly, her gaze slid to his and held. Her eyes rounded in something akin to hope, then narrowed as if she didn't believe him.

"Your strengths are my weaknesses and vice versa." He let out a measured breath. "I don't know where we'll wind up and I don't care what goes on around us. Just don't doubt me or what you already know to be true. We just started, honey. Please don't slam the brakes before we've even caught speed."

Her respirations were the only giveaway he'd gotten through to her. A steady pant, her chest rose and fell as she looked at him. Finally, she chewed her lip. "Do you mean that?"

"I've never lied to you."

She wrapped her arms around his waist and rested her cheek on his chest. "Counterbalance." She breathed a laugh. "I like that." Tilting her face, she smiled at him. "Did your parents really think we were dating all this time? That you'd proposed?"

He dropped a kiss to her forehead. "Let's go tease the crap out of them."

Chapter Twelve

From first stepping foot inside the Gaines' Napa Valley home two years before, Peyton had loved the place, and her opinion hadn't wavered since then. Four-thousand square feet of rustic chic in rural Italian style. Scents of lavender from the field blended with lemon from the grove, and wafted in through the open window to put her in sensory heaven. Little touches added charm, like the terra cotta tiled roof or the way they'd used an old barn door to design the dining room table.

They finished dinner and sipped wine around the table as Xavier's parents talked about their recent trip to Hawaii. With one hand cradling his glass, Xavier idly ran his fingers through the ends of Peyton's hair from the seat beside her, his attention focused on the discussion. He'd always been more comfortable in his parents' presence, but she'd never seen him this happy. No barriers. No hesitation. Just the real him, minus the strain.

She suppressed a shiver of delight at the ministration and his relaxed, easy grin. Since they'd gotten in the car hours ago, he'd found moments to connect. Minute things such as holding her hand or brushing his knuckles over her shoulder. It seemed ingrained and natural to him. But, for her, the gentle tenderness was something she'd gone without for so long. Both arousing and sweet, he kept surprising her with...affection.

One second she was tripping over desire, and the next she was sighing in utter girly contentment. To prove a point, the corded muscles and bulging veins of his forearm snagged her attention—again—as did his large hands. Idle details she'd not allowed herself to notice before kept surfacing. Like how he smiled with his eyes when he was too engaged to realize what he was doing. Or how touching her, in any form, seemed to pacify any lingering tension in his frame. As if she was a balm to him.

"She's been telling everyone she got lei-ed in Honolulu." Edward shook his head, a fond smile teasing his lips as he glanced at his wife.

Elaine shrugged. "I like the play on words. What can I say?"

Xavier's rich laugher filled the room. "Sounds like you had fun. Laid or lei-ed, either way." It was apparent he loved his parents immensely. They'd been a quiet beacon of support as long as Peyton had known him, and offered a great balance in understanding his quirks while subtly pushing him to do his best.

She set her wine aside and dropped her chin in her palm. "How did you two meet?"

To a lay person, Edward and Elaine were an odd pair, but despite their differences, they fit. And wow, they obviously loved each other more than air. Fond glances and sweet grins. Easy banter and casual touches. Watching them together had longing pooling in Peyton's belly. Her own parents had been like that before they'd died, and she yearned so, so much for that kind of love one day.

Elaine laughed. "We went to high school together. I was in nearly all his classes."

"Aw." Peyton sighed. "So you were childhood sweethearts?"

"Oh no." Elaine chuckled. "He didn't know I existed. I had braces and was in the glee club. He was handsome as hell and quarterback of the football team."

They sounded a bit like Peyton and Xavier, except with a role reversal. She'd been cheer captain and he'd been math club president. She'd tried to be friends with him back then, though. "So when did you start dating?"

Elaine tilted her head. "We went to separate colleges and ran into each other at our five-year high school reunion."

Edward slipped his hand in hers and grinned. "I saw her at the bar talking to old classmates and my heart stopped. Asked her to marry me two years later."

With a gasp, Peyton clutched her chest. "Well, dang. Be still my heart." If that wasn't the sweetest thing...

Xavier shook his head, a doting smile curving his lips. "Ever the optimist, Peyton." He glanced at his parents. "Before she starts spouting sonnets, maybe we should discuss the benefit." As if to prove he was teasing, he skimmed a hand down her spine and up again, his gaze affectionate.

"Yes." Elaine slapped the table, zeroing in on Peyton. "I was thinking a masquerade ball as the theme."

"How cool." Peyton could picture it now. Ball gowns and masks and dancing. "That might be even more fun than the roaring twenties from last year. Those flapper dresses and signature drinks went over uber well."

Ignoring the guys, Elaine leaned forward. "Champagne, low lighting for mystery, and a signature waltz. Perhaps some old-fashioned candelabras. What do you think?"

"I love it." A little unease curled in her stomach as she darted a quick glance toward Xavier. She lowered her voice to whisper conspiratorially to Elaine as if he wasn't there. "I don't think your son will care for the dancing part. Too much attention."

"Nonsense." Edward waved his hand. "He's—" At Xavier's subtle head shake, his father snapped his mouth shut.

Peyton narrowed her eyes, wondering what that was about. "Would you be okay with a dance or two? I could teach you a basic waltz and—"

Edward laughed, but the sound died as fast as it arrived when Xavier pinned him with an amused glare. An *ah ha* grin and nod from Edward cemented Peyton's suspicion they were up to something.

"Okay, what the heck? What aren't you telling me?"

Slowly, Xavier's gaze slid to hers. Held. Humor and affection were present where uncertainty usually resided, at least when they'd discussed charity functions in the past. "We've never danced together."

Huh. Her gaze wandered, trying to recall. They'd attended countless benefits, but no. They hadn't ever danced. Most of the events didn't have much by way of music and it had typically been an orchestra for background. Even if there had been dancing, she never would've encouraged him to participate.

"I can muster through a waltz or two, Peyton." Xavier's brows lifted, as did the corners of his mouth.

Edward laughed, amping Peyton's suspicion.

With a roll of her eyes, Elaine sighed. "Anyway, dear. There's this little boutique store we must go to while you're in town. They have the most exquisite selection. We can find you a dress. What do you say to shopping tomorrow?"

"You're on." Peyton held up a finger and looked at Xavier. "As long as someone trusts me enough to pick out my own gown." She clarified for Elaine. "Your son always chooses my evening wear for events. It's his thing."

Xavier leaned over the arm of his chair and brought his face close to hers. Heat collided with fondness in his bourbon eyes. "When have I ever not trusted you with everything?" His warm breath fanned her cheek as he kissed...the tip of her nose. "Pick whatever you like. You'll look amazing in anything."

Holy God. Desire ran rampant through her blood as she liquefied into a puddle of goo. Looked like someone got his way with words from his father, after all. If his parents weren't right across the table staring at them, she'd climb Xavier like an oak and demonstrate her appreciation.

He straightened in his chair and finished off his wine as if he hadn't just knocked her solidly into next week.

Shaking her head to clear it, she glanced at Elaine and Edward. "And you thought we were dating all along?" Without the chemistry from five seconds ago? One couldn't fake that or hide it. "Note the difference."

Elaine laced her fingers and set them on the table. "My mistake." Relief shone in her eyes. "I'm glad you are now, however." With a swift inhale, she waved the moment away. "Who's up for charades?"

Xavier groaned. "Hell no. You two team up and make Dad and I look like fools."

His mother tsked. "We picked easy terms for you to act out. Don't blame us."

"Easy," he repeated drolly. "Like *cow*? Dad guessed masturbation when I got that card."

Peyton slapped a hand over her face and laughed. At Elaine's giggle, Peyton nearly fell out of her chair. "I totally forgot about that." She fanned her face.

Edward scratched his jaw. "For the record, it did look like you were—"

"Stop right there." Xavier ran his tongue over his teeth. "I'm not playing. Period."

Twenty minutes later, dinner was cleaned up and they were in the living room mixing the homemade note cards for a game of charades. Xavier huffed from his seat between his parents on the couch while Peyton pulled her card from the stack the guys created.

Algebra. Had to be Xavier's suggestion. She smiled at him. "Yell timber now, X. You're going down."

He took the paper from her, glanced at it, and grinned. "No way Mom guesses that."

Peyton shook her head, feeling sorry for him. "Sixty seconds. Go." She nudged the neck of her sweater aside and fingered her bra strap.

"Bra!" Elaine shouted, leaning forward in her seat.

Nodding, Peyton pointed to her head like she was thinking, then pointed to Xavier. She pretended to write out an equation on her hand.

"Smart. Genius. Problem. Math." Elaine shot out guesses until Peyton pointed to her with the last answer. Elaine frowned. "Math bra? Oh! Algebra!"

"Bull." Xavier slapped his thigh. "You cheated."

Peyton took a seat beside Elaine and gave her a high-five. "I don't need to cheat. I'm just that good."

A gusty sigh, and Xavier rose.

Edward rubbed his jaw. "Just don't get a barnyard animal, son, and we'll be okay."

Peyton and Elaine laughed.

"Hardy, har-har." Xavier pulled a card, stared at it, and ground his jaw. "Seriously?" He tossed the card at them. "I'm not doing that."

Elaine turned the paper over and Peyton glanced at it. *Succubus*.

"Oh my God." She fell sideways into his mom's lap and laughed so hard she wheezed. "That's..." She heaved air. "That wasn't me. Honest."

Elaine joined the hysterics, and Peyton couldn't catch her breath to save her life. Her side ached and tears streamed from her eyes and her lungs burned. Xavier's droll expression and his mom's gasping hoots only added to the mix to send her straight into death by hilarity.

"Game over." Xavier wrapped an arm around her waist and threw her over his shoulder like a sack of potatoes. "Bedtime, giggles."

She blew out a breath and glanced at Elaine as Xavier carried her to the stairs. "Horseback riding before shopping tomorrow?"

"Sure thing, dear. Goodnight."

Halfway up the stairs, Peyton's cell buzzed in her back pocket.

"Your ass is vibrating." Xavier pulled out her phone and passed it over his shoulder to her.

She glanced at the screen and the text from Kate. *Is Moneybags being a gentleman? Remember, a self respecting girl can say no to sex.*

Peyton snorted and thumbed a response behind Xavier's back as he rounded the landing. *As if you'd know self-respect if it slapped you in the face.*

LOL. True.

She thought about their trip thus far, and typed another response. *He's been so sweet, Kate. Holding hands and saying nice things and kissing my nose. Gah.*

"Who are you texting?"

She blew her hair off her face. "My other boyfriend. He's wondering where I am."

He grunted as he strode down the upstairs hall toward the guestroom. A sharp, quick slap smacked her butt, and he rested his hand over the spot as if to soothe the heat.

"Kinky."

His laugh rumbled through her, and the rough, low sound had her panties damp. He smelled so yummy with his light cologne blending with the scent of outdoors. She wanted to breathe him in and never resurface. His hard muscles shifted against her and she was reminded all over again how mind-blowing it was to be in direct contact with him.

He set her down inside the doorway and crowded her against the frame. The lowlight from the dark hallway and dim lamp inside the guestroom cast shadows across the harsh planes of his face.

"I wish you'd sleep in my room with me." Leaning closer, he kissed his way across her cheek to her neck, his five o'clock shadow causing a delicious rasp.

A tremble tore through her and her breath caught. Any time intimacy was involved, it was like he flipped a switch and Alpha X took over. The complete imbalance from the man she'd known with the one he'd become when they were alone threw her in a constant state of flux. One second he had her smiling or content, and the next he had her all but begging.

"I don't think that's a good idea," she breathed, then moaned when his hands slid down her sides and up to cup her breasts. "I mean, I'm sure your parents know what sex is. I'm certain they've had it themselves, but—"

"Please do not put that visual in my head." Open-mouth kisses trailed from her throat to her mouth where he hovered inches from her lips. His heavy lids offered a slow blink. "We can just sleep together, you know. We've done it before." He brushed his nose against hers, his thumbs grazing her erect nipples.

"That was before I knew how talented your hands are."

He chuckled. "You haven't seen anything yet, honey." Studying her, he swallowed. "I agree our first time shouldn't be here, but do understand just how desperately I want you?" To emphasize his point, he thrust his hips and ground his erection into her belly.

Her legs nearly gave out. To level the playing field, she cupped him and stroked the long, thick length of him through his jeans. Holy wow. X had girth to him.

His eyes slammed shut, and he hissed. His body gave an involuntary jerk before his lips crushed hers. Firm, deft strokes of his tongue demonstrated what he obviously wished another part of him could to do with another part of her. He groaned a long, deep rumble into her mouth and the pressure on her breasts increased to a pleasure-pain combination.

Her cell vibrated in her free hand and she flinched. She opened her eyes to discover her glasses were fogged.

Xavier slid them off her nose and onto the top of her head, amusement warring with lust in his eyes. "Who are you really texting, anyway?"

Before she could protest, he snatched the phone and held it out of reach while pinning her to the doorframe with his body. After a beat, a wrinkle formed between his brows. "I'm not pressuring you to have sex, am I?"

Damn. "No. I assure you, we're on the same page in that regard." And if they didn't get there soon, she might combust.

He was still eyeing the screen as if he hadn't heard her response. "*He's being so sweet*," he mumbled, reading her message to Kate aloud. His gaze slid to hers. "Why is showing you respect and me liking to touch you so surprising?"

She opened her mouth and quickly shut it again.

Setting her phone on the dresser just inside the door, he cupped her cheeks. Intently, his gaze swept over her features as if trying to solve a riddle. "Answer me."

Helpless, she shrugged. If she were being honest, the white-hot heat between them was as shocking as his abject kindness. He'd been nothing but a fair boss and generous friend, but being in a relationship with him, short as it had been thus far, was just not what she'd expected. He didn't flaunt his lovers or trysts, yet she'd heard things. How he could be calculating and cold, inattentive and distant. That just wasn't the guy he'd been in her presence.

Concern twisted his mouth. "Should I be doing something different?"

She shook her head.

"Then, what?" His eyes darted back and forth between hers. "I realize Kate was just joking around, but I get the impression your response was more genuine."

"I'm not..." She sighed and stared at the ceiling, wanting to help him understand without adding guilt to the party. For some reason, he tended to take her every reaction and nuance like a direct hit. "I wasn't complaining in that text and you're right. I've been surprised by how things have gone with us."

He set one hand above her head on the doorframe and leaned into it. "Please explain that, because I don't—"

"I'm not used to this." She closed her eyes a moment and inhaled for a semblance of calm. Damn it, anyway. "Mark and I were together a few years, but he was deployed most of that time. We never really got to be a couple very much, and he wasn't the touchy-feely type. After his discharge, he couldn't even look at me. There's only been a couple quick relationships since then and..." She shook her head. "Let's just say I might not have been alone, but I was lonely. I've been by myself for a long time and I'm not..."

His exhale was as uneven as her pulse. "If you're trying to tell me you're not used to mattering to someone, I might just bleed out right here on the floor."

Double damn him. That's exactly what she was talking about. He took everything in regards to her like it was being done directly to him. She rubbed her forehead, avoiding his gaze. "I wasn't complaining, X."

"I never said you were." His gaze penetrated and held her in place. "Do you need space?" The way he paled, she assumed that was the last thing he wanted.

"No." She attempted to swallow and couldn't manage. "You...surprise me, I guess is what I'm trying to say." And ineloquently, at that.

He turned his face away, gaze distant. "That model I was with, Pamela? We broke up just before you started at Gaines Industries. She was my first true attempt at a relationship, public or otherwise. I'd had lovers, but nothing lasting." His brows furrowed as if coming to a realization. "I never had the urge to hold her hand or invoke any kind of touch outside the bedroom. Honestly, I wasn't all that comfortable in her presence, like I am with you."

His gaze returned to hers, wide open and gutting. "Around you, I just...act. You're like this—" he waggled his fingers as if searching for the right term "—extension of me. I want my hands on you all the time, and when they're not, I'm itchy. And I don't just mean sexually. Though, make no mistake, that's a fierce factor, too."

She reached up and smoothed the worry lines on his forehead, then cupped his jaw. "You didn't do anything wrong, X." The absent brushes and subtle caresses had been a direct current from him to her, relaying she meant something to him.

However, they were new in this endeavor and both of them had a lot to lose if things went south. Her, most of all. He'd been concerned about the company if they didn't work out. She'd lose not only him and possibly her job, but the few people she'd considered family the past two years. His parents had taken her in like a stray and treated her as if she were one of them. He was right about something. She hadn't mattered to anyone, not for a long time. Not until he'd come along.

Closing his eyes, he sighed. "I told you once before, I know what I'm doing in the bedroom, Peyton. Outside? Utter failure." He nailed her with a look bordering on feral panic wrapped in determination. "I can be myself in your presence. But if I cross a line or do something incorrect, you need to grade me on a curve."

"Grade you..." She wove her fingers through his thick chestnut hair and rose on her toes to speak against his mouth. "This isn't a test."

To prove he'd pass even if it were an exam, she pressed her lips to his and illustrated for him. The contrast of his firm to her soft and the coaxing way he took the kiss from sweet to hot to a thorough exploration had hope ramming the door of reality. No man had ever showed her such attention to detail.

His hand slid down her spine and grabbed her backside as he eased away. "I'm not feeling very tired anymore. How about you demonstrate this dance lesson you mentioned?"

"Tomorrow." She smiled. "Are you going horseback riding with us?"

He brushed his knuckles over her cheek, gaze following the movement. "I could be talked into it."

"Good." She slipped out of his arms and into the room. "Night, X."

He groaned and strode down the hall toward his bedroom. "Sweet dreams, honey."

Biting her lip, she closed the door and checked her phone to read Kate's text. *I'd tell you not to swoon, but he'd catch you, so never mind.*

Wasn't that the truth?

Chapter Thirteen

After his run, Xavier climbed the stairs and pulled out his earbuds, pausing outside Peyton's bedroom door. He was surprised she was still asleep and hesitated in waking her. She'd seemed exhausted lately and worn around the edges. But his mom was saddling the geldings and waiting for her. Plus, he really wanted to kiss her good morning without an audience.

He knocked, but she didn't respond, so he opened the door and stepped inside the guestroom. The drapes were parted over the balcony doors and early morning sunlight fed in through the glass. Her blonde hair poked out from under a heap of blankets and a purple, grape-printed comforter.

He walked closer and perched on the edge of the mattress by her hip, smiling. Curled on her side, she slept with one hand under her head and the other tucked to her chest. Her features relaxed, she looked like a sleeping angel with her round cheeks, long pale lashes, and hair light as a halo across the pillow. He fingered the quilt lower to expose more of her, grinning wider at her wineglass-patterned pajamas. Leave it to her to have themed nightwear.

"Peyton." Leaning forward, he kissed her temple and called her name again.

She opened one eye, blinked, and ran her gaze over his black nylon shorts and gray tee. "You're sweaty."

And she was utterly, devastatingly beautiful. Her sleep-roughened, husky voice wrapped around his throat and squeezed. "I'm just back from a run."

"How barbaric." She rolled to her back and stretched, thrusting her breasts out to tempt him. "What time is it?"

"Seven." Setting his iPod on the nightstand, he straddled her hips and set his hands by either side of her shoulders. "I'll bring you coffee in bed if you kiss me good morning."

"You had me at coffee."

Grinning, he dipped his head. He brushed his lips over hers until her warm breath fanned his mouth and she opened for him. He sucked a rapid inhale at the first stroke of her tongue and groaned at the second.

How insane was it that he wanted to do this every damn morning? Have his first task of the day be to sink inside her? He'd probably be more concerned at how quickly she'd invaded his every thought, but she'd been under his skin for years. Only now, she was burrowing closer to a certain organ that beat erratically behind his ribs. Truthfully, the only time in his life his heart ever leapt like this was when confronted with a social situation that tripped his anxiety.

Peyton had it pounding for an entirely different reason—like she'd given his heart a diverse purpose than simply a warning knell.

She issued a satisfied mewl and smiled. "There are better ways to get sweaty than running, you know." Her shocking cerulean eyes lit with amusement and nothing short of enticement.

He resisted the urge to rub his aching shaft. "Said the woman who kicked me out of her room last night."

"I did no such thing."

He grunted. "Lead me not into temptation, honey. My mother's waiting for you in the stables."

To be contradictory, she nuzzled his throat and licked a path from his neck to his jaw, her persuasive hum rippling across his skin.

His arms nearly collapsed. His lungs did. "Peyton," he warned.

"You came in my room, not the other way around." She—*have mercy*—nipped his earlobe and sucked on it.

"Guilty as charged." Hell, he'd gladly accept any sentence she enacted. But not now. When he took her the first time, there would be hours ahead of them to explore, divide, and conquer. And it would be in his bed back home. "You're killing me."

He rolled to his back and rose from the bed. She laughed.

Turning at the door, he took in her heavy lids, flushed cheeks, and body sprawled on the mattress. "You can get your own coffee since I need a cold shower."

He strode out to the sound of her laughing.

An hour later, his gaze was trained on her perfect ass as she rode Diablo across the lavender field ahead of him. Skinny jeans and Peyton Smoke should be a crime against restraint. Her fitted yellow shirt containing those breasts, too. She'd put in her contacts and left her hair loose to trail halfway down her back. Sunlight hit the champagne strands as she turned her head and smiled at something his mother said from the horse beside hers.

Like a battering ram to the solar plexus.

"What do you think?" She grinned at him over her shoulder.

About what? How quickly he could peel away her clothing and pin her to the closest lemon tree? How her hair would look spread over a field of lavender blooms? How he'd rather have her riding him than a horse?

Dad chuckled next to him. "Maybe you should repeat the question."

Peyton drew Diablo to a stop. "Your mom thought the thank-you gifts for the benefit should be personalized. She suggested cutting lavender from the field and suspending it in oil vials."

"Whatever you think." He was no good at this stuff, yet she always asked his opinion. Included him.

"Or we could press it between glass." Mom shrugged. "That might be less time-consuming. A little trinket for guests to take home with them."

"Oh." Peyton straightened in the saddle. "We should do that, but put a scripted note with it. There's this T.S. Eliot poem…" She snapped her fingers. *The Dry Salvages.* It uses a line about lavender that would fit our cause, too."

"I'll have to look it up." Mom's lips twisted in thought.

Peyton's gaze drifted. *"The future is a faded song, a royal rose or a lavender spray of wistful regret for those who are not yet here to regret, pressed between yellow leaves of a book that has never been opened. And the way up is the way down, the way forward is the way back. You cannot face it steadily, but this thing is sure. That time is no healer. The patient is no longer here."*

The breath seeped from Xavier's lungs, not only because her photographic mind was hot, but because that was exactly the perfect thing to coincide with their mission. If anyone knew the fallout of losing someone to war, across the ocean or at home, it was her. Both haunting and hopeful, the words would stay with guests a long time.

Mom wiped tears from her eyes. "I love it."

He cleared his throat. "Agreed."

After their ride, Peyton and his mother took off to go shopping, leaving Xavier and his dad to cut lavender for the benefit gifts under Mom's direct orders.

Straightening, Xavier wiped sweat from his brow with his forearm and eyed the basket full of purple blooms by his feet. Late afternoon sunlight beat down, and he never wished for a piece of technology so badly in his life. Fresh air was one thing, but he'd had enough.

And his mind kept drifting to what dress Peyton would buy. The color, cut, style. Part of him was always relieved she'd let him choose her gowns before. It gave him a semblance of control and eliminated the element of surprise.

"How much longer do we need to do this?"

Dad examined his full basket, then Xavier's. "They said until these were full. I think we're done."

Thank Christ. He smelled like a perfume factory and someone had stolen his man card two hours ago. They headed inside, where he showered and then waited on the back deck for the ladies to return.

Dad stepped out and handed him a beer, then claimed the Adirondack chair across from a short iron café table. "So, what was the deal with the dance nonsense at dinner last night? Are you really going to make Peyton teach you how to waltz?"

"Yes." Grinning, Xavier slumped in his seat and eyed the vast hills in the distance, coated in orange light.

The sun would be set in an hour, and he'd been hoping to drag Peyton to his favorite spot to watch it. The temperature was steadily dropping and cooling off as the day progressed, turning the upper seventies into the lower sixties. He stared at the small fire crackling in the outdoor stone hearth off the deck and imagined patient, tolerant Peyton with her arms around him, teaching him a box step.

The old man's brows lifted. "Even though you already know how? Your mother made you take ballroom dance lessons for two years in high school."

Xavier chuckled and took a sip of lager. "No harm in a refresher course."

"Or you just like the notion of a private tutor."

He laughed again. "There is that, yes."

When the ladies finally returned moments later, Peyton refused to let him see the dress she'd bought, so he took her hand and led her off the deck to show her what he'd been dying to do since their talk about Paris back at his apartment.

Weaving through the lemon and olive grove, they climbed a steep hill, where he tugged her to a halt by a mature lone maple tree.

She sighed, staring at the view. "This is amazing."

With the grove down one descent, a valley teeming with vines from a neighboring vineyard spread before them on the other side. Above them, there was only a reddish-orange sky fading to navy dusk. A barely-there breeze offered a variety of rivaling scents from lemon and red grapes to damp soil and cut grass. Crickets chirped and fireflies winked in the distance.

He couldn't conjure anything more settling or soothing than this, besides Peyton's presence.

He studied her profile, her features content and serene as shadows played over her face. Since she was the better view, he kept watching her, the array of emotions in her expression and the way she seemed to finally, if for just a moment, stop thinking.

She offered him an amused side-glance. "You're missing it."

"No, I'm not." He stepped behind her anyway, and pressed his face into her hair. Her sultry perfume rose over that of other scents and a peace he'd rarely known settled deep in his chest.

When the sunset had come and gone, she leaned against him. "You surprise me, X. All that genius inside your brilliant mind and you bust out with a romantic streak."

He smiled. "I'm not romantic." At her sound of disagreement, he amended. "Observing and appreciating one's surroundings isn't romance."

"No, but bringing me up here to a spot you've shown no one else qualifies. Or buying me a key charm necklace for my birthday to replace the one I'd lost does, too. Or carrying me to bed in order not to wake me because you knew I was tired. Should I keep going?" She glanced at him over her shoulder. "Standing sentinel all night when I hurt my head. Lying with me half the night after you found out my mind was restless. You, X, are a romantic."

Resting his temple to the side of her head, he stared at the stars and absorbed what she'd said. As a pragmatic, no one had ever accused him of being ruled by emotion. In fact, society as a whole saw him as a cold-hearted, unfeeling bastard. She'd done well to change their view since joining Gaines Industries, making him aloof and mysterious instead of detached and robotic. There wasn't one instance in her examples where she hadn't been directly related to said romanticism. For him, his actions were more about him giving a shit than sentimentality.

"I think maybe it's just you, Peyton." She turned in his arms, and he brushed a wild strand of hair from her forehead. Her confused expression battled with irritation, so he clarified. "I mean, I think perhaps you just bring out certain qualities."

She tilted her head. "Case in point. Only a romantic would say that."

He gave up. Let her think whatever she wanted as long as she was happy and he played a part in it. "I need a dance lesson." He reached around her and pulled her phone from her pocket. Behind her back, he swiped the screen and went through her downloads. Most of the songs he recognized. "What's this one? *Sad Song* by We The Kings."

She went still against his chest. "Um, it reminds me of you. It's a ballad, sort of."

Anything named *Sad Song*, followed by, *reminds me of you*, couldn't be a good omen. Concerned, he pressed Play and piano music drifted around them in the dark. The lyrics relayed the opposite of what he'd expected. Instead of implying he was pathetic, they talked about how, with her, he was alive and fearless, yet without, nothing but empty. Damn if that wasn't the goddamn most accurate rendition of his life.

At the chorus, he set the phone by the tree, the song still playing, and wrapped an arm around her back. "I have a confession."

Brows wrinkled, she cleared her throat. "What's that?"

"I don't really need lessons." Placing her hand in his, he set them in motion.

She stumbled, but quickly caught up to a basic waltz. When it was clear she knew what she was doing, he sped the steps along, making them more intricate, and glided her across the small hill. They matched each other beat for beat as if they'd done this a thousand times. He'd always wanted to dance with her, but never had the opportunity.

Her wide gaze met his and her lips parted in surprise. "Yeah, X. Because dancing in the moonlight under the stars isn't romantic at all."

He laughed at her dry tone and spun her. As the song ended, he tugged her flush against him. "I stand by my earlier statement. It's all you."

"I don't understand you." She offered a slight shake of her head. "If you had this kind of heart in you all along, why not let the women you used to date see it? Instead, you allowed them think you were cold, uncaring."

"I don't know." Yes, he did. They weren't her. Plain and simple. From the moment his former, awkward teenage self had encountered her charismatic grin in a school hallway between Freshman English and Intro to History, she'd sunk her claws deep and hadn't let go. Even all those years later, when they'd reconnected after lost time, she'd been one of the only people he could breathe around. "Doesn't matter now, does it?"

"I suppose not, but—"

He closed his mouth over hers and shoved his hands in her hair. He didn't appreciate her trying to fix something he didn't want fixed. If any of his previous lovers had given him cause to be half the man he was around Peyton, they wouldn't be here right now. Together.

On paper, their schematics might be all kinds of wrong, but he'd meant what he'd told her yesterday. They were the right counterbalance to one another. If things crashed and burned between them, life as he knew it would be over. Yet, for the first time since he'd raised his hands in surrender, he discovered he held the future in his grasp. Literally. All he had to do was avoid screwing it up.

She made a stunned noise in her throat and molded her lithe body against him. One hand pressed over his pounding heart, the other dipped under his shirt and skimmed up his back, sending a violent wave of need coursing through his hard drive. Then, the hand on his chest drifted south, past his abs, to wrap around his...

"Christ." He pinned her back to the tree and ate at her mouth, starving for what she alone could provide.

Hand to God, if he didn't have her soon, he was going to expire. Painfully. He'd spent an eternity desiring her, and he'd never gone this long between dating and sex. She was different than a conquest, and rushing things might derail what they had building. He wasn't even entirely sure what kind of lover she preferred. At times, the rougher side of him had her manic and breathless, but his more controlled self brought out a sensual, equally desperate response. He couldn't get a handle on what angle to attempt.

And that was the other thing. Sex had never been this important. Nor had he ever needed to think this hard. If he had confidence in two areas of his life, it was business and the bedroom. When a woman was under him, he could cut the power supply to his brain and pleasure her for hours. With Peyton, his body fired on all circuits and every cell was hyperaware. Nothing would properly reboot.

He settled for her skin against his and slid his hand under her shirt, over the smooth area of her taut belly, and cupped her breast. Her nipple beaded against the lace and pressed his palm. She was a handful and then some, and he was barely able to fit all of her flesh in his grasp. Hell, did he *need* her. Bad.

Shoving his other hand under her shirt, he cupped both breasts and ground his hips against her, seeking relief from the awful, wonderful ache behind his fly. He groaned from a place so deep, his ribs rattled. She gasped against his lips and arched into him, her own fingers attempting to explore.

Mercy, she'd kill him if she touched him again. He pinned her wrists to the trunk over her head with one hand and pulled away to stare down at her. Her heavy lids lifted to reveal lust-saturated navy eyes swallowed by her pupils. Breaths soughing, she bit her lip. And undid his hardwiring.

Keeping her arms pinned, he unbuttoned her jeans, watching her closely to check for any hint of objection. None. Her respirations increased, causing her pebbled nipples to rasp his chest. He slid her zipper down, the teeth releasing loudly to blend with the chirp of crickets.

He slipped his hand between the denim and the lace of her panties, and grazed his thumb over her clit. His lungs stalled when he found her drenched.

"Oh my God," she breathed, closing her eyes and thrusting into his touch. "Please."

Anything. He'd give her fucking anything.

Shoving aside the material, he parted her folds and drove a finger inside her wet, hot channel. She greedily clenched him and bucked, sending his pulse toward holy shit. Pressing his palm to her hard little nub, he bent to speak in her ear. "This what you want?"

"Yes." She moaned and wrapped a leg around his hips, sinking his digit deeper into her giving flesh.

He inserted a second finger and pumped, keeping pressure on her clit with his palm and licking the tendon on her neck where her pulse pounded. She jerked her hips in time with his thrusts and sent quiet whimpers into the night. She didn't take long. A few pumps and her walls tightened. Her breath caught.

He crashed his mouth over hers to contain any noise she might emit, and swallowed her desperate cry as she trembled and quaked against him. Unable to help it, he slammed his pelvis into her hip to cease the incessant throbbing, grinding until she'd gone lax.

Panting, he dropped his forehead to hers and withdrew his fingers, releasing her wrists. She'd yet to open her eyes, but watching her aftershocks subside was single-handedly the greatest thing he'd ever born witness to. Flushed cheeks and swollen lips and the slightest satisfied curve to her mouth. He wrapped his arms around her to give a buffer between her and the tree, hoping she didn't have marks from what they'd just done.

An eternity later, she offered a throaty laugh. "It's always the quiet ones." She stroked his jaw and buried her face in his neck. "Damn, X."

Color him crazy, but this was the most satisfied he'd ever been without coming. "Think you can walk, honey?"

"Yes, but…" She lifted her head. Blinked. "You didn't get to—"

"I'll take care of it later." While thinking of her. Probably repeatedly.

Chapter Fourteen

    Peyton bit her lip and, from bed, stared at the ceiling in the Gaines' guestroom. What a day. Horseback riding, shopping. They'd punched out most of the benefit weekend details and Elaine had even managed to get Peyton onboard for Xavier's surprise birthday party. He wouldn't be overly joyful, but he'd calm down once he realized it was a small affair.

    And, holy wow. Xavier had given her an orgasm up against a tree. Then, they'd headed back inside to eat dinner with his parents and drank wine like he hadn't...*given her an orgasm up against a tree*. With his hands. After they'd danced. Under the stars.

    God, that man.

    She rubbed her forehead and clenched her thighs, aching. She may have had her mind blown, but he hadn't gotten release. If she was still needy and wanting more, she could only imagine what state he was in.

    Glancing at the door, she mulled over her options. Thus far, he'd been the aggressive one when it came to intimacy. Though she was seeing less and less of his social anxiety, she just hadn't expected an alpha side. Sure, he was fair and confident in the boardroom. But nothing like the man he morphed into when he was turned on. Maybe she should take the initiative, just this once, in order to quell her ridiculous guilt trip about their one-sided exchange.

    Tossing the sheets aside, she climbed from bed and poked her head out into the hallway. His parents' master suite was down the opposite end and the door was closed. Xavier's was partially open, and light filtered onto the carpet through the crack.

    Okay, he was awake. Problem solved.

    Closing her door behind her, she quietly padded to his room and knocked. She ducked her head inside to find him leaning against the headboard wearing a white tee and flannel pants. His room was a mirror to hers, sleigh-style walnut furniture pieces and all, except his was in sage and earth tones versus burgundy and yellow.

He glanced at her over the rim of his glasses and set the tablet he'd been looking at in his lap. "Hey, can't sleep?"

"No." She shut the door and walked to the bed. "What are you doing?"

"Reading quarterly reports." He pulled the sheets aside in a silent invitation for her to join him.

Instead, she straddled his lap, earning a sharp inhale. "I would think that should make you bored enough to sleep."

He laughed, low and rough and yummy. "I guess not, since I'm still awake."

Taking the tablet, she set it on the nightstand, then slid off his glasses and did the same with those.

Hands on her thighs, he studied her with a mix of avid interest and wary censure. "What are you doing?"

Smiling, she leaned closer and kissed his neck, nuzzled the skin behind his ear. "Nothing."

"That doesn't feel like nothing." He groaned and tilted his head to give her better access. "I thought we agreed our first time wouldn't be here."

"Who said anything about sex?" She moved to the other side and licked a similar path. His chest rose and fell in rapid pants. Sliding her hands under his shirt, she worked the material up until it was over his head and on the floor. "I'm just returning the favor."

His head hit the backboard with a thunk, and he closed his eyes. "What?" His fingers clenched her thighs.

She hovered over his lips. "Don't you remember earlier? The tree?" Her nipples beaded painfully and the ache between her legs increasingly throbbed. The heat from his flesh seeped through her thin pajamas and his light, spicy cologne swirled around her.

Slowly, his lids lifted to reveal bourbon and fire. "Hard thing to forget, honey. You coming on my hand and the expression on your face as you detonated. Damn beautiful. But you don't have to—"

She cupped his hard length through his pants, and his hips jerked. He thickened with her ministration. "What were you saying?"

"I can't fucking remember." He grabbed the back of her neck and crushed his mouth to hers, demanding entry. Hot, sharp swirls of his tongue met hers as his hands slid north, up her belly to her breasts.

With a palm to his chest, she eased him away and switched off the lamp, bathing the room in moonlight from the balcony. He tried coming right at her again, but she shook her head.

"Nuh-uh. Your turn. You just lie there."

"Peyton..." He growled, the rumble vibrating from his chest into hers.

"Shh. You have to be quiet." She stilled for a fraction of a beat, never fathoming she'd have to tell Xavier Gaines that particular phrase.

She set his arms on either side of him and squeezed to tell him to leave them put. Kissing his jaw, she hummed in her throat at the abrasion from his outgrowth. The rasp from their skin connecting sent an electrical charge through her whole system.

At the office, he was always clean-shaven and neatly dressed in his expensive suits. The sexy billionaire cloaked in intrigue and control. Away from work, especially on the weekends, he rarely shaved, sported a semi-permanent case of bedhead, and wore jeans like they'd been designed for him—which gave him just enough of a dangerous, mysterious edge to pacify any bad boy fantasies.

He fisted the sheet by his hip. "I'm not known for being quiet. Or placid. I want to touch you—"

Slapping a hand over his mouth, she shook her head in warning. Figured the man was broodingly quiet everywhere except the bedroom. She shivered in delight. "Another time, you can make noise. Now, should I continue or go back to my room?"

His breath soughed against her palm as his hard, molten gaze nailed her.

"Good boy."

His eyes narrowed.

Smiling, she gazed down at him and set her hands on his sculpted, gorgeous torso. His stomach concaved at her touch, but he kept silent and unmoving. She lowered her head and swirled her tongue around the flat disc of his copper nipple, letting her fingers trace the dips of lean muscle on his abs, his narrow waist. Biceps bulged as he clenched his fists, and her grin widened.

"I freaking love your body." Corded, chiseled definition and hot, scented skin. She moved to the other nipple and nipped. Sucked hard.

He glared at the ceiling, his muscles tense. "The feeling is more than mutual, which I will demonstrate in the very near future, honey." His guttural tone was murmured through clenched teeth, and the knowledge she had someone like him at her mercy amped her desire.

She breathed a laugh and kissed her way to his navel. Dipping her fingers in the waistband of his pajamas, she peeked up at him. Their gazes locked, his so intense it bordered on savage. After a moment to seemingly process, he lifted his hips, and she nudged the pants to his thighs. Still watching her, he rested one bent arm behind his head.

And then, she glanced down, breaking the heated connection only to force back a gasp. The man certainly didn't lack for endowment. She'd touched him through clothing, but having at least ten inches of pulsing flesh millimeters from her face made her realize just how much she'd underestimated his size. He hardened even more under her gaze, veins popping and a bead of moisture seeping from the tip. No way was she getting even half of him in her mouth, but she'd make it good for him.

She wrapped her fingers around his length and stroked him from base to tip. He made a noise like the breath had backed up in his lungs. Her hair a curtain, she took his crown in her mouth and swirled her tongue on the underside of his shaft.

"Holy..." He clamped his mouth shut as if remembering to be quiet. His jaw ticked. With a gentleness his body didn't emanate, he used his free hand to thread his fingers through her hair. Eyes pleading, he nodded.

It had been a long time since she'd done this, but his response encouraged her. Using teeth and tongue, she teased him until she learned what he liked. His erratic breathing and groans told her he preferred a firm grasp and his head stimulated. With her hand around his base, she took him as far as she could and, when he nudged the back of her throat, she hummed.

He bucked under her, fingers clenching her strands. "Peyton, damn..." His bourbon eyes studied her as he carefully thrust into her mouth. With every roll of his hips, his lips parted wider, his brow furrowing deeper.

Gaze back on her task, she used her other hand to cup his balls. He hissed. She stroked him. He inhaled hard. She took him deep and hummed again. He choked and bowed halfway off the bed.

The heaviness in her breasts and pulsing between her thighs made giving him pleasure even more maddenly satisfying. She increased the pace, sensing he was close, and looked at him. His eyes flew open as if knowing she sought him, and the pleasure-pain combo in his depths felled her, heated her cheeks.

Controlled, contemplative, brilliant Xavier Gaines was on the brink of losing it, and all because of her. Pride coiled with need inside her belly and consumed. Though he'd had many lovers, she got the impression his wide open expression was something no one else had seen.

He whispered her name, his voice tight. "I'm..."

His thick lashes fluttered, and he threw his head back. Muscles bulged. Tendons strained. He barked a hoarse cry as the first jet of release came. Reaching up, she covered his mouth, never slowing hers, and pumped his shaft while his stiff body shuddered.

She eased up once he started to relax and lowered her hand while his breathing soughed. He flung an arm over his face, and she grinned. As he lay there, chest rising and falling, she reset his pants and kneeled between his thighs, waiting.

An eternity later, he jerked his head up, pinning her with shocked eyes wrapped in...absolution. Slowly, he shook his head, vaulted to a sitting position, and grabbed her behind the knees. He drew her onto his lap to straddle him and stroked her jaw. His gaze followed the movement and, after a few moments, it softened.

"Peyton." That was it, just her name, but the reverence had her throat tight. If she lived a hundred years, no one would ever capture the flurry of a thousand emotions in two syllables like him. He told a story simply by saying her name.

Closing his eyes, he dropped his forehead to hers, his large hands smoothing her hair. Then, he kissed her, not with passion or heat or need, but with tenderness. Feather-light, he brushed his lips across hers before he opened and, as if having all the time in existence, stroked her tongue. A caress. An unhurried narrative of patience and acceptance and some kind of deeper meaning she couldn't quite grasp.

Unsure whether to weep or sigh, she cupped his cheeks and held him pressed against her in a way that seemed much more intimate than the act they'd just finished. He could be such a contradiction that he left her reeling. Never harsh, forever observant, sometimes shy, often commanding, rarely indifferent, and always—*always*—considerate. Alpha and beta. Dominant and submissive.

He pulled away, holding her face, staring into her eyes. His mouth opened as if to say something, but he dragged his thumb across her lower lip like he wanted to pull words from her instead.

"What's wrong?"

A slight shake of his head, and he smiled. "This is going to sound moronic, but I'm finding the lack of something wrong disturbing."

Yeah, and then there was this Xavier—the side who would slice a vein for the sake of honesty because he trusted her that much. God, what was she getting into with him? Any deeper, and she might never climb back out.

He sighed. "I'm sorry. I shouldn't have..." He stared at her mouth, jaw tense. "Do you remember the day we met?"

Glancing over his shoulder, she tried to recall. It had been freshman year of high school, but to pin down an exact moment? She shook her head.

"You were standing by your locker in your cheerleader uniform." His smile grew wistful, and he tucked a strand of hair behind her ear. "I was between classes and about to pass by. I'd seen you before, but that was the first time you looked at me, never mind spoke to me." He cleared his throat. "You glanced up and, without so much as a hesitation about social order, you grinned and asked my name."

He let out a breath and idly traced a finger over her collarbone. "That was the first time in my life the craziness inside my head halted. There was the prettiest girl in school, talking to me. I should've been a bumbling idiot or wondering if I was being set up for a prank. My operandi back then was to keep my head down and just get through the days." He looked at her, a self-depreciating smile curving one corner of his mouth. "None of that mattered. You silenced the anxiety and, with a blink of those eyelashes, had me believe I could do anything."

She casually kissed his chin, even though her insides were mushy from his kind memory. "It was the cheerleading uniform. Short skirt and tight shirt. They're designed to make guys stupid."

His gaze went distant. After a moment, he grunted. "Don't get me wrong. You in that outfit? A ponytail, huge blue eyes, and blinding white smile? A boy would have to be dead not to react. But it wasn't teenage hormones. At least, not in that instance. You stopped my world when it had been uncontrollably spinning."

"An aphrodisiac?" Interesting.

His surprised laugh filled the room. "Something like that." He sobered, setting his hands on her hips. "My point is, that was the first time I remember it happening. I have moments with Joseph, definitely with my parents, but you? Fifteen years later, you still quiet my crazy, Peyton." He kissed one cheek, then the other. "No matter how turned on I am or what roadblock we pass while we evolve, I'm grounded."

"And it bothers you? The lack of...problems?"

He ran his tongue across his teeth. "When you put it that way, my concern sounds ridiculous."

She shook her head. "No, I get it."

He'd had to struggle all his life to adapt socially when his mind sought numeric order. A square peg in a round hole. Them being together or, rather, apart, could disrupt his balance. It was human nature to look for the out clause, and Xavier was the kind of man who took all factors into account. For him, their relationship seemed too good to be true. Maybe it was. Hadn't she been thinking the same thing?

"We've always had the honesty policy." He searched her gaze. "I don't want to hide things from you, professionally or personally. Thus, when these errant thoughts pop into my head, I want you to be aware." His thumbs stroked the skin on her waist between her shirt and her pants. "I trust you more than I trust myself. My life has been a series of near violent riots in my head. It's like you eradicated the chaos, and I..."

"You're looking for the next speed bump." For something to go wrong because, for him, something always would.

"Yes." He sighed.

She nodded, realizing how deep his feelings ran and unsure what to do about it. He'd always respected her in all aspects of their relationship and went out of his way to show appreciation. But she'd never known he'd considered her a beacon or...solace. Not on that kind of level.

"You and your parents gave me a sense of family I'd lost long ago." She chewed her lip, dissecting her thoughts. "I know I'm not blood, but I'd almost forgotten what it was like to have a support system, aside from Kate. I understand your concerns because I have them, too. We seem too ideal sometimes, even before we started dating."

She rubbed her forehead. "I think you need to cut yourself some slack. I can't take credit for all you've done with your life. At thirty, you own a Fortune 500 company, started your own charity, sold a software app for millions, and have the backing of government contracts. You earned your success without me."

"You're right. I did." He kissed her temple and spoke against her skin. "And I can walk into a crowded room and not break out into a cold sweat. I can speak in front of cameras and hungry reporters without clamming up. I don't have to think before smiling or moving or blinking. Because of you." He brushed her nose with his. "I'd rather have that than money or prestige or a top floor office."

God. Her eyes burned and her chest hitched. "X, I—"

"I know my accomplishments, honey. I can read about them in any newspaper or journal. What I'm most proud of is the man I've become since a certain blonde walked into my building and gave me the courage I never thought I had in me."

With a sound of duress she couldn't smother, she dropped her head on his shoulder and blew out a breath. "I love my job."

He chuckled and dragged his hand up and down her spine. "Good to know."

She buried her face in his neck. "I mean it. When I graduated college, this position is exactly what I'd been praying for. Decent salary, appreciation, friendly environment, a boss who gives a shit, working with people, and using my creativity. Plus...stability."

His hand paused mid-stroke. He tensed against her as if he'd drawn an unsavory conclusion. "Your job isn't at risk." When she said nothing, he eased away and looked at her. "Let me be clear. No matter what happens between us, Peyton, your job is not at risk."

Somewhere deep inside, she'd known that, but her nerves settled hearing him say it. "Okay." She wanted to bring them back to the light banter they had before. "Are you always this serious after sex?"

His eyes narrowed, but the smirk quirking his lips showed he knew she was kidding.

"I mean, that was just oral. I think I need to brace myself for the actual deed if—"

He smacked her butt, a grin splitting his handsome face. "Very funny."

"There you go with the kink again." She wove her fingers in his thick chestnut hair and basked in his cute, relaxed smile. She absolutely adored him like this—laid back and carefree.

"Serves you right for teasing me." He blinked. "Come to think of it, you're about the only person in existence who dares taunt me."

Poor, X. "Big, bad, broody Mr. Gaines. Always so solemn." She sighed. "Kate pokes fun at you."

He grunted. "No, Kate insults me, only she wraps it in sarcasm." He jutted his chin. "Joseph jokes around sometimes. Not like you do, though."

"Well," she said through a sigh. "Before I'm tempted to tease you in an entirely different way, I'm going back to bed." She gave him a quick kiss. "Goodnight."

His arms banded around her to keep her in his lap. "Where do you think you're going?"

"To my room. Favors have been returned and satisfaction abounds." She wiggled her brows.

"I want to know more about this other form of teasing. Demonstrations, please."

Throwing her head back, she laughed.

His too-talented mouth latched onto her throat. Sucked. Nipped. "I want my tongue on every inch of you." To illustrate, he licked and kissed his way over her neck to her ear and spoke against the shell. "I want to hear those needy little noises you made outside earlier." He held the back of her head as she gasped. Moaned. "Still want to go back to your room, honey?"

"No," she breathed, fighting the white-hot need building. What she wanted was his dirty bedroom talk followed by the dirtier things he claimed. God, all he had to do was speak naughty nothings in that gravel-rich tone of his and she was toast.

Still holding her head, he worked his hand between their bodies and cupped her breast. "I do believe it's your turn for a favor." He pinched her nipple between his thumb and forefinger, sending bolts of fire from the area to the apex of her thighs.

She trembled. "If we start this again, we'll be returning favors all night."

"I don't see the problem."

Oh God. They had to stop. She wasn't normally a vocal person in bed, but he seemed to turn her into one. And it appeared he liked to make noise, too. They shouldn't do this here, and if things progressed, she wouldn't be able to control herself. It was him who had said he didn't want their first time to be at his parents' place.

She twisted, flopped on her back, and groaned at the loss of contact. She threw her hand up when he reached for her. "Nuh-uh." Rolling, she got to her feet. "You, stay. I'm going."

A wicked, wicked grin curved his lips. "I will remember where we left off."

Knees? Jelly. "You do that." She strode to the door on shaky legs and turned as he called her name.

"Go out with me." When she frowned in confusion, his smile shifted and sobered from Big Bad Wolf to Sweet Xavier. "I'm not making love to you until we're back home and have had a proper date. Dinner? Next weekend?"

Gah. She had to clear her throat twice. "Yes."

Chapter Fifteen

Late afternoon on Tuesday, Xavier leaned back in his chair as Peyton strode into his office wearing a navy blue dress that made her eyes brighter and hugged every subtle curve of her body. He scanned her long legs before letting his gaze hover on her mouth. And sighed. Those red lips had been wrapped around a certain part of him a few days prior, and he couldn't shake the reminder whenever she was within a hundred feet of him.

"You ready?" She smiled, setting her hands on her hips.

Hell, yes. He was more than ready. For their date on Saturday and to take things to the next level. Damn, just to take her period. But that's not what she meant. The reporter and photographer from the magazine were here for his exclusive interview. He'd rather chew nails.

He rose and smoothed his tie. "Sure."

"Okay, just like we discussed, we're going to take photos with the heads of the various departments in the company, then sit down for the interview."

She stepped in front of him and adjusted the lapels of the suit she'd picked out. Something about the coloring and his eyes or whatever. "They want your solo pictures taken at night afterward, so we'll finish with that. This spread is more of a behind-the-scenes look than what we're used to, but I trust Daniel to keep it real. He doesn't have a rep for playing games. You can be a little candid for him."

She offered him a reassuring smile. "I know you hate these things, but this is a good opportunity to show the world who you really are behind the company. I'll be right there with you."

He stared at her and kept silent when he wanted to kiss her for the five-hundred and sixtieth time today. She always did this kind of thing before interviews—gave him a heads up on what would happen and reassured him she'd be close. In honesty, he loved that she still treated him carefully, even though he didn't need the kid gloves anymore.

In two years, she'd not given him any reason to question her decisions or doubt her intentions. Gaines Industries hadn't had a smidgen of bad press since she'd signed on. Moreover, because of their level of trust, he didn't freeze up when put in front of people because he knew she'd never drop him in a situation where he'd be vulnerable.

"All good?" She adjusted her glasses.

He nodded. "All good." Her preparation discussion popped to mind—how this magazine layout would be almost like a day in the life. The charity, his company, and a personal background were to be included. "What if they ask about us?"

She blinked. "Some of the media still like to query about a personal relationship, but most don't bother anymore. We nipped that in the bud."

"Except we are in a relationship now."

Crossing her arms, she shifted balance to her other foot and looked at him with an expression he couldn't read, yet left his blood running cold. "It seems too early to announce, and we agreed not to go public until we knew where or if this was headed somewhere. Besides, the article goes to print for the November issue—a month away. A lot can happen between now and then."

Dread settled heavy in his gut. Finally, he had an inkling of where her head was at, and he didn't care for it one iota. He'd been hesitant at first to cross the romantic line, but since they had, he'd been all in. For him, it didn't matter if they'd been together twenty-four hours or twenty-four years. He had the distinct impression she was it for him. If he'd not been so worried about screwing up, he would've known all along.

But Peyton? Though he trusted her with his life, his billions if it came down to it, she didn't seem to trust him. Not entirely. Logically, he couldn't blame her. As a teenager, her parents had been killed in a car crash. Her brother had died while serving their country. Her fiancé had suffered so terribly after returning from war, he'd committed suicide. Everyone she ever loved aside from Kate was dead. That had to screw with her head, never mind her heart.

He couldn't help but wonder if her particular form of survivor's guilt made her question if she was lovable or worth sticking around for. Mark's suicide being the most detrimental. Though he'd been sick, in a way, he'd left voluntarily, had chosen death over her. That wasn't true, of course, but did she see it that way? Xavier's own track record couldn't be helping the situation. It wasn't as if he'd had success when it came to dating.

She had such a huge heart and gave a piece of herself to those precious few she cared about. Her ability to empathize and make even the most hardened of souls comfortable in her presence proved she still had hope, meant life hadn't completely stolen her light. Right?

He clung to that tether and swallowed past the ball of apprehension in his throat. "I don't want to keep you a secret." Damn it, but being with her was the happiest he'd ever been, and he feared if they kept this up, she'd grow to think he was ashamed of their relationship. "We can still be discreet."

Her gaze dropped to her feet. "It's your decision. I'm just saying, that's a bell we can't unring."

It wasn't only his decision, and the fact she kept deferring to him regarding who knew about them only amped his suspicion this was all some kind of business transaction to her, that she wasn't an important factor. Or, at the very least, she wasn't capable of separating their two worlds.

She cleared her throat. "We have to go. They're waiting."

Nodding, he followed her out of the office, but he was determined to come back to this discussion later. He may have the hefty bank account and a company under his feet, but she held all the power. Always had.

In the lobby, the heads of various departments within Gaines Industries were being positioned in front of the company's logo mounted to the wall.

Peyton gave the reporter their names, proper spellings, and then introduced Xavier to Daniel, and the photographer, Mitchum. She glanced around. "Where do you want Mr. Gaines?"

Mitchum, camera in hand, rubbed his thick, white beard. "I was hoping for something a little less formal." He dragged a chair over to the group of Xavier's ten staff members and placed it in front of them. "Have a seat here, sir."

Xavier did as he was told. From there, Mitchum eyed the scene, seemingly not satisfied.

"May I?" Peyton raised her brows and the photographer shrugged.

She set the seven men and three women in a semi-circle behind Xavier's chair, then she directed Xavier to lean forward, forearms on his thighs, in a casual pose. She proceeded to position his employees' hands, each with one on his back, the other on the person beside them.

"I like it." Mitchum nodded. "Unity and demonstrates you're a team."

Peyton stood beside Xavier's chair and set a hand on his shoulder, squeezing to offer a silent issue of support. She cocked a hip and placed her other hand on her waist.

"That," Mitchum barked. "You, mimic her pose." He pointed to Xavier's human relations director on his other side. "Better. The few in the back, lean forward just a tad." He nodded. "Excellent. Now, I want laughing faces, not placating smiles." He clicked a few shots and frowned.

"Hold your pose, guys." Peyton cleared her throat. "I think we're going for true giggles here. Perhaps we could get Mr. Gaines to sing karaoke at this year's Christmas party. A little rendition of *I Saw Mommy Kissing Santa Claus?*"

Chuckles sounded behind Xavier, and he forced a grin as Mitchum fired off several clicks of the camera, moving slightly from side to side and crouching for a few.

He rose. "I think we're good."

Daniel nodded. "Thank you, everyone. I'll take Miss Smoke and Mr. Gaines for their interviews if someone could show Mitchum around the building? Get a few photos of the offices?"

Peyton tasked someone with the job and gestured for Daniel to proceed to the conference room. "Jackie, hold all calls, would you, please?"

Xavier gave Peyton a side-glance as they strode down the hall after the reporter. "Karaoke?"

She grinned, keeping her voice just as conspiratorially low to not be overheard. "It worked, did it not? Don't worry. I won't really make you do it."

"You couldn't get me drunk enough."

Her laugh drifted like an outer bank fog. "Was that a challenge?"

She stepped into the conference room and offered Daniel a seat. From there, she passed out bottled water and set down a tray of danishes before sitting next to Xavier. "Where would you like to start?"

Daniel put a recorder on the table between them and glanced at a legal pad. "Well, I was thinking I'd just mix up the questions between you both, since we're all together. Unless you'd rather do yours in private, Miss Smoke?"

"Now, Daniel." Her tone dipped to a sultry tease. "Are you implying I have something to hide?"

The guy laughed, which grated Xavier's nerves. The reporter was roughly in his late thirties, had dark blond shaggy hair, and was dressed in a suit that screamed style over class. His tie had pencils on it, for Christsakes. He'd flirted with Peyton on the phone, a fact Xavier only knew because she'd told him, and seemed to be carrying the torch in person.

Xavier eyed the two of them. This was a part of her job and her genetic makeup to be a crowd-pleaser, and she often straddled the line of professional banter into harmless flirtation to make people relaxed. It never bugged him until now.

"I wouldn't dare." Daniel grinned and glanced at his notes. "Let's start with your charity, Mr. Gaines. What made you join the cause with regards to veterans? Was there a vested personal interest?"

With a subtle nod from Peyton it was okay to answer, Xavier crossed one leg over his thigh. "Much of the technology we design here is best catered to the medical field, with a small part on weaponry. It made sense to shift into military contracts." He thought back to what jump-started his personal involvement and played the conversation in his head before responding. "Three or so years ago, I was in the airport waiting to board to head to a conference in Vegas when a woman sat next to me. She'd obviously been crying and, not wanting to intrude, I passed her my handkerchief and proceeded to check email on my phone."

He dug in his front pocket for the coin Peyton had given him and rubbed his thumb over the engraving to calm the trip of anxiety in his chest. He hadn't told anyone but his parents about this story, and it was more personal than he typically got in interviews.

"She wound up sitting next to me on the plane and, out of nowhere, started talking like she needed to unload on someone. As it turned out, her son had been injured in Afghanistan. He'd lost his arm in an explosion and hadn't adjusted well since being discharged. He'd taken to living on the streets and she'd just gotten the call he died. She was flying to Montana on a connecting flight through Vegas to claim his body."

Peyton's gaze settled on him, and he could feel her sympathy like radioactive waves.

He kept his eyes on the table in front of him, recalling the bone-jarring sensation in his chest from the woman's heart-wrenching story even after all this time. "I didn't ask how he died, and really, it didn't matter. He'd fought for our country, witnessed unimaginable horrors, only to come home and be left by the wayside. It got me thinking of ways to better track veterans to get them the help they need, and we shifted focus at Gaines Industries to do just that."

Clearing his throat, he glanced at the reporter, finding avid interest in his eyes. "Not long afterward, a friend's brother was killed in action, and her fiancé, who also served, committed suicide. I realized it wasn't only the men and women in the military that needed help, but the families, too. We were in a position to do something good. Thus, Fallen Veterans was born."

Silence hung for a few beats, and Peyton's fingers tightened on the chair arms until her knuckles turned white. He wanted to reach across the short distance and weave their fingers together, pull her to him and hold her, but now was not the time. There was nothing he wouldn't do to give her back her family or take away her pain.

Two years ago, it had been her idea to get more actively involved in a charity for his image. What she probably hadn't known was he'd already been playing with the idea, and it was her history, his connection to her, that had launched the entire thing. He hadn't been able to help those she'd loved before it was too late, but he could do something for others in similar situations. She'd been, and still was, the heart behind the project.

"That's amazing." Daniel made a few notes. "Miss Smoke, you do quite a bit for the charity as well, correct?"

"From a marketing standpoint." She smoothed her skirt. "It's a cause close to my heart, regardless."

Which was bull. She could name every single veteran on their list, along with their spouses and children, and not because of her excellent memory. Peyton gave a shit, even though she'd had all but no one to do the same for her in return. Once again, she was minimizing her role and importance.

Daniel nodded. "You started at Gaines Industries almost three years ago. What made you move from politics to corporate relations? And, as a follow up, what made you stay?"

She expertly wove around the first part of his question and breezed to the second. "Gaines Industries cares deeply about giving back, as indicated by Fallen Veterans. What the public doesn't see is the sense of community behind the scenes. Besides offering competitive salaries and job appreciation, the man at the top isn't just a figurehead. Mr. Gaines is actively involved in all departments. His employees aren't just a face to him, but a piece of the puzzle that makes the company a whole."

Leave it to her to switch focus right to him and make him come off looking like a saint. If not for her, he'd still be viewed as a robot who happened to make sound business decisions. She was the one who'd shown his human side, and was still doing it today every damn chance she got.

They moved onto other avenues such as what specific departments handle, and then shifted to personal hobbies and family life. Dusk descended and twilight peeked through the fog past the floor-to-ceiling windows. Xavier was anxious to get through the last of his questions and the dog and pony show photos afterward so he could down a finger of scotch to end this day.

Daniel scribbled notes. "Mr. Gaines, any special woman in your life?"

Xavier paused as Peyton stiffened beside him. He'd figured the question wouldn't be asked after making it two hours, but no such luck. He didn't want to lie, nor did he want to hide the relationship. Besides his parents, she was the best part about him, even before they'd started dating. These things had a way of getting out, too. Wasn't it better to control when and how? Yet her obvious distress over going public gave him heed.

"I mean, the two of you have always maintained a professional standpoint." Daniel leaned forward as if sensing juicy gossip. "Is that truly the case or is something more going on? The only plus one you've been seen in public with in two years has been Miss Smoke. There's an obvious chemistry between you, but is it all business?"

The hell with it. "I hired Peyton Smoke for her skills and expertise in media relations. She came highly recommended and with several references. Since then, she's lived up to the hype. She's efficient, dedicated, and can balance so many plates, it makes my head spin. The employees and our business associates adore her." He paused. "As do I. What started as a respectful working relationship has recently grown into…romance. She's smart, loyal, kind, and lovely. I'm only surprised it took me more than two years to ask her to go out with me."

Peyton's complexion paled several shades, and her profile gave no indication to what she was thinking. But her rigid spine and carefully controlled breathing told Xavier she was not pleased. The knots in his gut grew bigger knots and acid ate away at his stomach lining. Yet, a part of him was relieved it was out there.

Daniel eyed them with a smile like he'd already won a Pulitzer. "Interesting. So you're officially changing your standpoint, then?"

She brushed a nonexistent piece of lint from her skirt. "We have clear professional and personal boundaries to not interfere with work. The dating aspect of our lives is new. You're the first to hear about it, Daniel. We were a little concerned people would frown upon the relationship, but the heart wants what the heart wants. There's no reason to assume this will have any bearing on Gaines Industries."

Xavier ground his jaw. How fucking PC of her. Reasonably, her statement needed to be said, but he didn't care for her clipped tone or the way she'd seemed to shut down. He was the unemotional one here, not her.

Daniel nodded, his eyes alight. "You're keeping this on the down-low? Can I assume the article will be your announcement?"

"Correct. You have the exclusive." She rose. "Are we finished? We have your photographer waiting and it's getting late."

"Of course." Daniel stood and collected his things, setting them in a briefcase. "After you."

The next hour was spent in Xavier's office for the shoot. Mitchum had wanted several of Xavier in front of the windows, back turned, looking at the city lights in his suit. Casual poses came next on his couch, and when he couldn't relax, Peyton stepped in.

Without a word, she unbuttoned the first two notches of his shirt, rolled the sleeves to his elbows, removed his tie, and gave him a highball glass of scotch. She mussed his hair a tad and nudged him to lean back on the couch in a near slump, hand on his drink resting on the arm.

Once those were done, they directed Peyton to take the tidy bun out of her hair to let it down and remove her glasses. They leaned her against the front of his desk, facing the camera, hands gripping the edge at her hips, and Xavier perched on the opposite corner, back to the camera and head turned in profile looking at her. San Francisco at night was the backdrop, courtesy of the wall-to-wall windows.

He didn't see the end result, but the pose, low lighting, and after-hours feel gave the impression of intimacy, as did the hint of a smile they were repeatedly ordered to use. Sexy without actually touching.

Xavier waited for her in his office as she saw the reporter and photographer to the elevators, wanting to clear the air and talk to her before the irritated vibes morphed into a fight. Through the years, he could count on one hand the number of times she'd been upset with him. If he let this go, even for a night, he suspected he might not get her to see reason.

He glanced at his watch, wondering what was taking so long, then headed into the lobby. Empty. So was her office. Anger pounded his temples.

She'd left without so much as a wave or a goodbye. Hell if he'd stand for that. He'd flat out asked her before the interview what he should do if questioned about them, and she'd put the gauntlet at his feet. And he wasn't sorry about his response, either. Irrational as it may seem, announcing their relationship made it no longer casual in his mind, somehow gave credence to the issue and made them accountable.

Truth? She couldn't fucking pretend it wasn't happening now.

He grabbed his suit coat and rode the elevator down. He strode by Joseph waiting for him in the lower lobby and pushed past the exterior doors. His bodyguard followed. Saltwater from the Bay scented the air through a brisk breeze, but the temperature did little to cool Xavier's skin or mood. As they waited for the car to be pulled around, he glared in the direction of the parking garage attached to the building.

"She left twenty minutes ago." Joseph shrugged. "That's what the eye daggers are about, yes? She looked no happier than you do."

Xavier gnashed his molars to dust. "I'm going to wring her perfect little neck."

With a laugh, Joseph rubbed his bald head. "I'm no expert, but I don't think that'll help. Besides, I taught her self-defense. She can kick some serious ass."

The car pulled up, and he climbed in before his driver could round the hood. Joseph slid in next to him. Once they'd pulled away, Xavier barked an order to head to Peyton's apartment instead of home.

"Think that's wise?"

Xavier ran his tongue over his teeth and tried decide if talking to Joseph would be productive. Normally, he'd discuss these things with Peyton, not that Joseph hadn't been a decent friend. "I told the reporter interviewing us that we were dating."

His bodyguard was quiet so long that Xavier turned to look at him. Amusement shone in his eyes until Joseph sobered. "She's gonna kill you."

"She clearly said the decision was up to me."

"And you believed her?" Joseph hissed. "Women say one thing and mean another."

Not Peyton. He'd always known her to be up front, even when tact was called for. "She left without saying goodbye."

Which was really the arrow through the heart of his anger. And quickly downshifting into rabid fear. If she'd felt this strongly about the matter, all she had to do was tell him no, to wait, and he would have.

"Try to look at it from her perspective. You're her boss. How's it going to look to the world that you two are a thing? She's busted her ass in a male-dominated business to get where she is, and many are going to think she slept her way there despite her history otherwise."

So, then what? They stay a secret forever and never go public? That wasn't an ideal option, either.

The car stopped outside her building and he climbed out. "Go ahead and take off. I'll catch a cab back."

"Uh, no." Joseph slid out of the seat and leaned against the car. "Text me if you're staying the night. Otherwise, I'm waiting here."

Not bothering to argue, Xavier rode the elevator to her floor and strode to her apartment. She didn't answer his knock, but her feet shuffled on the other side of the door.

He gripped the frame and leaned into his hands. "Open up, honey. I can hear you thinking." Nothing. "I could use my key instead."

The door swung wide, and she stood in a pair of yellow ducky pajamas, her hair in a messy bun atop her head, and her glasses perched on the end of her nose. *"Ich bin nicht in der Stimmung—"*

"German. Hurray. You really are mad at me. English, please, or we'll be here all night."

"I'm not in the mood. Go home, X. We'll talk tomorrow."

How the hell was he supposed to stay mad with her dressed like that?

"I'll be quick." He stepped over the threshold, kicked the door shut, and pinned her to the entry hall. Setting his palms on the wall by her head, he hovered inches from her face and took in her cerulean eyes round in shock.

"First, I'm pissed you took off without bothering to talk this out. Communication has never been our problem, so don't make it one. Second, I get that you're scared. You're not alone on that life raft, honey, but we're in this together until one or both of us says we're done. And we're not done. Third, eventually our relationship was going to get leaked. Controlling when looked better than us trying to scramble our way out from under fire. We can get through any accusations they toss about your success by throwing logic back at them. In time, they'll see the truth, which is that we were inevitable, and our romance has no bearing on the company."

His gaze darted back and forth between hers as he studied her. Calm began to settle in his chest while he breathed in her light perfume, fading from the long day. Those eyes—those damn amazing eyes—looked back at him as if she didn't know whether to believe him or succumb. Her lips parted wider in surprise.

He cupped her cheek and rubbed his thumb over her plush lower lip. "Note the *we* in my argument, honey." It was almost as if she was waiting for an end instead of looking toward what could be. "Understand?"

She nodded, tears pooling, and blew out a ragged breath.

"Good. Allow me to show you how I really wanted to end my day."

He crushed his mouth her hers and pressed her against the wall with his body, pouring the last of his irritation and anger into the kiss. Need warred with compassion, but he battled both into submission in order to keep himself in check. Soon, he'd have her in his bed, and he could only pray she'd see reason through her doubt afterward. For now, he swallowed her shocked cry of arousal, followed it up with a groan of his own, and stepped away.

Chapter Sixteen

"Where's Moneybags taking you to dinner? Paris? Vienna? I'll bet a private plane is involved." Kate flopped sideways on Peyton's bed.

"He doesn't have a private plane." Not that he couldn't afford one. Using the vanity mirror, Peyton slid in hoop earrings. "And he wouldn't tell me where. Just said to wear a dress." Ergo, the little black cocktail number she'd put on. It seemed like the safe bet.

"He's being mysterious, huh?" Kate sat up, her red curls a flurry around her oval face. She traced a finger over the floral pattern on the comforter. "He seems to really like you."

Peyton turned and leaned a hip against the vanity edge. "Liking me was never a problem for us. We always got along great."

With a slow nod, Kate glanced at the window. "I mean, he *likes you*, likes you." Her gaze slid to Peyton's. "He's this self-righteous, privileged jackass most of the time, but lately...I don't know."

"X is..." Peyton rubbed her forehead, trying to think of a way to explain without breeching Xavier's trust. "Smart. Really brilliant, actually. People like that tend to have issues socializing. He's not cold, Kate. He's the opposite." She pressed a hand to her chest. "You should see him with his parents. Before I started working for him, he donated to a lot of charities, but I'm beginning to suspect he started his own because of me. Brian, Mark...he saw how losing them affected me. A jackass doesn't do those things."

"Yeah, maybe. That could all be for his image, though." Kate flicked an unruly curl from her cheek. "I'm talking about the things he's been up to recently." She ticked items off on her fingers. "The birthday cupcake, the attempts to protect you, tending to the bump on your head. Honest to God, I always figured he had a hidden agenda or something. But he's not even trying to get in your pants."

Oh, he'd tried, and she hadn't stopped him. But Kate was right. It wasn't about sex, though there was an awful lot of heat. "He's been doing little things like that the whole time I've known him."

"No. It's more than that." Kate whipped out her phone and her thumbs went flying over the screen. "Here." She held out the cell.

Peyton crossed the room and sat beside her, taking the phone. On the screen was a photo from the breast cancer benefit from a society page. They were standing off to the side, talking with a couple. Xavier's hand was low on her back, his profile to the camera as he smiled down at her.

"A guy doesn't stare at a woman like that if she's just a friend or employee, if he's only after sex." Kate took the phone and scrolled before handing it back. "There's hundreds of examples. Look."

The next picture was from last year for an autism awareness event. She had on a blue evening gown, him in a tux. His hand was on her elbow, guiding her while they climbed the steps. Again, his handsome face was in profile, warm smile directed at her. This had been taken long before the switch in their relationship, too.

Another showed him leaning on the bar next to her as she chatted with someone. Seemingly unaware of the camera, he wore a contemplative expression as he watched her, a barely-there curve of his lips. Desire and fondness were clearly etched in his eyes.

Heat pooled in her belly and warmed her cheeks. Xavier had mentioned earlier he'd always been attracted to her, but Kate was right. This appeared to go beyond attraction, and had for some time.

Kate took the phone back while Peyton's pulse tripped. "He cares about you. I didn't notice until that night we went out for your birthday, but he cares. Around you, he...defrosts." She sighed, studying Peyton. "I've known you since college, and not even Mark got under your skin like Xavier does. A month ago, I would've warned you off him."

Unnerved and anxious, Peyton reached for her heels by the nightstand and put them on. "And now? You're cutting back on the death threats and making voodoo dolls in his likeness?"

"Now, you smartass, I'm telling you that you'd be an idiot not to go for it. With him. I think I'm jealous."

Her gaze jerked to Kate's so fast, Peyton got whiplash. "Do you have a fever?"

"Nope. I'm not drunk, either." Her best friend's expression softened in a way Peyton had rarely seen. Compassion and understanding filtered through her eyes. "I was there when you lost

Brian, when Mark died. I laid in bed with you while you cried and would've given anything to make it better." She sighed. "You've got a second chance for happiness. Take it."

Misty-eyed, Peyton waved her hand in front of her face. "I love you."

A knock from the front door stopped any more conversation, and she rose. Kate followed her down the hall and waited as Peyton opened the door.

Xavier, dressed in a white button-down shirt and gray slacks, held out a bouquet of pink lilies. "Hey." His gaze skimmed down the length of her, approval in the depths. "You look amazing." He stepped in and kissed her cheek.

"Thank you." She took the flowers and grinned over her shoulder at Kate. "Flowers."

"I see them. They're pretty." Her friend gave her a hug and moved toward the door. "Well done, Xavier. Pink's her favorite color, too."

He did a double take. "Is she drunk?"

Kate paused on the threshold, brows pinged to her hairline. "Not yet, but the night's young."

He grunted. "You gave me a compliment and called me by name."

"Yep." She winked at Peyton. "I won't wait up. Mostly because Joseph's coming over." At Peyton's gasp, Kate grinned. "Did I forget to mention we hooked up while you were in Napa? Silly me."

Giddy and happy for both her friends, Peyton bounced on her toes. "I want details later."

Xavier held up a hand. "I don't, for the record."

"Huh." Kate tilted her head. "He made a funny." With that, she stepped into her apartment across the hall and shut the door.

"I'm totally grilling Joseph, too." Smiling, Peyton headed for the kitchen to put the flowers in water. "These are beautiful."

"Well, they're fitting then. So are you."

She paused, the vase halfway full from the running faucet, and faced him. Hands in his pockets, he looked at her as if he'd just said something about the weather and not called her beautiful. Through the years, he'd always been generous with compliments, but this felt different. Aware instead of responsive.

Setting the flowers in the vase, she turned and placed them on the kitchen table. Then, she rose on her toes, threaded her fingers through his hair, and kissed him. He paused a moment, then slid his arms around her and tilted his head. He kept the kiss soft, light, and smiled when she pulled away.

"What was that for? Not that I'm complaining."

She traced her fingers over his jaw and the dark shadow covering it. Gah, she loved it when he didn't shave. "For calling me beautiful."

"If this is how you react to obvious statements of fact, I'll have to do it more often."

Dropping her head on his chest, she laughed. "We better go or I might do more than kiss you." She eased out of his arms and grabbed her clutch on the counter. "Ready?"

He'd brought his Jaguar to pick her up, and once they were enroute, she asked again where they were going.

"Figured we'd start at *La Nourriture est Amour*." Eyes on the road, he reached for her hand and kissed her knuckles.

"But you hate French food."

"You love it, though. Besides, hearing you order in French is incredibly hot." He flashed her a quick grin. "I don't even know what the restaurant name means, never mind what you say, but it's worth it."

"It means food is love, and I can speak the language anytime. We should go some place where you'll enjoy dinner, too."

He didn't respond, other than a shake of his head, and they were quiet the rest of the short drive.

The restaurant was a mix of fine dining and elegance with low candlelight on white tablecloths and chandeliers from a lattice ceiling. Various black and white photos of the Seine and a brick-laid floor added to the atmosphere. She and Xavier had a rare business meeting here with clients once in awhile, but it had been some time.

They were seated at a corner table by the terrace and Xavier glanced at the wine menu while the waiter stood by. "This one's from the vineyard next to my folks' place. You prefer sweet white and not dry, correct?" At her nod, he ordered and smiled at her as the server left. "You can order the meal. Just don't get me snails."

With a laugh, she opened the menu. "Seeing as you don't know most of the lingo, I could be really mean. Sure you want me to choose?"

"You don't have a mean bone in your body."

True. She decided on *Magret de Canard* for him—a duck dish—with roasted potatoes and steamed carrots, and *Fricassee*—chicken with mushrooms, peas, and potatoes in a heavy sauce—for her. Once the food came, he shifted conversation from work stuff.

"Now that I got my fix of you speaking French, where else do you like to eat? I know some of your lunch hangouts, but not date stops." He blinked at his food. "This is really good. What is it?"

"Duck. And I'm not picky about food. I'm happy wherever."

"Surely you have a favorite spot, though. Where did you and Mark frequent?"

She studied him over the rim of her wineglass and realized he might be nervous. They'd known one another what felt like eons, but they'd never dated. "Mark and I didn't go out often. When he was on leave, we usually got a pizza and ate on the couch." Setting her glass down, she contemplated how far to take this conversation. Discussing past relationships wasn't exactly first date material, but she and Xavier didn't fit the normal mold.

"Does it bother you? To talk about him?" He stared at her, all hint of amusement gone.

Guilt shifted in her belly. "No." She smiled to soften his severe expression. "It's just...you and him are very different."

The last thing she wanted was for Xavier to compare himself to a relationship that had ended in the worst possible way. In the darkest recesses of her mind, she often wondered if her and Mark would've made it down the aisle if he hadn't died. She'd loved him. Very, very much. But they'd had so little time together and she'd often gotten the impression she'd been more of a crutch to him than a soul mate.

"I'm sorry. Forget I said anything."

God, now she'd made him doubt himself. "Hey, you can ask me anything." She covered his hand with hers. "There's not much I can say about Mark that'll make a lot of sense to you."

He stared at her a tense beat, then turned his hand over and laced their fingers. "Try me."

She chewed her lip and figured if anyone would understand, it would be Xavier. He'd spent his adolescent years awkwardly getting by and most of his adulthood questioning who he could truly trust. Or, rather, who liked him as a person versus just for his money.

After a sip of wine for courage, she opened a door she'd closed long ago. "Brian and Mark met in boot camp and came up the ranks together. My brother brought him home on leave, and we just kind of...came together. There wasn't a moment or anything, he was simply there. I think I was convenient at first. At least, in his mind. A few weeks later, they reported for their first tour, and I got to know him better through emails than we did face-to-face." She smiled, gaze lost on her plate. "I fell in love with him through the computer. Is that stupid?"

"Not at all." He frowned, jaw ticking. "Go on."

Since he seemed more concerned than tense, she rubbed her forehead. "We continued the relationship for a couple years. We'd see each other on leave, and sometimes it was hard to get into a rhythm in person since we were used to having an ocean between us. We'd be watching TV or talking, and I felt more like a friend than a girlfriend. But then he'd do something to make me believe he was in it for the right reasons. He'd trace patterns on my arm with his finger or reach for me in the middle of the night, and I stopped doubting."

Xavier brushed his thumb over her knuckles at her pause, encouraging her without saying a thing, waiting patiently like always.

"When he proposed, my first reaction was why. I mean, we loved each other, but...I don't know. We had comfort and familiarity, yet lacked passion. I thought about how Brian was all I had, and I could do worse than a handsome man who treated me well, wanting to marry me." She shrugged. "I said yes and the relief on his face nailed me right in the gut. Like I'd just handed him the world or something."

In the silence, she took another sip of wine and glanced at Xavier. Brows knit, gaze unrelenting, he stared at her. The bombardment of emotion in his eyes gave her heed. Wounded. Hesitant. Sad, even.

She set the glass down. "What is it?"

He lowered his gaze to the table and drew a deep, slow inhale. Finally, he cleared his throat. "You are one of the most passionate people I know. Whether it's issuing a press conference or kissing me or simply walking into a room, you do things with everything you have inside yourself. The idea of you marrying a man who didn't give you the same passion, who might've dulled that eternal light, makes me physically ill."

Closing his eyes, he pinched the bridge of his nose. "This isn't coming out right." He exhaled and nudged his plate aside, leaning forward. "I'm not trying to diminish his memory. Mark was obviously brave and smart and a lucky son of a bitch to have you. So am I. You said he and I were different, but I'm not seeing it from your perspective, honey. I—"

"See me." How could he not get the vast, immense differences?

He snapped his mouth shut, gaze just shy of frantic.

She squeezed his fingers. "You see me when I don't think he ever did. Yes, he was brave and smart. He was more than that. He was also funny and the best friend my brother ever had, but how I am with you is not how I was with him."

His throat worked a swallow as his gaze cut away. Again, with the jaw tick.

"Mark is gone and I don't like comparing. All relationships are different." She took in his sharp profile, this man she knew so well and, sometimes, not at all, and tried to conjure a way to explain that wouldn't leave her eviscerated in the process. "You can go an entire day and speak maybe five sentences in total. But you say so much without opening your mouth."

Slowly, his gaze slid to hers and held.

"I can feel your eyes on me from across the room with a hundred guests present. Nothing I do escapes your attention. You buy me cupcakes and key charms and flowers because you see me, not just a person. I can count on one hand the number of people who've managed that, and three are dead." God, sometimes she missed her family so much it gutted. But Kate and this precious man in front of her were a damn valid filler of the void. "Whether we are dating or not, I'm never alone when I'm with you. Do you understand?"

Instead of answering, his gaze swept over her face as if he were memorizing her features or trying to recognize who the strange anomaly was before him. She couldn't say what, but something about him...changed. An internal switch flipped or a mental door slammed. Something. His eyes flickered, his chest quit moving air, and he sat so motionless, she would've questioned if he'd fallen asleep had his gaze not been pinning her to the seat.

The waiter came by and she tore her attention away to address him. In French, he asked how they'd enjoyed their meal.

"Everything was delicious. Thank you. You speak French?" She smiled at the adorable guy. He had to be fresh out of high school and had dimples to add to his sandy blond, shaggy haircut.

"Second year. You're very fluent."

They chatted a bit in the language until he asked if they'd like dessert. She glanced at Xavier and did a double take. His sole focus was still on her, and he hadn't twitched so much as an eyelash.

"Uh, do you want anything else?" She offered a hesitant smile hoping he'd blink or breathe or...anything.

"I want to take you home. Right now."

She sucked a rapid inhale. Holy cow. Had lightning just hit her? Probably. Okay, well... She looked at the poor waiter and raised her brows. "Perhaps just the check. Pretty please."

He smirked, rolled his lips over his teeth, and nodded before walking away.

After blowing out a careful breath, she refocused on Xavier. "Geez, X. I'm all hot and bothered."

Resting his forearms on the table, he leaned forward so fast she flinched. "I'll clarify." His low, hoarse tone sent shivers over her skin. "I want to take you home right now and make love to you until the sun comes up, then do it all over again until your only recourse is to sleep for a week to recover. That should eradicate whatever lingering doubt you have that you're not passionate, and will hopefully erase my suspicion no one's ever taken the time or cared enough to show you said passion."

Her mouth opened, but all that popped out was a winded squeak. Holy cow again. And *all* the barnyard animals. Throw in the whole farm to boot. She'd never been so turned on in all her life. Her lungs burned and...heck. What was she supposed to say? *Please, God, yes?* "Um..."

"I'm not done." His hot bourbon eyes dilated. "I simultaneously have the urge to forego making love and screw you right into the next fiscal quarter. Between that dress and you speaking French in your sexy as hell voice, I can't see straight."

Heart pounding and dizzier than a disco ball at Studio 54, she grabbed the table edge and clenched her thighs. She was certain her cheeks had caught fire two syllables into his diatribe. And she panted like a beast in heat. Where had this controlled, outspoken, alpha guy been all this time? Because he needed to come out and play more often.

The waiter returned with the check. "Here you go. Take your time—"

"Standby." Without glancing away from her, Xavier pulled out his wallet, put some bills into the check fold, and handed it back to the server. "Keep the change."

"Thank you, sir. Have a great evening."

"I intend to." Xavier rose and held out his hand.

She took it, stood, and he wrapped an arm around her waist. Which was probably a good thing since she was uncertain if her legs were functioning. Once outside, she took a deep lungful of air and let the crisp breeze cool her cheeks.

Xavier passed a ticket to the valet and pulled Peyton flush against his hard wall of a chest while they waited on the wet sidewalk. Dropping his forehead to hers, he closed his eyes and held the back of her head. After a moment to seemingly collect himself, he met her gaze. "I didn't ask what you wanted."

Surrounded by him—limbs and hands and torso and his light cologne—she found it a little difficult forming a logical thought. "I'm good with your suggestion. All of them."

He brushed his nose with hers, lips millimeters from making contact with her mouth. "Are you sure? We can wait, honey. It'll be painful on my end, but I—"

"Mis bragas son húmedas," she breathed.

His fingers clenched her hair. "You could've told me I kiss like a goat and I wouldn't know the difference. I'd still be harder than—"

"I said my panties are damp. Does that answer your question?"

"Mercy." He groaned, brows knitting. "Your apartment is closer."

"The bed in your house is bigger."

Chapter Seventeen

With one hand on the wheel, Xavier rested his elbow on the window well and rubbed his lips in thought while he drove his Jag through the rain-soaked streets. A yellow glow from the lampposts hit the drops on his hood and windshield. Somehow, it escaped his notice it had stormed while they'd been in the restaurant. He supposed he'd had his own storm brewing.

Peyton had forever and always maintained the ability to clobber him with the equivalent of an emotional battering ram. Yet, the stuff she'd told him tonight about her former fiancé sat like battery acid in his gut. Not only had her whole family been wiped out and she'd lost a man she loved, but Xavier was starting to get a full HD view of the extent of her loneliness. And it had begun long before Mark shot himself.

Xavier was no expert, but he'd been raised by two parents who loved each other to the ends of the earth. He'd been surrounded by affection. How Peyton described her relationship with Mark didn't sound like love. It leaned toward companionship with a side of contentment. He always figured if he ever fell face-first into the emotion himself, it wouldn't be all that different from how he'd been brought up. Respect. Safety. Trust. Compromise. Desire. Throw in hand holding and adoring gazes, and there was his how-to handbook straight from his role models.

Christ. And Peyton had almost settled for...what? The next best thing? Had she been that desperate for someone she would've married for less than she deserved? Or had she not even been aware of the fact she'd been in like, not in love, with the guy?

Xavier shook his head, not understanding in the slightest. She had the hugest bleeding heart, comparable to no one else, and was a hopeless romantic. She didn't walk around in la-la land spouting sonnets, but under her skin, in her bones, she was a romantic. Why would she ever consider anything but the real deal?

And just what in the hell was wrong with the men she'd dated? Peyton was gorgeous. Gigantic cerulean eyes, flawless skin, champagne hair that wove through daydreams as easily as the strands wrapped around his hand. Her legs went on for decades, her ass begged to be grabbed, and if one looked up perfection in the dictionary, there would be a picture of her breasts. Delicate hands and a stop traffic smile and the cutest damn button nose to offset all the sexy. Librarian fantasy in daylight and seductress by night.

Seriously. And those were just her physical attributes. Never mind her personality, which was ten times as sweet as how she tasted. Funny, open-minded, generous, witty, brave—

"I'm on birth control."

He jerked his gaze to her long enough to notice she was glancing out the passenger window. "What?"

"I'm on the pill and I'm safe. I'm assuming you are, as well."

It was a damn good thing it was anatomically impossible to swallow one's tongue. "Okay. Yes, I am." He white-knuckled the wheel until his joints popped.

"I figured we'd have the protection talk now, so we don't ruin the mood later. I'm simply letting you know. If you wanted to have sex without a condom, I trust you and I'm guarded from pregnancy. My partners always used one."

He nearly swerved from between the dotted lines. And he was wrong. It was possible to swallow his tongue. Something was choking him, at least. Lust, most likely. The idea of being buried inside her was exquisite torture enough. Take a condom out of the equation and he was about to bust his inseam.

Peyton Smoke. No barriers. Nothing but him and her and...

Mercy. "Whatever you're comfortable doing, honey." He paused. "I've never had sex without one, either." Hell, he wanted to so badly, the visual metastasized as pain.

He glanced at her and back to the road. She was biting her lower lip, an indication she was thinking or nervous. His heart tripped behind his ribs. "I repeat, we don't have to rush, Peyton."

"I'm not having second thoughts. It's just...this is a little surreal, isn't it? You and me, after all this time?"

She'd know surreal intimately after he was through with her tonight. Guaran-damn-teed.

If they ever got home.

The hills made way to quieter streets in his gated community and he nearly wept as he pulled into his expansive garage. As the bay door closed them in, he climbed out of the Jag and rounded the hood. Without a word, she took his hand and he led her past his car collection into the house.

They stopped in the dark kitchen, where she set her purse on the counter and slipped out of her black heels. The gold hoop earrings came next and were placed on the island, her gaze focused on them.

Moonlight filtered through the rain-speckled bay window, casting her skin in ambient patterns. He let his gaze roam since they were finally alone, and fire roared through his veins. The sleeveless black dress molded to her curvy body as if painted on and stopped just shy of her knees. The neckline had been playing peek-a-boo with the swell of her breasts all night—a game he was damned determined to win. Her hair framing her face and in a curtain around her shoulders made him itch to wrap the strands around both hands until she gasped from those full lips.

Heaven help him. He never desired a woman so intensely as he did Peyton.

"Where's the staff?" Her quiet voice was like a siren in the room.

"I gave them the weekend off." He rubbed the back of his neck, trying to summon manners when caveman tendencies threatened to overwhelm him. "Do you want anything to drink?"

"No, thank you."

Right. Now that pleasantries were out of the way... "Hold onto me."

Her wide eyes lifted to his while he closed the meager distance. "What?"

Dipping his head, he spoke against her lips. "Hold onto me." He crushed his mouth to hers, grabbed her thighs, and lifted her off the floor.

She wrapped her legs around him and wove her fingers through his hair. Every glorious inch of her molded to him as he deepened the kiss and pivoted for the living room. Blindly, he found the stairs and climbed while she sent him into cardiac malfunction with her tongue alone. By the time he rounded the landing and made it down the hallway, he was shaking with uncoiled need.

The little vixen kissed like she did everything in life—heart strong and with fervent attention to detail. One second she was tender and endearing, spilling her guts, the next she devoured as if she'd been starved for attention. She probably had been, knowing what he did now. Shock and longing and relief and satisfaction battled between them until he couldn't tell which emotions were his own.

In his bedroom, low light from the lamp he'd left on warmed the tone of her skin. He kicked the door shut and pinned her to it in order to free his hands. Which he used to grab her perfect round ass. She hummed into his mouth, her fingers working the buttons on his shirt. He couldn't resurface from the kiss long enough to care she was stripping him first. Hell, he'd be lucky to get her dress off before he lost it.

She tugged the material down his arms to the floor and reached for the button on his pants. He hissed and came to his senses. Barely.

Spinning her around, he pressed her chest-first against the door and swept her hair off her neck. The sultry scent of her perfume invaded his sinuses, wrapped around his throat. It was the same brand she'd worn on her interview years ago, and still had the power to obliterate thought as he knew it. Berries and musk with a slight floral undertone. Sensual. Distinct.

He grazed his teeth along her nape and licked a path to her ear. "Your scent drives me to the brink. Have I ever mentioned that?" He sucked her earlobe. "I want to bite you every time I catch a hint in the air."

She dropped her forehead to the wood and pressed her hands there, fingers curling. A whimper, and she thrust her ass against his aching shaft. He siphoned oxygen through clenched teeth and prayed for patience.

Finding the zipper on her dress, he slid the tab down, exposing her back and the elegant column of her spine. She trembled against him. He nudged the straps off her shoulders and let the garment fall to the floor. She trembled again while he got caught up in the black lace of her panties. No bra. The breath rasped from his lungs as his skin heated.

With a hand gently on her throat, he brought her flush against him and palmed a breast. Her hard nipple grazed as he squeezed. She threw her head back and moaned. Sucking the tendon on her neck, he slid his hand south, stopping over the soft skin of her taut belly, and dipped his pinkie into the waistband.

"Am I going to find you wet, honey?"

"Go ahead and see for yourself." Her breathy whisper was his undoing.

Hands on her hips, he spun her again and crouched in front of her. Leaning on the door, she watched through hooded eyes as he lowered the lace. Past her hips, down her thighs to her ankles. She stepped out of them.

He drank in the sight of her. She stole his heartbeat and resuscitated him in the same blink. He'd be lying if he claimed to never have imagined her like this, and somehow even his grandest fantasies were no match. Peaches and cream skin that blushed with arousal. Full breasts pushed out, rosy nipples peaked and begging to be sucked. A slight hourglass curve to her waist that segued right into hips a man could hold onto, that could take punishing thrusts.

Leaning forward, he kissed one thigh, then the other. On her mound, she had a small triangle of hair just shades darker than the strands on her head. He pressed his lips to her belly and looked up at her. She all but begged him with those navy eyes to put his mouth between her legs, right on her core.

He ran a hand down her calf and wrapped his fingers around her ankle, encouraging her to rest the back of her knee on his shoulder. Never taking his gaze from hers, he did the same thing with her other leg until she was suspended with only the door and his hands on her lush bottom for support, leaving his face wedged between her thighs.

Then, only then, did he drop his gaze. He groaned as his dick twitched in his pants. Wet, pink folds and a hard little nub. Beautiful.

"Brace yourself, honey."

He closed his lips around her clit and she bucked. Gasped. Grinning, he widened his crouch and kneeled for better balance, then licked a trail from her opening to her bundle of nerves, which set her off. Her head hit the door, she curled her fingers in his hair and made the most delicious, needy noises.

Damn, he loved how responsive she could be. He never had to guess her tastes or likes or preferences. Her body told him everything. From her flushed skin, erect nipples, and wandering touch, straight to her lip bite, tremors, and soughing breaths—she said it all. And, hell. The knowledge he not only could but did have her? Pride inflated his chest, surged through his system.

Like she'd done a week before up against the tree, she splintered with little encouragement. This time on his tongue and without the necessity for quiet. She climaxed with her whole body, as well. Quaking, moaning, arching. Eyes pinched tightly, lips parted, she came undone. Over and over. He eased his pace and rode out the currents with her until her muscles stopped contracting and she slumped against the door.

He lowered her legs from his shoulders and held her waist as he rose so she wouldn't collapse. Then, he swept her into his arms and carried her to bed. He tugged the comforter aside before laying her down and stood bedside to watch her.

Seeing her champagne hair over the pillow, her lithe body against his dark green sheets, pulled a groan from deep in his chest. How was it possible she was here with him? The number of times he'd imagined her... He shook his head. She was the only woman he'd ever brought home. The first he'd be making love to in his own bed.

Her sleepy lids lifted and she smiled, stretching like a contented, sated cat. Best part? There was no shyness about her. Arms over her head, one knee bent, she laid there like a centerfold imploring to be ravaged. There was nothing hotter than a woman comfortable in her own skin and unabashedly confident.

"That was only a precursor, honey. We haven't hit round one yet." He stroked his aching shaft through his pants.

Her grin widened. "Then why are you standing by the bed?"

He had no clue. To savor? Download this exact moment to his memory in case he was dreaming?

Stripping out of his pants and briefs, he crawled across the mattress and straddled her. Her satisfied smirk punched the breath from his lungs. "You're really beautiful, you know that?" Weight on his arms, he leaned down and kissed her throat, her chin.

"I do now," she panted, tilting her head to give him better access.

He saved that comment to ask her about later and kissed his way to her breasts. He could spend a decade on her chest alone. He took one beaded tip in his mouth and sucked hard. She wrapped her arms around his head as if to hold him there.

Like he had any plans to move.

Testing her, he bit her nipple, wondering if she wanted fast and hard or long and slow their first time. She'd responded to both his reckless, desperate side and his more gentle, controlled one, but that hadn't been during sex. Normally, he'd take his partner's cues. Except, Peyton wasn't just anyone, and this...mattered.

He switched to her other breast to repeat the process, and he got his answer. She made a strangled sound and banded her arms around him until his face was buried in her soft flesh and oxygen was a distant memory. She cried his name, and a part of him snapped off at the root.

"Christ, the things I want to do to you." He crashed his mouth to hers in a hard-drive deleting kiss that sent reason straight to the recycling folder, never to return.

Lowering himself, he covered her body with his and ground his erection against her belly. If it were physically possible to climb inside her, he might've done it right then. As it was, her skin against his and the way she undulated under him had him coming apart at the seams.

Her hands explored, adding to the holy shit. Across his shoulders, down his biceps, tracing his pecs. She raked her thumbnails over his nipples and he barked a hoarse shout into her mouth. He wasn't going to last ten seconds inside her without losing himself in the process.

And he couldn't wait.

He grabbed her wrists before her hands could descend any farther, pinned them over her head, and threaded their fingers together. Tearing away from the kiss, he looked in her eyes as he shifted his pelvis between the cradle of her thighs. Her irises had gone navy with lust.

With her arms stretched toward the headboard, their bodies were aligned in perfect sync. Skin caressed skin. Her nipples grazed his chest. His hard muscles were pillowed by her supple softness. Each inhalation from her met his exhalation as if timed in harmony. Her head was framed by his biceps, his face hovering over hers, and there wasn't an inch of available anatomy space where he didn't cover her body...yet it was her who was wrapped around him in every possible, conceivable way.

Not wanting to release her hands, he rocked his hips, gliding the crown of his shaft through her drenched folds until he nudged her opening. "I think I may need to hold onto you this time."

He eased inside her and was immediately surrounded by hot, giving flesh. He groaned, pressing forward. Nothing had prepared him for this utter, utter annihilation. Having never gone without a barrier, there was no protection from the over-sensitization or her tightness. He suspected it wouldn't matter anyhow. She'd kill him either way. A thin sheen of latex wouldn't make a damn bit of difference.

Her breathing escalated and her lashes fluttered closed, blocking his view of her eyes. He paused, and she looked at him again. All that blue assaulted him with hunger and endearment and revelation. What conclusion she'd garnered, he had no idea. But if it was anything like his, she'd found heaven and hell wrapped in a tidy bow.

As he sank fully inside her, they shared air, and he shook with restraint. "Damn, Peyton." Just...damn. "You feel amazing." He couldn't pull a stronger adjective, genius IQ or not. "Fucking amazing." That was better. Closer to the truth, at least.

She brushed her nose with his and offered a soft sweep of her lips in a bare kiss. Something about the tender move devastated him. All he could manage was to stare at her, torn between drawing out this moment and sending them both over the edge.

"Xavier..." Her brows furrowed, and she strained against his hold.

He immediately released her hands and cupped her face, using his forearm to raise himself a little. "Are you okay?"

"Yes." She swallowed. "No. I need..." She whimpered and rolled her hips.

Oh hell. He knew just what she needed, all right. So much for giving her a moment to adjust. He pulled out until only his tip remained, then thrust back in and saw stars. Comets. Planets. Whatever...it was cosmic. He repeated the motion with more force and she gasped.

"Is that what you want, honey?"

She held his tense jaw, lifting her head from the pillow to rest her forehead against his. "Yes." She made desperate... breathy...noises that rumbled from her chest to his, bathed his face, and he drove faster. One of her legs tangled with his and she raised the other, digging her heel into his lower back as if to gain leverage. "Ah, yes. There. More."

Mercy, her voice. If she didn't kill him, he'd donate his billions to saving some endangered creature.

Keeping the near breakneck speed, he thrust with everything he had, encouraged by her moans and whispered pleas. The connection was so incredible his throat burned. And he was going to detonate if she didn't come soon. A looming orgasm tingled in his lower back, squeezed his balls.

To get her there faster, he cinched her leg higher up his waist to stroke her spot and make sure he ground her clit with his pelvis while he thrust. She arched, surprising him, and nearly rolled them to the side. He kept them at the odd angle because her hips pistoned and she pressed her face to his neck. She muttered his name against his skin, her lips grazing his already raw nerve endings.

Holy hell. He grabbed her ass, supporting her and holding her to him for each punishing plunge. "Come, Peyton. Sweet Christ, come for me." He tugged her hair in order to get to her mouth and kissed her, his tongue stroking hers, mimicking the motion of their bodies.

Her lips parted in a silent scream a fraction of a second before her walls gripped him in a vise. She went rigid, trembled, then quaked with such force, she ripped his release from him.

Jarred, he ground out a sharp expletive against her temple and said her name like a goddamn oath. Atoms split and it was entirely possible his bones fractured. He spilled inside her, wave after wave of near violent convulsions locking his joints. She hugged him to her as she came down and he let go with blinding vigor.

Heaving air, he closed his eyes and buried his face in her hair. Aftershocks involuntarily shook him. Or her. One of them was still experiencing a 7.0 on the Richter. It didn't matter. She was wrapped around him like a bandage and he was too injured to move or care.

Panting, too, she ran her hand down his back and up again. "Wow. That was..."

"Biblical," he said mid-groan.

Her chuckle expelled like smoke and vibrated through him. "Not to repeat myself, but it's always the quiet ones." She kissed his cheek. Nuzzled his ear. "You're not so quiet, though, are you?"

He lifted his head, which took much effort, and smiled at her. "Neither are you, Miss *Oh God* and *Right There* and—"

She swatted his arm and laughed.

His heart flipped over in his chest, shifting ribs. Her lips were swollen from his kisses, her cheeks were infused with so much pink, she glowed, and somehow her hair had tangled into knots. Not unlike their limbs at the moment. She was so gorgeous, it hurt. He stared into the bluest eyes in creation, framed by thick, pale lashes, and found his safe haven.

All he could do was shake his head and say her name.

"Hmm?" she hummed as if he'd asked a question.

He tucked a strand behind her ear. "Nothing." Or everything.

Chapter Eighteen

Perched on the vanity counter in Xavier's bathroom, Peyton swung her legs and waited while he took out his contacts. She'd already removed hers and brushed her teeth. He'd thrown on a pair of black briefs and had her slip into his button-down shirt he'd worn earlier. The casualness of their undress, plus the domestic scene of their toothbrushes beside one another's, kept tripping her mental focus.

It wasn't as if she hadn't been in a relationship before. It had just been a long time. Mark's toiletries had shared space with hers, but he'd been gone so much that it hadn't seemed real sometimes. He'd been as much a ghost in her life as her parents' memory.

This...was different. Every experience with Xavier was different. From the way he touched her to how he spoke, he gave the impression she wasn't simply someone beside him sharing oxygen or a warm body to pass time. Rather, he saw her, the woman. Inside, out, up, down, throughout...and every crevice in between. And he apparently liked what he'd encountered because here they were. Together.

For a guy who was intensely serious at the office and was uncomfortable with crowds, he'd always been at ease in her presence. But after what they'd just done—that amazing, holy cow, knock-her-socks-off act of love-making—it was as if the last of whatever wall he'd erected had crumbled.

"I think you look better in my shirt than I ever did." With a lazy smile, he stepped between her thighs and set his large hands on her waist. Sexy geek was back since he'd donned his glasses. "I can't decide which version I like most. Your sophisticated and elegant in ball gowns side, polished and stern in business suits, or the sex kitten."

Smiling, she rubbed her thumb along the rough stubble on his jaw. She completely understood his dilemma. Sleek billionaire at work, the laid back version in jeans at home, or the hot tumbled mess? "You say the nicest things."

A wrinkle formed between his brows as he tucked a strand behind her ear. "When I asked if you knew you were beautiful, you said *I do now*. What did you mean by that?"

She glanced over his shoulder. "I don't know. You make me feel beautiful, I guess."

"Has that been an issue? Not feeling attractive?"

Her gaze darted to his and her belly fluttered. The concern in his eyes was completely unexpected. "No, not really." She chewed her lip and thought it over. "It never crossed my mind." She considered herself good-looking. Not striking or anything. More like pretty or appealing. Though not vain, self-esteem hadn't been a problem for her.

"Which tells me you don't hear it often enough."

She thought about that, too. "Brian used to say it a lot." She smiled, remembering. "Actually, he used to tug on my hair and say, *stay adorable, lil sis*." God, she missed him.

"And what about your previous lovers? Mark, for instance?"

Gaze lost in the past, she scrambled through memories and came up empty. Her former fiancé hadn't been big on compliments. Not that she'd needed them.

"Exactly," he said as if she'd proven his point by not responding. "You're beautiful, Peyton." He brushed his knuckle down her cheek. "Inside and out."

Well, damn. Eyes burning, she tried to blink through the sudden wetness and cleared her throat. "Thank you."

He kissed her forehead, letting his lips linger, and the simple act shredded her heart. Whereas a peck on the cheek could be informal, construed as a greeting or dismissal, a kiss on the forehead relayed so much more. To her, it meant deep intimacy, told a story. It said *you're mine* and *I care*, while hinting at protection and fondness.

Throat unbearably tight, she closed her eyes, needing to lighten the mood. "This wouldn't be a ploy for round two, would it? You don't need compliments. Just ask." She smiled at him, but he stiffened.

He glanced heavenward. "Please don't do that. Don't make fun of me right now."

Oh God, no. How could he...? "I'm not—"

"I know I'm the serious one." He held her face and glared at her like he was nearing the end of his rope. "I realize that I'm not quick to joke or laugh, and I won't ever be the life of the party. Most view my responses as cold or insensitive, see me as heartless and shrewd. But that doesn't mean I don't feel."

Gah. "I know—"

"That's just it. You do know everything, know me. And therein lies the problem." His gaze roamed her face. "When just about everyone else keeps me in the callous column, you add subheadings and amendments to prove them wrong. But I don't think you're adapting to..."

Trembling, she stared at him, her heart somewhere near her knees. "To what?"

"Change." He sighed. "Maybe you're stuck in the place we used to be or perhaps locked into habit from prior relationships. I don't know. I get the sense you don't...believe me."

Her stomach bottomed out. "You're not a liar, X. I trust you—"

"Do you?" His brows pinged even as the concerned torment remained in his eyes. "I'm completely, utterly free around you. What we did tonight? It only added to the calm you bring me, sealed our connection in my opinion." He inhaled, jaw ticking. "I've lost the last of my filter with you and can just say what's on my mind. You don't get how rare that is for somebody like..."

Suddenly, he closed his eyes and stepped away, severing all contact. "Never mind." He offered a weak smile before lifting his lids, gaze focused on her necklace. "Go ahead and finish up in here. I'll meet you back in bed."

She opened her mouth, but he stepped out before she could protest. Shocked immobile, she wrung her fingers and stared at the tile floor. She didn't understand him or the rapid shift in mood.

Rubbing her forehead, she rewound the conversation. Aside from Kate and perhaps Joseph, there was no one else except Xavier she trusted entirely, without bounds. Yeah, sometimes she had to grill him to get his thoughts, but he was always honest with her. How could he think otherwise?

And what about that change nonsense? The two of them had been nothing if not in a constant flux the past month. They'd gone from a respectable working unit and tentative friendship to dating. Now, lovers. Chemistry and passion. Open communication and compromise. They'd done that together and she was right here, in his house, with him.

Her belly twisted. Somehow, she'd hurt him, had rendered his feelings moot. Xavier was the last person she'd ever want to cause pain. Especially because there were so few people he let into his real world.

Well, he'd had his say. She'd get hers.

Hopping off the vanity, she cut the light switch and stepped out of the bathroom. Lying on his back in bed, he trekked her movement in the dark moonlit room until she stood beside him. He had one arm bent under his head and the sheets pooled at his waist. His expression was unreadable as he stared at her, and it was like a knife to the chest that he'd skilled himself blank.

God, he was magnificent, though. Lean, rippled strength. Dips and contours. Perfect symmetry of muscle and bone. Expressive eyes and wide jaw. Long lashes, thick chestnut hair, and full, firm lips. When he smiled, he could silence congress, and when he laughed, it was rough and from the gut. Add his quiet power, a compassionate heart, and brilliance, and there was no one else like him.

Without a word, he pulled a corner of the comforter aside as an invitation, his eyes still warily watching her. She climbed in and, on instinct, straddled him, then removed his glasses to set on the nightstand. Keeping one arm behind his head, he set his hand on her thigh, gently stroking with his thumb.

And they stared at one another with only the moonlight through the balcony for illumination. Hours, days, years passed. She couldn't tell what he was thinking, but his tender touch and unwavering gaze held her captive. Sometimes, he could level her without doing a thing.

"I wasn't making fun of you." She tried to swallow and couldn't through the guilt lodged there. "I'd never do that."

"That was a poor choice of words on my part." He expelled an uneven breath. "I meant you were making light of the situation."

Slowly, she nodded. "You're right."

"Why?" He paused a beat, long enough for his walls to come back down. Understanding and fondness shone in his eyes as if he already knew the answer. "Tell me. Why, honey?"

Why? Because for the first time in years, since the last of her family had died and her fiancé had permanently checked out, she garnered hope. If there was one cruel reality she'd learned in her almost three decades on earth, it was that hope could erect or destroy her very existence. In a blink, it gave her a reason to smile, to get out of bed, to dream. And with no warning, it could be dashed away, ripped from her clutches as if a punishment for believing.

"You scare me." Okay, there. She'd said it. "Things between us escalated so fast and you make me feel..." Happy. He made her happy, damn it. "I'm not used to your kind of attention, I suppose."

"Get used to it." A determined edge darkened his eyes. "Be scared all you want. Lean on me if you need to. Hell, it's about time I returned the favor. But I refuse to go back to censoring every syllable when I'm finally near someone I can be myself around. Moreover, I will not stop complimenting you or showing affection. This isn't a game to me. This relationship isn't a casual affair in my book. You matter to me, and I'm not ashamed to tell you that."

Had she said scared? She meant terrified. Because when he said things like that, when he took charge like he'd been waiting for the day he'd be able, it sent her skittering right past falling and straight toward splat.

Sitting up, he wrapped his arms around her and set his hands low on her back. His face inches from hers, he took in her features in one fell swoop. "I've been drowning, Peyton. For twenty-nine years, three-hundred and thirty some days, and a handful of hours, I've been under water. And then, I kissed you."

Holy...what? Her jaw dropped. His nostrils flared with a harsh inhale like he approved of her reaction.

"And I touched you." He clutched the front of her shirt, lips in a firm line and heated gaze locked on hers. With a fast jerk, he ripped the material open, exposing her and sending buttons pinging across the room.

While her pulse stroked out, he cupped her breasts, dragging his thumbs across her erect nipples before reaching around and grabbing her backside. She gasped. Her skin grew hot and her core ached and, oh God, she might die. But his groan was proof he wasn't done.

"And I was inside you." His fingers twitched, then both hands clenched the flesh of her ass like a brand. He thrust against her damp folds. The momentum of his hips surging while he held her in place sent a tremor through her every fiber, the cotton from his briefs a meager barrier from his thick shaft.

She whimpered, putty in his hands, and threw her head back.

"No, look at me." He waited until she did as asked, and the smoldering inferno in his bourbon eyes made her feel like kindling in his wake. "I don't want to keep holding my breath. You pulled me to the surface, now stay here with me."

"I am here," she whispered, ready to splinter apart in his arms. She didn't understand what he was talking about. She'd admitted she was scared. He was dangerously close to consuming her heart and soul. What else did he want?

"Are you?" His gaze penetrated until all she could do was nod. "Show me." He traced her lower lip with his thumb, then slid it into her mouth. She hummed around his finger, and he hissed. Teeth bared, he growled. "Prove it."

She gripped his wrist, shoved his hand away, and crashed her mouth to his. Hunger ate away at her control and they devoured one another. Sharp, fast strokes of the tongue and hands searching for purchase. He raised his hips and shoved his briefs down his thighs. They fumbled positions, mouths sealed, until he tossed them aside.

He laid her out on the bed, raised his head, and looked at her with confusion and desperation. A barely perceptible shake of his head, and he flipped her onto her front and covered her back with his body. Every...inch.

"You drive me out of my ever-loving mind." He brushed her hair to one side and nipped her earlobe. "Do you feel it, too, honey?" His mouth latched onto her neck. His tongue and teeth scraped her nerve endings and sent goosebumps across her skin despite the heat he generated. "Tell me."

"Yes." God, the way he spoke to her. Like years of frustration and bindings had broken free, and he needed nothing more than to dominate.

He kissed her nape, her shoulders, and raised himself only enough to create space with little margin for error. His hand slid down her spine, past her crevice, and between her legs. He groaned as he spread her slickness, coated his fingers. "So wet for me."

"Yes." She ground against his hand, needing more, yet he avoided where she wanted him most. A sharp tingle shot through her. "Xavier."

He removed his hand and she whimpered in protest. "Shh. I know what you want." The thick head of his shaft rubbed between her folds. He surged forward, filling her in one deft thrust, and stilled. "I know what you need."

Fuller than she'd ever been, she pressed her face into the mattress and fisted the sheets. Even with the slight ache from him stretching her, it was so, so good. He knew what she wanted? Needed?

Absolutely. Beyond all doubt. And like no one else.

With his thighs, he spread hers wider and covered her once more with his body. His hands skimmed up her sides, then between her and the bed. Hot, hard flesh pulsed inside her as he settled into position. One hand cupped her breast and the other descended until his fingers scissored around where they were joined.

The heel of his palm ground against her clit. She cried out, bucking under him. He had her pinned and at his mercy. The oddest sense of protection and safety surrounded her even as she struggled to roll her hips to chase pleasure. "Xavier, please."

"I love the way you say my name. It's like you're marking your territory and begging at the same time." His warm breath caressed the shell of her ear. He shifted behind her and the next thrust had skin slapping skin. "Say it again. I'm yours, honey."

She barely got his name past her lips and he was moving. Taking her. Filling her. Hard, shallow strokes that sent reason and logic into a different hemisphere. Each plunge caressed from within while his graceful body moved in an eloquent, sacred dance against hers. There was no part of her he didn't touch, didn't surround. Even his light cologne wrapped her inside his embrace.

Although his hips pistoned and coiled need echoed in his grunts, something about the lack of tension in his frame had her thinking he wasn't making a mad dash toward the finish line so much as he was unable to contain his desire. Like they were one damn person trying to remerge, to regain something once lost.

"You are mine." He followed his hoarse, whispered declaration by pressing his face against her neck as if he hadn't meant to say it aloud.

Emotion burned her eyes, and she pinched them closed. She struggled to hold out, to keep this feeling forever, but he had the reins. Between his palm circling her swollen clit, his shaft gliding along her sensitive walls, and the hard planes of his body, she began to come apart.

"That's it, honey." His mouth opened wide against her skin and a low groan emerged. Words of encouragement were muttered against her nape.

An orgasm tore through her, and she gripped the sheets tighter. Toes curling, she ducked her head and choked out a pleasured sob with her face smashed into the mattress. Not a part of her wasn't affected, and she wasn't prepared for what it would do to her. Blood boiled in her veins and her muscles locked and a scream raked her throat. His motions never slowed, despite how she bowed, quaked, and thrashed. Both anchoring and catapulting her, he never let up. The release went on forever, violent and beautiful, until finally, the tremors became aftershocks.

Just as she found it safe to open her eyes, he jerked. His thrusts slowed, halted, then rocked anew as he came. He said her name, yelled it, and spilled inside her. If possible, his arms banded tighter, and he dropped his forehead to her temple, panting.

"Mercy, Peyton."

She offered a moan/laugh combination and stretched under him.

Breaths soughing, he eased out, rolled to his back, and reached out an arm. Limp, she had no recourse but to let him haul her on top of him. They stayed like that, catching their breath, and her like a blanket covering him. She wanted to crawl inside his embrace and never venture out again. His warm skin and sexy scent and hard muscles...a safe haven.

Sated, she closed her eyes while he untangled the sheet by kicking his legs, then draped it over them. He skimmed his hand down her back, the other sliding into her hair. Not that she minded, but he was very affectionate after sex. So far, anyway. Gentle ministrations and kisses on her face like he feared losing contact.

"For the record, this is the biggest thing about you that scares me." She ran her fingers over his chest, wondering if she should've said anything at all.

He was quiet a long moment, then went back to playing with her hair. "Are you referring to the sex or afterward?" His hoarse, low voice rumbled his chest and vibrated her cheek.

"Yes."

His hand stilled. "Explain, honey. I'm drawing my own conclusions and—"

"We're good together." She bit her lip, unable to look at him. "At work, at home, in bed..." She sighed. "It sounds stupid, I know. It's scary, though."

The arm around her back cinched her tighter, then released. "Know what scares me?" He drew a deep breath and massaged her scalp. "That you'll walk away."

His response hit a nerve. She couldn't pinpoint why, exactly, but in the deep recesses of her mind, a part of her wondered if the connection he felt with her wasn't gratitude. Would he still want her or be attracted if she hadn't come to work at Gaines Industries? If he didn't see her as a balm for his social anxiety?

And even bringing the hint to her subconscious had guilt coagulating in her stomach. She was inserting facts not in evidence and he deserved better than that.

She lifted her head and set her chin on his pec. His golden brown eyes zeroed in on her, and never in all their time together had he ever looked at her with such abject openness. Concern, hope, fear, and surrender shoved together in his gaze.

"Take away my company, my wealth..." He shook his head. "What's left besides a brain that refuses to shut down or guy who can't stand crowds?"

"Are you being serious with me right now?" Irritation pounded her temples. When he didn't answer, she rose up on one elbow. "What's left? The things that matter, X. Your heart. Your dry, shy sense of humor. Compassion for others and the ability to see beyond the normal spectrum." Since she was getting pissy, she drew a calming breath. "There's the way your ass looks in jeans, too. I wouldn't underestimate your abs, either."

He ran his tongue over his teeth, then appeared to take her bait. One corner of his mouth curled. "What I meant was, you keep pointing out our differences. If the factors that brought you to me were suddenly gone, what's to keep you here?"

Sometimes, she could wring his neck. "*Für ein Genie, können Sie ziemlich dicht.*" She held up a hand before he could ask for a German translation. "For a genius, you can be pretty dense."

Up popped the other corner of his mouth. "There's my point. What scares me makes no more logical sense than what frightens you. Yet, there they are, irrational or not." A ragged exhale directed at the ceiling, and he closed his eyes. "Just trying to be honest."

Chapter Nineteen

Xavier strummed his fingers on the chair in Peyton's office and waited for her to finish a phone conversation with his mother. They'd been at it twenty minutes, going over the final details for the Fallen Veterans fundraiser tomorrow, and he'd forgotten why he'd come in here in the first place.

"The mask is beautiful. It matches the dress we picked out. I can't wait for you to see it." She laughed into the receiver.

He eyed the ceiling. No matter how many times he'd asked over the past few weeks, she'd refused to even tell him so much as the color of her gown. He understood why curiosity killed the cat. Whatever the style, she'd look better out of it.

They'd both been busy as of late, only able to hook up on the weekends, and it was driving him batshit. Every morning, he woke up without her in his bed, and it only cemented the notion she should move in with him. The conversation had been on the tip of his tongue since they'd made love but, for whatever reason, he'd remained silent.

He kept picturing her in various places in the mansion late at night when he couldn't sleep. Reading in the library. Drinking coffee by the patio door in the kitchen. Watching the sunset from his bedroom balcony. Kicking his ass at Halo in his media room. The vision of her in his shower was his favorite.

She laughed. "No, his tux is back from the cleaners and at his house. The media kits are at the ballroom..." Another laugh that tugged at his balls. "Right? They're perfect. The lavender was a great idea."

Joseph strode in the room, brows drawn, and moved right past Xavier to stand in front of Peyton's desk. He snapped his fingers, indicating his visit was urgent.

Eyes wide, she held up a finger. "Elaine, something's come up. I'll see you tomorrow. Yes, thanks." She hung up and rose. "What's wrong?"

Joseph rubbed his bald head, sending Xavier's pulse thumping in concern. "We've got a teenager in the lobby asking for you. She's upset over something. Been crying since she got here ten minutes ago. No appointment, and she insists she'll only talk to you. It raised warning bells for Jackie, so she called me up to deal with it."

Xavier clenched his hands into fists. "What's her name?"

"Juanita Jefferson."

"Oh." Peyton clapped a hand to her chest. "Send her in right now."

After a brief pause, Joseph nodded and strode out.

Peyton came around her desk and leaned on the edge. She smoothed the pleats of her red dress. "That's Marcus Jefferson's daughter. He's one of your first beneficiaries at Fallen Veterans. Below the knee leg amputee after his unit drove over an IED in Iraq."

Xavier nodded, recalling the soldier but not the girl. What would she be doing at Gaines Industries, in tears, no less?

Moments later, Joseph escorted a girl into the room and shut the door behind them. At roughly seventeen, her chubby cocoa cheeks were tear-stained, but she looked no worse for wear. Her black hair was pulled back in a frizzy knot and her yellow dyed jeans were clean, as was her Hilfiger t-shirt. She certainly didn't appear threatening.

She went right for Peyton and wrapped her arms around her waist. "Thanks for seeing me, Miss Smoke."

Xavier rose and stood in the corner with Joseph to give them some space.

"Of course, sweetheart." Peyton patted the girl's back and held her at arm's length. "What's got you so upset? Here, sit down."

They pulled the chairs until they faced each other, and Juanita sighed. There was something world-weary and heart-wrenching about the sound. "I know this is last minute, but do you think I could..." She ducked her head, staring at her lap. "Could I sing at the picnic on Sunday? For my dad?"

The Fallen Veterans event ran the entire weekend. A charity dinner would be held the night before, garnering most of the donations and throwing society's elite together. A picnic the next day was more of an appreciation family-type thing. It wasn't unusual for the soldiers' kids to get involved with games and entertainment.

Concern wrinkled Peyton's forehead. She exchanged a quick glance with Joseph and refocused on Juanita. "Is he all right? Has something happened?"

"My mom died last month. Breast cancer."

Shit. Just...shit. Xavier rubbed the ache in his chest.

Peyton reached forward and clutched the girl's hands, her eyes suspiciously wet. "Oh, sweetheart. I'm so sorry."

Juanita nodded, seeming much older than her years. "It happened fast. One second I was filling out college scholarship forms, the next we were setting up hospice. It was, like, two months after they told us and she was gone. Something about it spreading to lymph nodes or something." She shook her head. "Anyway, Dad's been taking it hard. I wanted to cheer him up."

"I understand." Peyton's soft tone nailed Xavier right between the eyes. "What would you need from us to perform? There's a gazebo in the center of the park grounds. Would that work?"

"You'll let me do it?" For the first time since she entered the room, Juanita's eyes lit up with something other than grief and, in a flash, she was just an excited kid. "Really?"

Peyton glanced at Xavier as if seeking permission just in case, and he nodded. "Heck yeah. I've heard you sing at your choir practice. You're amazing. Your dad will love the gesture, too."

Xavier watched them, having no clue what Peyton was talking about. He knew she sometimes got involved with the families, attending graduations and whatnot, but she obviously did more than he ever anticipated if choir practices were involved. Every time he thought he had a read on her, she smacked him with something else.

"I usually use a keyboard, so I can bring it with me. We can't afford a piano." Juanita frowned. "It needs to be plugged in, though."

"That can be arranged. No problem." Peyton skimmed her hand over the top of Juanita's head. "How are you holding up? Losing your mom had to be tough. I was about your age when mine died."

Xavier closed his eyes and fought the tugging, push-pull of emotions in his chest. They'd been seniors in high school when her parents were killed in a car crash. He hadn't a clue what to do for her, and they hadn't been as close back then. He also didn't know this girl from Adam, but realizing she was going through the same thing as Peyton once had just...sucked. Being a teenager was difficult enough without losing a parent.

"Some days are better than others." Juanita sniffed.

Peyton looked close to losing it. Her throat kept working a swallow and, if she blinked any more, she'd create a tornado from the flutter of her lashes. "Is your dad still working nights?" At Juanita's nod, Peyton chewed her lip. "Why don't we go get an early dinner? I'll take you home afterward and you can play me your song."

"Yeah? I don't want to be a pest or anything."

"You're never a pest, sweetheart. Give me twenty minutes to finish up and I'll meet you in the lobby, okay?"

Joseph saw the girl out, and the door had barely shut behind them when Peyton doubled over, grabbing her stomach. She flung her glasses off and whipped them toward her desk, then pressed her palms to her eyes.

Damn it. Xavier ate the distance and pulled her against him. Her shoulders hitched in a sob, and he felt like a useless ass doing nothing but holding her. It was a rare sight, her in tears, but he'd rather have a hot poker shoved under his nails than watch her cry. He was pretty sure a unicorn died every time the phenomena occurred.

"I didn't know she was sick. I could've attended the funeral. We didn't even send flowers." Her voice cracked, and she buried her face deeper into his chest.

Leave it to her to feel guilty. He ran his hand over her back, wishing she had her hair down so he could sooth her by smoothing the strands. She seemed to like that best when they laid in bed. But she had it in a severe bun like she always did at work, so he held the back of her neck and banded his arm tighter.

Her fingers gripped the lapels of his suit as she let out a quiet sound of duress. "God. To have her mom taken like that, and after almost losing her dad while he served. He's just now starting to get used to a prosthesis and a new job."

It couldn't be any easier than burying both parents at age seventeen, a brother a handful of years later, and a fiancé months after that. Life was a big ball of shit sometimes. "Shh." He closed his eyes and kissed the top of her head, letting his lips linger. "She seems to be doing okay."

"Yeah." She let out a watery exhale and lifted her head. "I'm sorry. I got your tie wet."

As if he cared. He pulled a handkerchief from his breast pocket and wiped the mascara smudges under her eyes. Other than that, she seemed no worse for wear. Unlike him, whose chest had gone through a meat grinder.

"Are you all right?" He stretched to grab her bottle of sweet tea on the desk, handing it to her.

She sipped the tea and recapped it. "I'm good. Sorry again."

"Quit apologizing." He remembered why he'd come into her office and retrieved her glasses for her. "Since you have dinner plans, how about we meet up afterward? I can pick you up?" He needed her. In more ways than one. They couldn't get touchy-feely at work, and the last time he'd held her, aside from this brief crying jag, had been five damn days ago.

"I can't. I need to stop by the ballroom to approve table settings, the staging area, and decor. They got it done this afternoon. Tomorrow morning, I have to stalk the caterers and florists to be sure they're on task. Somewhere in there, I must make myself presentable." She rolled her head to stretch her neck. "I'll meet you at the event like we did last year."

He despised that plan. Immensely.

Yes, they periodically had to meet at a function separately, and yes, she had a lot on her plate. But he had the urge to stomp his foot like a petulant child. They were ten days from going public with that article and it might as well be ten years. He wanted the world to know now, wanted to stop hiding. And every second they were apart was like an eternity.

"What's wrong?" She pressed her finger between his brows as if to smooth a worry line.

He was way past simply caring about her and headed toward forever, that's what was wrong. Or not wrong, but too soon. He'd known her a long time, yet they'd only been dating six weeks. He'd had chips in his pantry longer than that. And it wasn't like he'd ever been in love before. How the hell was he supposed to know if this was it?

Who was he kidding? He'd probably fallen before his lips had ever met hers, before she'd come to work for him, and before he'd tutored her in high school. No doubt, the exact moment could be pinpointed to the second she smiled at him in a cheerleader uniform by a locker.

"Move in with me." And hell. He used to have tact.

Her jaw dropped, and she blinked. Once. Twice.

He sighed. "Let me start over. I miss you when you're not around and I'm sick of sneaking moments with you. My house is unbearably empty without you there. I think about you constantly. Please consider moving in with me." Not so much as a muscle twitch. Great. He'd rendered her catatonic. "Blink once for yes or twice for no."

Well, she didn't blink, but she did press a hand to her forehead and say "Oh God" somewhere in the vicinity of thirty times. She stalked to the other side of the room and paced. The click-click of her heels matched his heart rate.

"Would you say something, at least?" Panic tripped his pulse. "And I don't mean *Oh God.*"

"We haven't even..." She waved her hand as if unable to conjure words.

"Haven't what? Gone public? Vacationed together? Skydived out of a perfectly good airplane?" He ran a hand through his hair. "Help me out, honey. You're usually the calm one. I'm not liking the role reversal and—"

"We haven't declared our feelings." She closed her eyes, sighed, and dropped her arms. Her hands slapped her thighs. "I don't know, X. It seems prudent to drop the L-bomb before we share closet space and argue over sofa patterns."

Struck stupid, he tried to grasp a tangible thread on how he felt about that. Instead, his brain detached from his mouth. "I don't care what fabric you pick out."

A cat-like rumble shot past her clenched teeth and she fisted her hands. If it hadn't been so adorable, he might've been worried. "*Frustrierender Mann.* Frustrating, frustrating man."

German. Not a bad sign. Angry was better than...

Then again, she used it when scared, too.

He almost told her right then he loved her. Not out of desperation, but because he had very little doubt he did. The only woman he could see a future with was her. She was the frenetic beat of his heart and the balm to his soul. Nothing made sense without her. Hell, nothing had meaning without her. If that wasn't love, he'd eat his flash drive.

But a sliver of warning wove up his spine, telling him she might not be ready to hear it yet. Or she might think his declaration was because of the current conversation and not based on true emotion. The very last thing he needed was for her to grow so nervous she walked.

"Hey." He closed the distance and held her face. "This was crappy timing. I'm sorry. There's no rush. Think about it, all right? You don't need to decide today or even next week. Just understand, this is what I want. You and me."

Her shoulders deflated and, just like that, his Peyton was back. "Okay." She gave him a brief kiss. "I have to go. I'll see you tomorrow."

"Will you spend tomorrow night with me, at least?"

The grin hit her cerulean eyes. "Deal."

He stood in her office a good ten minutes before heading back into his. At the computer, he logged into the secure server for Fallen Veterans and pulled up Marcus Jefferson's address, then strode into the lobby.

With a nod at Joseph in a waiting room chair, Xavier rested a hip on Jackie's desk. "Do you know where Miss Smoke usually orders floral arrangements?"

"Yes, sir." She smiled and brushed a strand of her neat blonde bob away from her face.

"Good. What flowers are appropriate for a funeral?"

Her lips twisted in thought. "I'd say callas. They call them peace lilies."

"Could you order a pot and have it shipped here?" He handed her a scrap of paper with Jefferson's address. "Have the card say *Sorry for your loss from Gaines Industries.*"

"Sure thing. I'll do it right away."

"Thanks." Then, he recalled something Juanita had said. He couldn't give the girl back her mother, but he could make her smile. "Where can I buy a piano?"

"Uh...that I don't know. Hold on. I'll check." Her fingers clacked over the keyboard and a search engine popped up. "This place is close by and has excellent ratings."

He turned her desk phone around and dialed the number on the screen. After a greeting from the salesman, Xavier introduced himself. "What's the best piano brand?"

The courteous male cleared his throat. "That would be a Steinway. We carry two selections and the other top nine craftsmen, as well."

"If I purchase in the next hour, can you have it delivered today?" When the guy made a sound of hesitation, Xavier cut in. "I'll double your fee. When can you have it delivered?"

"Oh. Well, six o'clock should work."

"Excellent. Standby." He glanced at his watch and pulled his cell out of his pocket, then texted Peyton. *Can you get Juanita home before six?*

Her response was almost immediate. *Yes. Why?*

He thumbed a response. *She's got a delivery coming. Try to get her there by then.* He put the phone back to his ear. "I'm sending a representative to your store now. Have it delivered by six."

Not waiting for a reply, he hung up and dug in his wallet for a credit card. He waved it at Joseph. "Go buy a piano."

Rising, his bodyguard walked over. He glanced at Jackie's screen, assumingly to get the address, then Xavier. With a shake of his head, he took the card and moved to the elevator. "And they say you have no heart."

When he was gone, Jackie smiled. "Who's the piano for? If you don't mind me asking, sir."

"I don't mind. The girl who just left? She's into music and can't afford one." She blinked at him, and he wondered if he had a God-given gift to shock women mute. He was two for two so far today. "What?"

"That was very kind of you, Mr. Gaines." She pressed her lips together.

Uncomfortable, he shoved his hand in his pocket and rubbed his thumb over the coin Peyton had given him. "Don't tell anyone. People might think I really am nice."

She yelped a surprised laugh. "You are nice, but your secret is safe with me. I won't squeal that you're funny, too."

Funny? Maybe she needed more caffeine.

"Excellent." He strode back into his office and finished a few tasks that couldn't wait until Monday, then he stood in front of the windows and watched the city.

Fog hovered in the distance near the Bay and the daylight was beginning to wane. Office lights petered on as cars bustled twenty floors below. He'd taken in this very view thousands of times before Peyton had come back into his life, had observed the melee as it whooshed by him, never once realizing how lonely he'd truly been.

It wasn't just social anxiety that had kept him from engaging, but the disconnect he'd latched onto, as well. Safer that way. Until she'd shown him the world. The ugly and the beautiful. That it was okay to feel. And that he not only should, but had an obligation to take part. Because of her, he no longer existed. He lived.

Christ, he yearned to give back a fraction of what she'd offered. To share something more than an office and a house. A family, most of all. Perhaps not to replace the one she'd lost, but to build a new one.

Having no idea when these desires had arisen, where they'd come from, or what the hell to do about them, he rubbed the ache in his chest. It had been a matter of weeks since they'd started dating. He'd gone from sexually frustrated to holy shit in one season change. Yet, all his instincts, every last one, told him to grab hold of her with both hands and fight with everything in him not to let go.

And she'd freaked out when he'd asked her to step up the relationship.

At the knock on his door, he turned to find Joseph. "Hey. Did you get the piano ordered?"

"Yep." His bodyguard took a few steps into the room. "Are you done for the day or do you need more time?"

Rubbing his neck, Xavier glanced at his desk. "We can go." He grabbed his suit coat from the back of his chair.

On the ride home, Joseph eyed him. "Shame about that girl's mom."

Xavier rested his head on the seat. "Yeah. Hit Peyton pretty hard, too."

"I noticed." Joseph glanced out the window.

"I asked her to move in with me."

His bodyguard's brows shot skyward, and he glanced at Xavier. "What did she say?"

"Not a whole lot." He watched other cars zip past, gaze lost in the glow from streetlights. "She looked at me like I'd punched her in the face."

"Do you love her?"

Heaven help him. "Yes."

"Have you told her?" When Xavier shook his head, Joseph nodded. "Does she love you?"

"Fuck if I know." She hadn't said the actual words, but sometimes, he'd swear she felt the same riotous, bone-jarring way he did.

His cell pinged, and he pulled it out of his pocket. Peyton had sent a text, along with a video. *You did this, X. Thank you.*

He hit Play, and the video showed Juanita from behind as she opened a door. After a few seconds, she squealed and jumped up and down. Peyton's shot followed the girl out onto the lawn, where two guys were unloading a piano from a box truck on the street. They had her sign for it and she continued her excited dance as she took the pen. After two more minutes of similar activity, the clip ended.

Grinning, he re-pocketed his cell.

Chapter Twenty

With an hour to spare, Peyton climbed out of the car Xavier had sent, adjusted her dress, and snuck in the back entrance to the Fallen Veterans masquerade ball. She'd had him do the same thing thirty minutes ago when he'd arrived to avoid any rumors that they hadn't come together. The press liked to pounce on any little thing and twist a story. Tonight was about charity.

She worked her way through the back rooms and into the upper foyer, handing her coat and purse to an attendant. Behind her was the main lobby. Ahead, the ballroom was down a set of marble stairs and surrounded by a wrought iron terrace on the second level. From her position, she glanced below at the open floor plan and smiled.

Lovely. Just lovely.

An enormous chandelier rained from a vaulted ceiling, the lighting set low. A platform was up front with a podium and a couple chairs. Pictures on easels displayed previous events and some of the soldiers they'd helped. In front of the staging area was a small dance floor and, beyond that, tables. Lavender stems and floating candles dotted the white linen.

Quite a few people were already milling about and, to the left, Xavier stood at the bar with his parents. Face clean-shaven, he smiled at something his father said and sipped from his drink. Scotch, no doubt. The sight of him in a tux never failed to create a flutter in her belly. The man knew how to fill a suit with his broad shoulders and narrow waist. But the simple black mask framing his eyes added a sexier, mysterious edge to his polish.

She spotted Joseph walking her way along the upper railing where a few other security members were perched. He met her at the top of the stairs and grinned.

"Well, well, blondie. Aren't you a vision."

"Aw. Thanks." She glanced at her dress. Deep lilac and sleeveless, it hugged her chest and waist, then flowed in a loose, ankle-length skirt. Over the purple silk was black lace. She'd loved the elegant sexiness of it from first glance at the boutique in Napa. "Everything looks great, doesn't it?"

"How could it not? You planned the shindig." He winked at her. "I hear Xavier asked you to move in with him."

Yeah, that. Her head was still reeling. "He did. Is this the part where you caution me not to move too fast?"

"No." His smile slipped in varying degrees. "This is the part where I say you've had enough loss and hurt for three lifetimes. No one will love you or treat you better than him."

The breath seeped from her lungs. It wasn't as if she didn't understand. She'd wanted them to move forward, start dating, and she didn't regret the decision. And fast or not, being with him felt natural. Right. Yet, something kept hovering near the fringes of her mind. Not quite a warning. More of an awareness to be careful.

She sighed. "What about you and Kate? Things seem to be progressing nicely."

He laughed. "I'm half in love with her. I can handle Red just fine, blondie. But we weren't talking about me." Stepping closer, he took the mask from her hand. Carefully, he undid the strap and lifted the purple satin and black lace to her face. Placing it over her eyes, he tied the mask behind her head. Before she could adjust her hair to cover the band, he did it for her, then took a step back. "I think you should do it. Move in with him, I mean."

In the pretense of checking her mask placement, she smoothed her strands, buying time. All she could come up with was... "Why?"

Up went his eyebrows. "Because you'd be hard-pressed to find someone who looks at you like that." He glanced over her shoulder. "You showed the world he has a heart. Don't break it."

She turned and followed Joseph's gaze. Down below, Xavier was watching them, his drink halfway to his mouth. The several hundred feet between them shrank to one. Heat, awe, and...love shone in his eyes. *Love*. She tried to catch her breath and couldn't. Perhaps Joseph was right. Xavier's expression indicated he had fallen. She certainly had. Craziest thing? She had no clue when it had happened.

In all her years, she'd had only a precious few who'd truly loved her—romantic or otherwise. Most were gone now. But no one, not even Mark, had gazed into her eyes, held her captive, and sent such abject longing right back at her like Xavier could. One glance, and a multitude of meaning slammed into her full force, with the impact of a mountain.

"I wouldn't break his heart," she whispered to Joseph, unable to look away from Xavier. He didn't move, not a tick, but a storm raged in his eyes.

Pleading. Understanding. Lust. Need. Affection.

"Not on purpose." Joseph shifted, and she finally tore her gaze away to face him again. "Like I said, the way he looks at you says enough."

"Why is no one worried about him breaking my heart?"

He shook his head. "You're the first person he's opened his up to, Peyton."

True. In a romantic sense, anyway. She took in Joseph's bald head, wide shoulders, and wry grin. "Are you adding guardian angel to your resume?" She smiled. "You could pull it off."

He laughed. "Sure, blondie. Just call me divine intervention." He jerked his chin. "I'll be over there watching if you need anything."

Pivoting, she headed downstairs, Xavier tracking her the entire way. It almost felt like a twisted form of foreplay between the masks, the growing crowd, and their inability to act like a couple in public.

"Peyton." Elaine sighed dreamily. "You were absolutely right. That gown is perfect."

"Thanks. You look amazing, too." Elaine was always the pillar of elegance. Tonight, decked out in a sequin black dress. Peyton hugged his parents and smiled at Xavier. "Very handsome, Mr. Gaines."

His eyes narrowed to slits. "And you are beautiful as always, Miss Smoke." He leaned close to her ear and lowered his voice. "That dress is toast when we get home. By the end of the night, I'll have bitten a hole clean through my tongue in order to not react."

Rawr. She cleared her throat and hoped her cheeks weren't as red as they were hot. "The photographer's here. Are you ready to walk around? Be pleasant?"

He ran his tongue over his teeth. "After you."

They made the rounds together, chatting with attendees. Elaine stole Peyton from Xavier after an hour to introduce her to a society couple she'd yet to meet. By then, Xavier was trapped by the governor, so Peyton made her way back to the bar with his mom.

His dad passed her a champagne flute. "I do hope you'll save a dance for an old man."

She adored his parents so hard. "If you find an old man, let me know."

As Edward winked at her, a tall, slim brunette sidled up next to them. Her gaze bypassed Peyton and landed right on Xavier's mother. "Elaine, thank you for the invitation. I'm looking very forward to a private chat with Xavier."

Elaine's smile was as cold as the arctic. "All in the name of charity. I don't recall sending you an invitation, though."

The woman's dress was a silver slip of a thing that bordered on pornographic. She was nearly as tall as Edward, and her lips couldn't be natural with that kind of sultry pout. She ran her finger along the neckline as her gaze slid to Xavier's father. She seemed familiar, but Peyton couldn't remember from where. Whoever she was, Elaine was very unhappy the woman had attended.

Edward slipped his arm around Peyton, and it took her a moment to realize it was a show of solidarity. "Pamela, have you met Xavier's girlfriend? This lovely creature is Peyton Smoke."

She tensed at the informal address, plus the blatant disregard for their privacy. She thought his parents understood the need to keep the relationship quiet. "Nice to meet you."

Pamela gave her a once over, lip curling. "Her? His girlfriend? Pah-lease." A frown line shoved its way through the botox and wrinkled her forehead. "Wait. Peyton, Peyton," she chanted as if trying to summon why the name was of significance. Then, she rolled her glittered, charcoal-lined eyes. "The personal assistant. That makes sense. You're the affair."

Peyton's jaw dropped, but nothing of intelligence passed her lips.

Elaine's spine stiffened. "Peyton is a marketing director, not an assistant, and she's no affair. They've been together quite some time. After you, other pastures were bound to be greener. I'd say she's emerald by comparison." Every insult dripped with sarcasm, but was spoken with so much saccharine, they could've passed for compliments.

Peyton's head hurt and...what the heck was happening? Elaine wasn't a mean person. Certainly not when Xavier's charity was at stake or in public venues.

Pamela. Where did she know that name?

Oh. *O-o-h-h*. She remembered now. As in, Pamela Squire, the model who'd dumped Xavier years ago after she'd publicly spouted crap about him to the press. The woman was a world-class, grade-A bitch, and Peyton had no idea what he'd seen in her. Well, besides the stunning body and perfect face and sultry voice. Or her fame. And money.

Edward cinched Peyton closer to his side. "Our girl here also did most of tonight's planning."

"It's nice to meet you," Peyton croaked, then swallowed a groan because she'd already said that. Sucking in a breath for courage, she summoned her backbone. "You'll have to forgive me. Xavier rarely brings up past regrets. It took me a moment to put the face to a name. I also haven't seen you on many advertisements lately. How are you enjoying retirement?"

Edward chuckled under his breath.

Pamela scoffed, which ended on something close to a screech. "I'm not retired." Her gaze dragged over Peyton. "And you won't last long." With a huff, she stormed away.

"Drama queen, three o'clock." Peyton shook her head in disbelief. "How did Xavier last three months with that woman?"

"Alcohol?" Edward gave her a last squeeze and dropped his arm. "I'm sorry if I misspoke. I suspect she's going to try to get my son back."

"Eh, let her try." Which, apparently, the model was already attempting. Plastered to Xavier in the middle of the room, she walked her fingers up his chest. Xavier, jaw tight, stared balefully at her. A couple feet away, the photographer snapped shots. "Crap. I'll be right back."

Peyton made her way over and hooked her arm through the photographers'. "James, you talented devil. You're doing a wonderful job."

"Thanks, Miss Smoke." His ruddy cheeks blushed. He was a good foot shorter than her and had two strips of gray hair over his temples. The rest of his head was bald. "I was thankful for the opportunity to come back this year."

"Well," she rolled the word off her tongue, "I wanted no one but you. Could you do me a teensy-weensy favor? Delete the shots you just took of that awful model and I'll give you several better opportunities of Mr. Gaines later."

"Oh, sure thing." Clearly flustered by her flirting, he played with the settings on his camera. She glanced at the digital screen as he sent five pictures to the trash bin. "All done."

"Perfect. You're the best." She kissed his cheek. "After dinner, be ready when the dancing starts." She patted his arm and strode away, but stumbled when she caught Xavier's pissed off bourbon eyes on her. Pamela was nowhere in sight, so Peyton walked up to him. "Hi."

If possible, his jaw clenched harder. He stared at her two tense beats, then sucked a harsh inhale. "While I'm doing my best to send my ex away with some dignity, you're off hitting on someone else?"

Jealousy. Interesting. And, jeez. He was sexy all worked up.

"For your information, I was flirting my way through getting the photographer to delete the shots he'd taken of you and said ex." She raised her brows. "You're welcome."

He stared at her—hard—but his shoulders sank. After a moment, he glanced away and swallowed. "I'm sorry. I don't know where that came from."

"You're the only man I'm interested in, X." His gaze jerked back to hers, and she smiled. "If we weren't surrounded by people, I'd show you."

His chest quickly rose and fell, nostrils flaring. "I really want to kiss you right now."

"Plenty of time later." She grinned. "Come on. They're getting dinner ready."

The meal consisted of a veal or duck option, chosen by Elaine, and Peyton spent the entire hour imaging all the naughty things she'd be doing later while trying to hold a conversation with their tablemates. By the time Xavier had gotten through the speech she'd written for him and taken her hand for a dance, she was aching.

Xavier tugged her to his chest, one arm around her back, his other hand clasping hers. He set them in motion and glanced at her as they waltzed. "I wanted to ask you to prom. Did you know that?"

"No." She tried to keep up with his intricate steps, but her head was all over the place.

He grunted, a smirk teasing his lips. "Never had the guts. Thus, the only time we've danced together was the one time by the tree in Napa. A pity, that."

She laughed. "We're dancing now." Glancing over his shoulder, she spotted Edward and Elaine on the floor, as well as a few other couples. Then, she realized what tune the orchestra was playing and looked at Xavier again. "Interesting song choice."

His grin dissolved her insides to goo. "I was wondering if you'd notice. I requested it."

Sad Song by We The Kings—the one he'd pulled up on her phone that night at his parents' place. "I dare you to tell me again you're not a romantic."

He laughed, gliding her over the floor. Damn, but he was graceful for a computer geek.

The photographer knelt at the edge of the seating area, lens pointed at her and Xavier. Several other guests were watching them, as well. Nerves fluttered in her stomach, but she battled them back, keeping her expression pleasantly serene.

Next weekend was his birthday party. The Tuesday after that, the article about him in GQ. They'd no longer be a secret. Unsure how she felt about it, she lost herself in the melody, in the scent of his light cologne, and the way his arms held her like a protector.

"You've zoned out on me." He spun her away from him and pulled her back. "That's better. Have I told you how goddamn gorgeous you look tonight?"

Gah. "Yes, thank you. Behave or you'll make me blush in front of all these people."

"I can't wait to make you blush without all the people." His low, hoarse tone sent a shiver of need up her spine. "Like that, do you? Shall I tell you what else I'd like to do, Peyton?"

And the territorial way he said her name? Total panty melt. "Payback's a bitch, X."

He grunted. "It doesn't bother you? The way I speak to you while aroused?" Though his expression was blank, avid interest and concerned curiosity radiated in his eyes.

"Not at all." It was hot as hell. She wasn't used to it since none of her previous partners were vocal, but that just proved to be another defining factor between Xavier and other men. "You surprise me."

His gaze roamed her face as if trying to spot a lie. "How so?"

She shrugged. "I guess I didn't expect your alpha side. The way you go after what you want and speak your mind when we're alone."

Slowly, he nodded. "I haven't been that way with other women. Assertive, yes. Encouraging with sounds and praise in the bedroom, sure. But not like how we are together. I'm not sure I can shut it off, actually."

Be still her heart. He killed her sometimes.

"Don't shut it off." Chewing her lip, she thought up ways to counter his naughtiness while the song changed. He tugged her closer and slow-danced versus the formal waltz they'd just finished. "When we get home later, I'll show you how much I like the way you talk to me."

His chest rumbled against hers with a quiet groan. "I'm going to regret asking this, but how will you show me?" He looked down his nose at her, heat and interest in his eyes, amusement in the curve of his lips.

She lowered her voice in case another couple was standing close enough to hear. "I'd start by unbuttoning your shirt. With my teeth."

He cursed and closed his eyes.

She laughed, loving his response. She'd never really done this sort of thing and felt a little silly. And turned on. "Can you feel my tongue on your chest as I lick my way down to—"

"Mercy." He shook his head as if to clear it. "I'm not going to be able to walk upright off this dance floor if you don't pause this conversation."

She laughed again. "What should we discuss, then?"

"Nothing. Your voice alone gets me aroused." He grinned at her, sending her pulse into hyperactive.

"I love your smile." His steps slowed, and worry ate at her stomach. "What's wrong?"

His mouth opened and closed twice before he responded. "I don't think I've ever heard that phrase in reference to me." His shell-shocked gaze wandered over her shoulder. He tilted his head. "In fact, I'm sure I haven't."

Sympathy wrapped around her throat and squeezed. Sure, he was cautious and reserved with other people, and there was a blinding difference between his smile and the grin he'd just flashed, but how was it possible someone hadn't complimented him until now?

Jeez. It stalled her lungs when he was wide open, carefree, and without the emotional safeguards. His smile? Lord help her. But his grin? Stick a fork in her.

"In that case, like you, I'll repeat myself. I love your smile."

A tiny wrinkle formed between his brows. His hand slid from her lower back, up her spine, and stopped under her hair at the base of her neck. Possessive. A claiming. His fingers clenched hers, but it seemed involuntary, judging by the intense concentration in his eyes.

Bourbon and fire looked back at her, then simmered to amber and affection. "I have to tell you something. It's important, but it shouldn't be said here. So, later, do try to remember this very second as the moment I wanted to say it and couldn't."

Was he...did he mean...? Holy God.

The air in her lungs evaporated, and she froze. Her heartbeat stuttered. She didn't know why she was reacting this way. She'd just had a discussion with Joseph about this very thing. Peyton was certain Xavier loved her, as she did him. They hadn't said the actual phrase yet, however, and something about the formality of it was frightening. New. Real. Lasting.

"May I have this dance?" Edward held out his hand, gaze darting between the two of them. "Looks like I came at a good time, too."

Xavier cleared his throat and stepped back, gesturing at Peyton. "Be my guest." His gaze lowered to the floor before he turned toward Elaine. "I'll take Mom for a spin."

Edward clasped Peyton's hand and held it to his chest, his other resting on her upper back. He set them in motion and she followed his rhythmic sway. "Everything okay?"

"Yes." Up in the air, a little scary, but okay. She smiled. "Xavier must've gotten his moves from you, too."

"I take it he mentioned at some point he really didn't need dance lessons."

A laugh bubbled in her chest. "I figured it out." She watched Xavier and his mother a moment. "The benefit turned out very well, I think."

"Have to agree with you there." Edward glanced around, then back to her. Xavier resembled his father so much she got an inside peek at what he'd look like in thirty years. Not a bad deal. "I'm a happy man, my dear."

"Oh really? Pray tell."

His cheerful grin melded into a contented smile. "I married the love of my life and my son finally noticed his. Life doesn't get much better than that."

Double damn. What was with the Gaines men and their abject romanticism? Talk about knocking a girl off her feet.

She playfully shook her head at him, attempting to keep the conversation at a light banter. "Aw. You think he loves me?"

"No. I know he's *in love* with you." A grin split his face and, without warning, he dipped her. Keeping her suspended, he bent over her. "We men folk can be dolts, but we know a good thing when we have it." Once she was upright again, he sighed. "Elaine's already planning a summer wedding. Be warned."

She laughed. How could she not with this man? "Your wife wouldn't be right in the head if she weren't planning something." She sobered a fraction as unease wove through her belly, cooled in her veins. "We shouldn't rush things, though." Heck, love or not, she and Xavier had barely begun. Then again, it seemed like they'd been together forever.

"Rush? If my son moved any slower, he'd be going backward." He squeezed her fingers, drawing her gaze to his. "When the time comes, I do hope you'll let an old man walk you down the aisle."

She stopped. Stared at him. Pressed a hand to her chest. God. Just...God. Blinking repeatedly, she tried to bat back the tears welling. Fruitless. Her eyes burned and a hot ball of emotion clogged her throat. The breath caught in her lungs as her lip quivered.

It would be an outright lie to claim she hadn't thought about her wedding day. What woman hadn't? Her engagement to Mark had set ideas in motion long ago. But even though she had a vague idea for a dress and flowers and a venue, her plans always drew up suddenly short of the mark with regards to fantasizing.

Because she had no family. No one to sit on her side of the church. To give her away.

As if sensing an emotional breakdown, Edward stroked his thumb over her knuckles and gingerly swayed to the music. "I hope you have chocolate cake. None of this yellow or marble nonsense."

With a watery laugh, she dropped her forehead on his shoulder.

Chapter Twenty-One

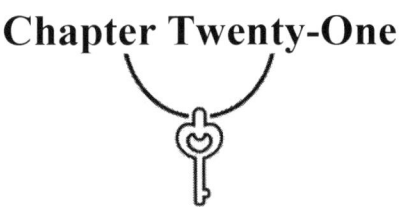

After they'd dropped off Joseph at Kate's apartment, Xavier glanced at Peyton in the backseat as his driver wove them through the dark city streets. She hadn't said much thus far, and her contemplative, lost expression was poking holes in his chest.

He took his mask off and tossed it aside, glad to be rid of the thing. "Come over here."

She turned her head and blinked as if she didn't understand.

Concerned, he leaned over and wrapped an arm around her waist, depositing her sideways on his lap. He untied her mask and dropped it on the seat, then cupped her cheek. "Are you tired?"

"A little." She smiled as if to null her acknowledgement. "I had fun dancing with you."

"Same here." He watched shadow and light play across her pretty face and got trapped by the dark navy of her eyes. "You and my father seemed to have quite the discussion."

"Ah, yes." Her breathy laugh washed over him. "It would appear your mother is already planning our wedding."

Not sure how to react, he studied her. If anything, she appeared amused. "And you thought they'd hate the idea of us dating." If that didn't tell her she was loved by more than him, he didn't know what would. Other topics he'd wanted to discuss popped to mind, and she'd left the opening. "What kind of wedding would you like when the time comes?"

Damn. There was the hesitation he'd grown to despise. Right in the twist of her lips, in the distance in her baby blues. Not quite panic, but uncertainty just the same.

"I don't know. We haven't even agreed to live together yet."

Refusing to back down, he catered to her anxiety the way she'd always done for him. "In abstract terms, then. What kind of wedding would you want?"

Her eyes rolled as if she were thinking it over. "Something outside. Small, but traditional. White dress, flowers, yada."

Breathing easier, he smiled. "And kids? Do you want them?"

Her lashes fluttered. "Do you?"

Just like her to turn the tables on him. Fine, he'd play. "If someone had asked me that a year ago, I would've said I don't know. The concept is appealing, but I'm not good with little people. For the most part, they make me nervous." He swallowed hard and gazed into her eyes. His safe place. "Now? I want children if they're yours."

Her jaw dropped. She shook her head as if unable to believe her ears. And if her eyes grew any wider, they'd pop from her skull.

"You'd probably teach them ways to defy me in four different languages, but it would be worth it." He shrugged. "I'd simply make them learn to reprogram all the electronics to get back at you. Win-win."

She pressed a hand to her forehead. A shocked, choked laugh skated past her lips.

He drew a deep breath and smoothed her soft, champagne hair as his stomach rioted. They were going to get nowhere if he didn't first tell her... "I love you."

A whimper, and her hand slapped over her mouth. Eyes welling, she stared at him. With hope, thank Christ.

"Living together, getting married, having kids?" He brushed his nose against hers and breathed in her familiar perfume, finding calm. "It doesn't matter to me when they happen, Peyton. But they do begin with I love you." Honesty, always.

She exhaled an uneven breath and held his jaw. "Ask me again to move in with you."

He wondered where she was going with this and frowned. "Will you move in with me?"

"Yes." The solitary word was spoken against his mouth, her lips feathering his and causing his heart to crack ribs. "Ask me why."

Damn, but happiness was rattling his cage, pounding at a locked door. "Why, honey?"

"Because I love you, too." Tilting her head, she sealed her mouth to his.

Hands shaking, he held the back of her head and sank into her kiss. His tongue stroked hers, his fingers threading in her hair, and he nearly died right there in the back of his limo. Aside from his folks, no one had ever told him they loved him. He suspected it had been too long since she'd heard the words, too.

He eased away and looked into her sleepy eyes. "Say it again."

A sexy, wanton smile curved her lips. "I love you. No living together until we're public, though."

"Okay."

"You might change your mind after you see how many shoes I own."

"I won't." He kissed her temple, her cheek, her mouth. "I love you, footwear and all." The car rolled to a stop, and he glanced out the window. Home. "By the time I'm done with you tonight, you won't be able to walk, never mind require shoes."

She laughed as his driver opened the door, and Xavier lifted her in his arms while he climbed out. A cool breeze went right through him and he wished he'd given her his jacket. Her dress didn't have sleeves. Leaves crackled and whirred with another gust, and he cinched her higher up his chest so they could head inside.

Tilting her head back, she looked at their driver upside down, her hair a curtain over Xavier's arm. "Goodnight, Archie."

He offered a mock bow and chuckled. "Good evening, Miss Peyton."

Carrying Peyton, Xavier climbed the front steps and strode past his butler, holding the door.

"Hi, Sam I Am." She grinned. "Lovely night."

"Yes, it is, Miss Peyton."

Xavier wove through the foyer and turned for the staircase. "Take the rest of the weekend off, Sam. Archie, as well."

"Yes, sir."

Wasting no time, Xavier started up the stairs while she nipped and licked his jaw. "You're always carrying me up the stairs."

And she was always trying to make his legs give out while using her mouth. "It's my pleasure."

She hummed. "I can walk, you know."

"I'm well aware. I watch you half the day and incalculably enjoy it." *Uhn.* She went to work on his throat. "I prefer not wasting time. Friendly as you are, you'd stop to talk to dust bunnies along the way."

Her husky laugh knocked him from interested to harder than steel. "Can we get a puppy?"

He paused halfway to the landing and looked down at her. "What?"

"My complex doesn't allow pets. I always wanted a dog." She shrugged.

Heaven help him. "Yes, we can get a dog."

She went back to assaulting the nerve endings in his neck while he continued to the second floor. "And a kitten?"

His laugh ended in a groan when she sucked his earlobe. "Yes. A kitten, too."

"What about a pony?"

The facetious little brat. He strode into his room and kicked the door shut. "Peyton, I'll buy you Saturn and all its rings if that's what you want."

He set her on her feet by the bed and skimmed his lips over her bare shoulder. Mercy, her dress tonight. He'd lost count of the number of times he'd thought about getting her out of it.

She moaned, shoving her hands in his hair. "You should only agree if you want them, too."

"As far as planets go, I've always been partial to Mars." He moved to the other side, used the tip of his tongue to trace the tendon by her pulse, and reached behind her. "Where the hell is the zipper on this thing?"

A throaty laugh, and she pulled away. "On the side." Holding his gaze, she reached under her arm and slid the tab down. "Shall I take it off?"

"Yes," he growled. He slipped out of his tux jacket and tossed it on a chair. The tie followed and, as he pulled his arms from the shirt, he noted she hadn't moved. Her forearm was crossed over her chest, holding the material to her breasts, and he changed his mind. "Stay like that."

She bit her lip while he toed off his shoes, dropped his pants, and kicked them aside. He sat on the edge of the mattress, holding her gaze, and shucked the socks. Instead of stroking his aching shaft, he crooked his finger for her to come closer. Without argument, she stepped between his legs and blinked down at him.

Sex between them so far had been passionate and sometimes animalistic. Not that he was complaining, but they hadn't taken their time. Explored. His need for her had driven out reason, common sense, and...sensuality. Truth be told, he'd never made love to another woman. Not in the slow, adoring, bonding sense of the term, anyway.

Reaching over, he switched off the lamp his butler had left on, drowning the room in moonlight from the balcony. When his eyes adjusted, he fingered the neckline of her dress just above the swell of her breasts and encouraged her to move her arm.

The dress fell to the floor, and he nearly wept. He was the luckiest bastard on the planet. Purple lace panties, bare breasts, and nothing else but his Peyton and the key charm necklace he'd given her.

Christ, she stole his breath. Legs that went on for decades. Taut belly and an hourglass flare of hips. Lush breasts almost too full for his hands and rosy-tipped nipples. Peaches and cream skin scented with her berries and floral perfume. The elegant column of her throat that led to her oval face, pert nose, and stop traffic eyes.

Never, never would he tire of looking at her.

Leaning forward, he set his hands on her waist and kissed her stomach. She trembled and wove her fingers through his hair, encouraging him. He looked up at her and took a nipple into his mouth while he slid her panties down her thighs to the floor. Keeping their gazes locked, he switched to her other breast and groaned when her lids grew heavy.

White-hot lust threatened to choke him, but he kept himself in check, going slow. He even quieted the words scraping his throat, begging to be said—what he wanted to do to her, how, and to what extent. He'd show her instead.

He grazed his knuckle up her inner thigh, pausing just before reaching her core. It took very little to arouse her, something he adored immensely, and her body's response to him was completely in sync with his desires. What she asked for, he delivered. What he needed, she provided.

She trembled against him, one hand kneading his shoulder, and he slipped his fingers between her slick folds. Panting, she closed her eyes and threw her head back. Knowing her, she was spiraling toward detonation already.

Rising to his feet, he pulled her to him and laid her out on the bed. With one arm under her back, he placed her in the center of the mattress and hovered over her. Every instinct wailed for him to plunge inside her, bury himself so deep he'd never resurface. Claim her, brand her, prove she was his and his alone.

But her eyes opened, and there was nothing except tenderness looking back at him. Unlikely as it seemed, he only had to meet her gaze to see himself, see how she viewed him. To her, he wasn't weak, awkward, or shy. He wasn't only a suit with an above average intellect who happened to be rich. She had no clue what a rare gift she was to him. To be able to bring out his best side when even his greatest attempts at normal had failed. A version that probably wouldn't exist had she not been a part of his life.

Her declaration of love came back to him, and his throat closed. The words he wanted to say wouldn't come because nothing would encompass the sensations swirling in his chest. He kissed her instead and raised his arms, caging her face between his biceps in order to grab the headboard.

She guided him toward her entrance and tilted her hips. Slowly—so damn slowly, he thought he'd die—he filled her. Buried, surrounded, crushed, he stilled and lifted his head. Sharing air, they stared at each other while his chest cracked wide fucking open.

He didn't understand it, this pain-pleasure combination, and shook against her. His sinuses prickled, his eyes grew hot, and he didn't notice until his breath hitched that there was a sheen in hers. Or was it his?

"Peyton?"

"Open your eyes."

He hadn't realized he'd closed them, but he did what she said.

Her hand settled on his jaw, and her warm, delicate fingers stroked his cheek. The other caressed his back in a soothing, circular motion. "I love you."

There. Yes, right there. Like she'd always done, she climbed inside his mind and ceased the chaos. Filled the dark, empty spaces.

Keeping one hand on the headboard, he slid his other arm between her and the mattress and sunk his fingers in her hair. Gaze pinned to hers, he pulled out and gradually thrust back in. The pace was so measured there wasn't an inch of him that didn't suffer the torment. In awe, he repeated the motion, and knew this was what he'd been missing. This was the difference between mere physical release and having his whole system engaged. The result being sheer, unadulterated bliss.

She closed her eyes and turned her face toward his arm. Her hot breath fanned his bicep as her chest rose and fell in a steady pant. He dropped his forehead to her temple and watched the way her lips parted and how her expression contorted while she sought her release. Helpless, needy sounds of pleasure filled his ears, and he opened his mouth wide against her cheek to contain his own.

He took her body with deliberate, shallow thrusts, owned her the way she did him. Her fingers dug into his flesh like she was marking him, clawing her way inside, when she'd really done that eons ago. Though he had her pinned, her hips surged to meet each plunge, and he ground his pelvis against her clit to ensure she got everything she needed to teeter off the brink. Their legs tangled and his spine prickled and she...

Came on a silent scream. Her inner walls fisted him as she vibrated beneath him. He chased his own white light and kissed her with his eyes wide open while she quaked, scratched, and bowed. The second her lids lifted and their eyes met, his orgasm tore him in half. Mouths fused and gazes locked, he emptied inside her.

Still shaking, unable to break the connection, they remained trapped in a holding pattern. His breath soughed between his teeth and hers puffed against his lips. Head pounding, he lost sight of her for a second through a watery haze, but he blinked and there she was again.

An eternity later, his heartbeat decelerated and, with his arms around her, he rolled them to the side. She shimmied, covered them with a blanket, and burrowed next to him.

The next thing he knew, he was alone in bed. A glance at the balcony doors proved it was still the middle of the night. The bathroom light was off. Where the hell was she? He craned his head around to check the clock. Two a.m.

He climbed out of bed and stepped into a pair of flannel PJ bottoms, then went in search of her. They had the big benefit picnic tomorrow to cap off the Fallen Veterans weekend. She should be sleeping. As he strode down the hallway, he peeked into the guestrooms, but she wasn't there. Nor was she downstairs in the living room, library, or media room.

Just as panic began to clutch his chest, he found her in the kitchen. Her back to him, she faced the patio doors to the deck, wearing his white tuxedo shirt and nothing else. Her hair was a golden wave between her shoulder blades and damn if she didn't look...frail.

"Hey." He stepped into the room and stopped by the island. "What are you doing awake?"

She turned and smiled. Except it was smile number forty-seven in her arsenal—the one she used when distracted or lost in her head. "Just getting some water." Her glasses were perched on the end of her nose and she'd removed her makeup.

And there was no cup in her hand or on the counter.

A barely perceptible sigh, and she glanced out the doors once more. "I forgot how big your estate is, X. It's pretty at night with—"

"Peyton, honey. Why are you out of bed at two in the morning, staring at my backyard?" She didn't move or answer. "What's wrong?"

She ducked her head. "I wish I knew."

And...shit. His heart stopped beating so fast, it left skid marks. "Talk to me."

Rubbing her forehead, she turned around. "Is it always like this?" She waved her hand, indicating them. "Love. Is it always this...consuming? Volatile?"

Perfect? Fulfilling? Because those were the adjectives he'd use if given the choice.

"I'm not exactly an expert." He ran his hand across his neck, wondering what in the hell had happened in the short time since he'd fallen asleep to hollow out her eyes. "I hope so."

After all, love erected kingdoms, started wars, and was the focus of many of the best literary works since the dawn of time. One would think the emotion was supposed to bring people to their knees.

"It's never been like this for me," she whispered and pressed a trembling hand to her chest.

His first thought? She needed a ring on her fourth finger. The second being, he hoped to all that was holy she'd say yes when he put one there.

"With Mark, I didn't feel this..." She sighed. "I don't know. Deeply, I guess. I did love him but, looking back on it, I think it was more of a choice than something that chose me. Our relationship is different and all I keep thinking is, if his death hit me that hard, what the hell am I going to do if...?"

Well, damn. "If I died, too?"

Her breath caught and her eyes filled. She shook her head, lowering her lids as tears trailed down her cheeks. Setting her glasses on the counter, she pressed her palms to her eyes and rolled her lips together.

If she'd taken an axe to his chest, it might've been more preferable. For as long as he'd known her, Peyton and crying had been akin to napalm on his control. He didn't know why. Perhaps because he could only imagine the number of times she'd had to do it alone. Or maybe it was a sure sign she wasn't all light and rainbows. No doubt, it was due to the fact her pain had always been his.

Whatever the reason, he had to resist the urge to haul her against him and make her stop. This irrational fear of hers wasn't something he could fight. He had absolutely no defense against fate.

"I know it sounds stupid." She sniffed and wiped her cheeks. Her gaze pinned him with such misery and helpless desolation, his gut clenched. "It's stupid and I can't stop the picture from forming in my head."

"It's not stupid." In fact, given her circumstances, it made a lot of sense. He took a calming breath and erased the distance between them in two strides. "You're the one who taught me how to thrive, Peyton. Better than anyone, you should know this is no way to live."

She looked away. "You're right."

He tucked her hair behind her ears and cupped her damp cheeks. "I can't promise you I won't die tomorrow after accidentally ingesting coconut any more than you can claim you won't get hit by a meteor crossing the street. What I can vow is that I'll love you every second until that time comes."

Hopefully, they'd be eighty-five with two kids and six grandchildren. If he had his way, she'd go first, and on the night of her funeral, he'd slip into bed and follow her in his sleep. But life came with no guarantees and it was hardly ever ideal.

Plastering herself against him, she wrapped her arms around his waist and pressed her face into the curve of his shoulder. "Deal."

Chapter Twenty-Two

Peyton pulled her car up to Xavier's garage and cut the engine, then turned in the passenger seat to face him. Yep, still brooding. Sexy as sin in jeans, a gray sweater, and a little scruff, but brooding just the same. Poor, X. "It's just a surprise party."

"I hate parties. And why did this have to be at my house?"

She patted his arm. "Because my apartment's too small."

"Smartass." Almost a smile. "Now I know why I never let you drive. You taking me all over Kingdom Come today had my life flashing before my eyes."

All over Kingdom Come meant a quick trip to buy him a few ties and lunch afterward to allow his parents time to set up and welcome guests. To avoid laughing, she rolled her lips over her teeth. He was too damn cute when he sulked. Had she said broody? She meant pouty.

"Good thing you got rid of my old deathtrap and bought me a car with extra airbags."

He ran his tongue over his teeth. "Speaking of, there are no cars here, either." He turned and glanced at the circular drive.

"Your mother has Archie parking the guests' vehicles on the road until you arrive."

He strummed his fingers on his thigh. "I hate parties."

"The sooner you go in, the sooner it'll be over. Let's practice your surprise face." She mimed an exaggerated shock expression and waved her hands.

His golden gaze gave her a once-over. "I'm not doing that. I'll look constipated."

Slapping her hand over her face, she laughed until her side ached. Then, laughed some more. "Okay, look. This is a small affair and your mom went to a lot of trouble. If you smile and behave, I won't withhold your gift."

His eyes narrowed. "Are you my present? Naked in my bed with a giant bow? Otherwise, it might not be worth it."

Gah, this man. She reached in the backseat and snatched the package holding his custom-made book. Inside were pictures of people he'd helped with his charity, along with personalized signed notes thanking him. She held up the blue-wrapped box with a green bow.

He glanced at the gift, then her. "You won't fit in there."

"When everyone leaves, I'll crawl naked in your bed with nothing but this bow on. Deal?"

"Our bed." He leaned forward and brushed his lips against hers. "In two days, the article goes live and we're officially public. Next weekend, you're moving in. Thus, it's *our* bed."

Jeez, he was good. "Our bed." Tilting her head, she kissed him and wove her fingers through his thick chestnut strands. Before he could turn the heat dial to scorching, she pulled away. "Party first. Naughty later."

He rolled his eyes. "Fine. Let's get this done."

Climbing out of the car, she adjusted her long, pink sweater and checked her black leggings, assured she was presentable. A crisp breeze scented with rain from earlier caught her loose strands and whipped them into chaos.

"I changed my mind." He gave her a side-glance. "Just you, the bow, those boots, and our bed."

She grinned. So, Xavier Gaines had a thing for knee-high boots, did he?

An hour later, he was being a good sport. Elaine had invited his immediate family, including a few aunts and uncles, plus cousins. On Peyton's end, she'd invited Kate, Joseph, Xavier's secretary Jackie, and the ten members of Gaines Industries' division heads. All in all, roughly twenty-five people. She knew he was used to attending events and functions, but having all the focus on him was different. She'd make it up to him later.

He walked around the grand living room and talked to guests. She supplied him with scotch and mini-quiches. By the time he was halfway through opening presents, she could tell he was near the end of his rope. In front of the fireplace, he stood stiffly beside his mother as one package after another was passed to him.

"From Kate." He glanced around the room and stopped on her, standing beside Peyton by the far wall. His eyes indicated he was more than a tad concerned. "Thank you."

"Please tell me you were nice," she whispered.

Kate patted her chest. "You wound me. I get awesome gifts."

He tore into the paper and stared at the contents. After a dramatic pause, he closed his eyes and chuckled. He showed everyone. The box displayed a white container with the words *Retirement Fund* scratched out and *Cookie Jar* scrawled instead. The room laughed accordingly.

"Cute." Peyton grinned at her friend.

"I have my moments." Kate popped a peanut into her mouth. "He's not easy to shop for."

Peyton's present was last. As he set the wrapping aside, he glanced at the book, a frown marring his forehead. Slowly, he paged through, not stopping long enough to read, but to get the gist. She was pretty sure he wasn't breathing. The silence was deafening, and she grew concerned he hated the gesture.

After a tense beat, he rubbed his chest and cleared his throat. Twice. "Go ahead and pass it around." He handed the book to his father and looked at Peyton. *Thank you*, he mouthed.

She expelled a heavy sigh of relief. He didn't hate it. He was just moved and too emotional with this many people around. Shoot. Maybe she should've waited to give it to him in private.

Peyton turned to Joseph on her other side. "Do me a favor. Take him into the library or something to give him a breather."

"You got it, blondie."

She waited for the two guys to leave before joining Elaine in the kitchen to help with the cake. Leaning on the counter, she checked out the design while Elaine put candles on top. White frosting and numbers in icing, interlocking together. Very Xavier-ish.

"I love it. And thank you for using number candles and not thirty separate ones."

Elaine brushed her hands together. "He only turns thirty once. Thanks for keeping him away from the house. Too bad he wasn't surprised." She raised her eyebrows knowingly.

Peyton batted her eyelashes in feigned innocence. "I have no idea what you're talking about."

With a grin, Elaine hugged her. "You're a terrible liar. He seems to be having fun. Not like his tenth birthday party. Only two kids showed up, and they only stayed long enough for the grab bags." She pursed her lips. "Come to think of it, that was the last time I threw him a party."

Jackie stepped into the room before Peyton could respond, setting the gift book on the counter. "Peyton, this is so cool."

"Ooh, let me see. I didn't get a chance when he opened it." Elaine skimmed through the contents. She paused over the picture of her and Edward from last year, and the one of Peyton sandwiched between Brian and Mark. Peyton had been able to get more than a hundred Fallen Veterans' recipients to send in photos and sign the book. "Darling, this is the sweetest thing."

"Kinda makes the tie I gave him pale in comparison." Jackie smoothed her red blouse.

"I love that tie." Peyton set her hand over Jackie's. "Elaine, have you met Jackie, Xavier's new secretary? She's awesome wrapped in awesome."

"Yes." Elaine folded her hands. "I've heard wonderful things about you." She eyed Peyton. "And I'm grateful that dreadful Fern is gone." She shuddered.

"Aren't we all?" Peyton rubbed her temple, having a shadow pain from the stapler incident. "Should I go fetch Xavier?"

Elaine nodded. "Go ahead. I'll take this in the dining room."

Leaving Jackie to assist Elaine with the cake, Peyton made her way out of the kitchen and down the hall toward the library. Above the dark walnut chair rail, family pictures were displayed, some dating back to Xavier's great-grandparents. She found it really neat he had this much history to tie to his roots. It made her wish she'd been able to find or keep more portraits of her own before her parents had died.

Xavier and Joseph's voices rumbled the closer she drew.

"Well, she's moving in next weekend. There's that."

She halted near the doorway at the sound of Joseph's low tone and the reference to her. She peeked in the room, finding Xavier leaning on the small desk by the window with his arms crossed and Joseph standing close by, hands in his pockets. She straightened, staying out of sight, and chewed her lip.

"Yeah." Xavier sighed. "I feel like a fucking jackass. I mean, the guy fought for our country, came back injured, and I hate him for leaving her the way he did. He had severe depression and PTSD, and I know my reaction makes no sense, but there it is. I hate the guy." He paused, and a *thwap* filled the silence as if he'd slapped his thigh. "He did this to her, knowing she had no one else. And now she's afraid I'm next. How am I supposed to look her in the eye and reassure her I'm not going anywhere?"

She pressed her fingers to her lips. A chill started in her belly and spread. She had no idea he'd felt that way about Mark. Yes, it made sense because Xavier cared about her, but Mark hadn't been responsible for his actions. Not with as far gone as he'd been in the end. His death wasn't what put the fear of loss inside her, was it?

"I hear you." Clothing rustled. "I think you're doing everything you can. She's not fighting the relationship."

"No, that's not it. Sometimes I get the sense she's pulling away from me, but I believe her when she says she loves me." There was a pause, and she swallowed past the lump in her throat. "It's just...I'm contending with ghosts. I have this wonderful family and I want to give one back to her, you know?"

Tears sprang to her eyes so quickly, she couldn't blink them away. Never, not ever, had she wanted to hurt Xavier. But it seemed she had somehow made him think he wasn't enough. Worse, he appeared to believe it was up to him to return something she'd lost. It made her question if she was, in part, an obligation.

"Damn, Joseph. I can't do this without her." Footsteps padded the floor like he was pacing. "Everything that makes sense in my life, that flows right, is because of her. The office, my charity, and even things at home."

Clapping a hand over her mouth, she stalked away from the doorway before they heard her sob. Unbearable pressure filled her chest and tears streamed hot paths down her cheeks.

From day one, she'd had this niggling sense about his true feelings. She didn't doubt he cared about her, loved her. It was the *why* that tripped her mental switch. He'd gone his whole life as an outcast, struggling to fit in. For whatever reason, her presence soothed him. He'd latched onto that calm in times of need, but had he misguided himself into thinking appreciation was love?

No. Maybe. Everything he'd told her up until now said otherwise, that they were the real deal in his eyes. Yet, how could she be sure? How could he?

Blowing out a breath, she carefully wiped her eyes and fanned her face. Now wasn't the time for a breakdown. He had guests and his mom was preparing the cake. She'd talk to him later. Communication had always been their strength. Most of the things he'd told Joseph she'd already known through their discussions anyway, even if the context was different.

When she thought she was presentable, she called Xavier's name and stepped in the doorway. "Knock, knock. It's cake time." She beamed a megawatt grin like her heart hadn't taken a severe blow.

From the corner, Xavier faced her, and the tension in his expression dissolved. "Thanks for giving me a minute. I was going nuts." He closed the distance and kissed her forehead. "Ready?"

"Yes." She turned to Joseph and gestured for them to precede her.

If his tight smile was any indication, Xavier hated being sung to more than he'd hated opening gifts for an audience. By the time guests left an hour later, she was wrung tighter than him. Their upcoming discussion kept playing through her head and her stomach was in knots.

"Success." Elaine hugged Xavier and squeezed his shoulder. "That wasn't so bad, was it?"

"Nope. Can we skip the hoorah for my fortieth, though? I'd rather have a root canal." His nose wrinkled and he sobered. "Thanks, Mom. For the party and everything."

"You're very welcome."

Peyton brushed the hair from her face and fisted her fingers when her hand shook. "Can I help you clean up?"

"No, no." Elaine waved them away. "Go sneak off and be alone."

Wasting no time, Xavier grabbed Peyton's arm and headed for the stairs.

She dug in her heels. "Can we talk? In the library or media room?"

His gaze jerked to hers. The longer he studied her, the more he paled. She pressed a hand to her mutinous stomach and led the way, stopping only when she got by the desk in the library.

He quietly closed the door and shoved his hands in his pockets. "You haven't even said anything yet and I'm scared to death."

That was the crux of both their issues, in her opinion. His fear of losing his anchor and her fear of being alone. She'd been just seventeen when her parents died. Ever since then, she'd played it safe. So safe, she'd been ready to marry a guy she didn't love with her whole heart. And years later, she was about to go all-in with a man who owned her soul, but who may not love her for the right reasons. It wasn't fair to him for her to stay with him if he was another safe bet.

"Peyton?" He stepped forward and stopped, concern and tension wrinkling his brow.

It came to her, suddenly and like a blow, what they should do. He was going to flip out, but it was the right thing.

She rubbed her forehead and focused on his chest. "I know its last minute, but I'm going to take off work next week. Use a few of my vacation days."

"Okay," he hedged and crossed his arms. "Why? Do you need to pack up the apartment so soon?"

"No." God, her heart thumped so hard the room spun. "We need some distance."

They were constantly together—in the office, at home, during functions. It muddied the waters. The only way to know for sure if what he felt was genuine, and the only way she could get over her abandonment issues and trust him completely, was to create separation.

Chest heaving, gaze furious, he stalked toward her. "Are you kidding me? The article releases in two days." He grabbed her shoulders and ducked to meet her eyes. "What in the hell is going on, Peyton? Better yet, where is this coming from?"

Gently, she took his wrists and stepped out of his hold. "I overheard your conversation with Joseph."

Hands on his hips, he distractedly glanced past her as if trying to remember. "And?"

"And while I'm gone, I think you should ask yourself two questions. Am I an obligation to you, and is what you feel love or gratitude?"

He went so rigid, she thought he'd snap. His jaw ticked and cold fury turned his bourbon eyes glacial. "You've lost your ever-loving mind."

"Have I?" She fisted her trembling hands over her heart. "Think about it, X. Pick apart what you told him." Closing her eyes for a quick moment, she took a cleansing breath. "This isn't just about you. For years, I've taken the path of least resistance. You told me something similar when we discussed my wanting to travel, remember? I may have surrounded myself with people most of my adult life, but alone is different than lonely. You shouldn't have to contend with ghosts."

He flinched. "Christ, honey. That's not what I meant."

"I know. But it's not far off the mark." Her lip trembled as her eyes filled, and she bit her tongue to get through the last part. "I love you. I'm not calling it quits or breaking up or ending things. I simply want us both to take time and evaluate."

"Evaluate," he dully repeated. "Evaluate?" In his wide gaze, terror pushed anger aside. He shook his head, posture wooden. "I love you and you want to walk out? You claim to love me and you want time apart?" He raked his hands through his hair and stalked away. Came back. "Don't do this. Whatever you think is wrong, we can fix it right here."

That's just it. They couldn't. "I'll be back on Saturday."

"You're supposed to be moving in here with me on Saturday!" He slammed his lids shut, nostrils flaring. When he opened his eyes, his tone softened. "What about the article?"

"I haven't retracted it." And she'd be leaving him alone for the fallout. Another test, of sorts.

Cruel as it seemed, he needed to realize he could do this by himself. She'd worked with him to build courage and had taught him how to cope with his anxiety. There was so much more to him than a bank account and a brilliant mind. He'd never understand his capability if she didn't step back.

He ran a shaking hand over his mouth, his jaw, and stared at her like he was at his wit's end. "You're already gone, aren't you?"

Her throat closed, and she couldn't stop the outpouring of tears if her life depended on it. "No. I'm right here and I'll be right back here after—"

"After we've had time to think?" His brows rose. "I don't need to think, Peyton. You're breaking my goddamn heart. Think about that. Think about all the times and ways you've shown the world I had one. I'm right back to square one if you walk out that door. There is no heart without you."

Oh God. That's exactly why they needed this break. His heart had always been ten times the size of hers. But he refused to separate his actions from her help. "Xavier, please. I—"

"Go." He clenched his jaw and closed his eyes as if looking at her another moment would level him to the ground. "Take this time you say we both need. Just go."

She did. Before she lost her nerve, she left on shaking legs.

Chapter Twenty-Three

By the end of the workday on Monday, Xavier had given Peyton all the space he was going to allow. She hadn't been joking when she'd said she was taking off this week. At his arrival in the office this morning, her schedule had been cleared. In preparation for tomorrow's magazine article release, she'd left instructions for the front desk not to patch through any press calls to his secretary.

That was that. Nothing else. And he'd had to hear that little amount from Jackie.

He pounded on Peyton's apartment door and waited with his clenched fists on his hips. Two days, and he was losing his mind. She hadn't answered one text or voicemail. He hadn't slept more than a handful of scattered hours, never mind having an appetite.

When he received no response, he pounded again and yelled her name. He knew she was home. Her car was in the designated parking space. He'd checked. Yesterday and today.

"She's not here."

He whirled to find Kate standing in the doorway to her apartment across the hall. He glanced at her yellow pantsuit and loose red curls. As an attorney, her hours were pretty close to his and she'd probably just gotten home from the office.

"Where is she?" He ground his teeth, temples pounding.

"I don't know." Instead of her usual fire, Kate looked just as weary as him.

"Don't play games with me."

"Shh. Keep your voice down." She grabbed his tie, dragged him into her apartment, and shut the door. "Swear to God, Xavier. I don't know where she is. On Sunday morning, she packed a suitcase, snatched her passport, and had me drop her off at the airport."

Wait. Passport? "She's in another damn country?" Just exactly how much fucking space did she need?

"Apparently."

At a loss, sick to his gut, he glanced around. Kate's place was a mirror to Peyton's. Except instead of neutral tones, books, and plants, Kate's was dripping with color, blankets, and figurines of...mermaids?

He shook his head. "What airline?"

Kate raised her hands in surrender. "I don't know that, either. She had me let her out at the main terminal."

Pinching the bridge of his nose, he paced. "If you have no clue where she is and I have no clue where she is, how do we know if she's okay?" That was, what? Two out of the three people close to her? And that sent a whole slew of what-ifs tearing through his head. None of them pleasant and all of them making the acid churn in his stomach.

She'd told him once she'd wanted to travel, but was too afraid to go alone. Was this some kind of test for herself? A way of breaking out of that safety zone she'd claimed?

"She texts me twice a day." Kate took a seat in a lime green chair. Between the fabric and her yellow suit, she resembled half a bag of Skittles. "She never responds to my questions. Just claims *I'm alive and okay*. That's all." She tapped a finger to her lips like she was debating what to say next. "If she doesn't send a message at our allotted time, her itinerary is in the safe in her bedroom. She asked me not to open it unless something was wrong. Or to tell you that tidbit because you'd chase her."

Something *was* wrong. Very, very wrong. His Peyton wasn't here, and now he was worried frantic because she was on another continent. Alone.

He rubbed the ache in his chest, needing to punch something. Much as he wanted to chase after her, he couldn't break Peyton's trust and go into the safe. He shouldn't put Kate in the middle, either.

"You really do love her, don't you?" Kate's gaze was filled with something he'd never witnessed from her—understanding. Compassion.

"I didn't realize that was in doubt." He dropped in a purple chair across from her and strummed his fingers on his thigh. Make that nearly a full bag of Skittles. Who owned purple furniture, anyway? Or green. Hell, her couch was orange. "She seems to think

I love her out of—" what were the words she'd used? "—gratitude and obligation." Ridiculous.

"Is it true?" At his glower, she shrugged like that had been a legit question. "If she wants you to think about it while you're apart, then maybe you should. Are those the reasons you love her?"

He sent her a seething glare that would've made anyone else run screaming while pissing themselves.

Kate merely lifted her brows as if bored.

Screw this. She'd never been on his side and made no qualms about disliking him. She was the last person he should be around. For all he knew, Kate had planted this crap in Peyton's head. Rising, he strode to the door.

"He never made her feel the way you do."

With his hand on the knob, he turned.

Kate leaned forward, forearms on her thighs. "Her whole family was dead and she latched onto all she had left. She sleepwalked through that whole relationship. No passion, no spark. She never once opened her eyes. And then, he died, too. She blames herself. Did you know that?"

No, he didn't. But it made a lot of sense, knowing her personality, and the awareness wasn't helping the riot in his chest.

"His family blamed her, too. For not doing more, not being there. Take your pick." She waggled her fingers and let them fall in her lap. "If she had loved him more, could she have saved him? I assure you, she's asking herself that very thing. She wears guilt as armor."

She rose from her seat and crossed her arms. "Given your history, it's not that crazy she's dissecting your relationship. Try to look at it from her point of view. Imagine her reaction when, years later, she does fall in love. The real thing and not the version she had in her head. She's doing everything she can to protect you."

"Me?" He didn't need her protection. He just needed her. "From what?"

"From making the same mistake she almost did."

With information overload threatening his download percentage, he stared at her. More insane was, Kate had a point. Several, actually.

Peyton had been his quiet champion for a long time. It would be just like her to erect distance for the sake of protection if she believed that's what he needed. Mercy, he'd give up every red cent to have her here right now, if for no other reason than to assure her Mark's death hadn't been her fault. To hold her and...

Damn. Holding her would be enough.

He rubbed his neck. "You must be one hell of an attorney."

"Duh. I'm also her friend." She cocked a hip. "Prove her wrong about your motives like you proved me wrong."

"Why are you helping me?" Until very recently, Kate hadn't exactly had his back. About anything.

"Because I love her and I'm not stupid. You love her, too." She sighed, closing her eyes. When she opened them, tears brimmed, and he froze like it was the first sign of the apocalypse. "You make her happy. She hasn't been genuinely happy in over a decade." She tilted her face heavenward as if to collect herself before refocusing on him, her eyes clear. "Snark is my armor. I was wrong about you and I'm sorry."

Hand to God, if he got rammed by any more emotional battery, he wouldn't be responsible for his actions. "Bygones. I'm glad she has you."

She huffed a laugh that somehow managed to sound sarcastic. "Bygones," she agreed.

The next morning, due to the magazine article release, Joseph had to direct Archie to change course and go through the private parking structure just to enter the Gaines building. The press was that thick out front. A shitty way to start Xavier's shitty day on this shitty week. And it was only Tuesday.

In the elevator, he shook his head. "I'm going to wring Peyton's perfect little neck the first chance I get."

Joseph smirked. "Right after you kiss the hell out of her?"

Touché.

They stepped off the elevator to a frazzled Jackie with a phone to her ear, her hand on her forehead, and the lines—plural—ringing off the hook. She glanced up and set the receiver in its cradle. "The article's live." She smiled with false cheer. "And in print."

Xavier took the magazine from her outstretched hand and glanced at her phone. All thirty lines were lit up. "I thought Miss Smoke directed the front desk not to patch media calls through."

"Those are just the ones slipping by. It's been like this for over an hour." She ran her hand through her blonde bob, then smoothed the strands. "What would you like me to say to them, sir? We've been going with *no comment*."

He glanced at Joseph and thought it over, trying to figure out what Peyton would do. The only way to reach everyone at once was to hold a press conference. They'd still get inundated with calls and emails, though, and... Wait.

"I have an idea." Xavier pulled his cell out of his breast pocket. "Don't answer the phone, Jackie. Let it ring." He connected with his mother. "Do you have any pictures of me and Peyton from Napa? She has one in her apartment."

"Yes." Mom clicked her tongue. "Let me have a look and—"

"I'm slammed over here. Please email what you have to my corporate account and we can talk tonight. Love you." He hung up and looked at Joseph. "Tell the front desk to send someone outside and announce we'll have a press conference in one hour. Put a security guy with whoever goes, please."

Joseph nodded and jumped back on the elevator.

Xavier turned to Jackie. "Let's go in my office." They strode down the hall and he pulled a second chair around to his side of the desk for his secretary. "Have a seat."

She complied, and he booted his computer. He'd give his mom credit. She'd sent four pictures of him and Peyton already, one being the shot she had in her living room. He logged into the account for Fallen Veterans and scanned through the pictures from a week ago, finding a photo of them dancing. Then, he went into the corporate system's mainframe.

"It's done." Joseph strode in and parked himself in a chair across the desk. "What's the plan?"

"First, I'm going to stay in the apartment here this week to avoid the circus coming and going." Xavier typed as he spoke. "Second, I'm creating a new company email address. When I give the press conference, I'll direct them to that for an official statement. I'm setting it up to auto-reply with my message and making sure recipients are unable to respond. It'll just bounce back if they try."

He scooted his chair aside and pointed to his monitor. "Does this sound okay?" He glanced at Jackie as she read the screen.

Press Release

Gaines Industries announces confirmation of a romantic relationship between Founder, Xavier Gaines, and longtime Media

Relations Director, Peyton Smoke. Xavier Gaines goes on record to state: "She's the other half of my whole. I recommend everyone try this love thing."

He'd also put the picture of them dancing at the charity event and the one from Napa in the body of the email to give the media something to use for articles.

Jackie nodded. "It looks good. Short and sweet. No typos. I'd just add a copyright credit under the photos." She smiled at him. "And if I may get personal...Aw."

Shaking his head, he grinned as he inserted her suggestion. "That should keep the phone from blowing up too hard. I'll let the front desk know not to send any more calls up here and to direct the press to the email." He rubbed his chin. "Let's cancel whatever I have on the calendar today and reschedule for later in the week."

"You got it, sir." She rose from her seat. "Did you need anything else, Mr. Gaines?"

"Yes. I'm giving you a raise and promoting you to personal assistant for myself and Miss Smoke. I'll have HR hire for a secretarial position."

They could use the extra hands and he'd been on Peyton to get an assistant. Some of her work could be delegated and, when she got back from wherever the hell she was, he planned to spend as much time with her as possible. He trusted Jackie. Plus, she was smart and efficient. She was too talented to waste answering phones. Problem solved.

Her jaw dropped. "Um, thank you, sir."

He nodded, and she went back to her desk up front. He glanced at Joseph and did a double-take at his smirk. "What?"

"You're all grown up now. My, they get big so fast." Joseph mock-sniffed and pretended to wipe a tear from his cheek.

Xavier narrowed his eyes. "I'm not amused."

"Okay, seriously." Joseph leaned forward. "Blondie asked you to evaluate. The way I see it? You're more than capable of handling yourself without her, which is all I think she wanted—for you to separate your worlds for a moment and look at the two parts. Knowing that, do you love her any less?"

No. If anything, he loved her more.

And later that evening, sprawled on the bed in his apartment hidden inside Gaines Industries, he thought about the other things she'd said, too. About him loving her out of gratitude and her being an obligation to him. For her sake, and because he always listened to her, he dissected their relationship starting from the day they'd met.

He didn't know what it was about her that quieted the crazy. Maybe he'd never know, but it had begun outside her locker at age fifteen. Before he'd earned billions, before anyone knew who he was, she'd been there. Yes, there were many years between that time and when she'd come to work for him, and yes, his initial draw had been the shock of calm she'd instilled. But that's not why he'd stayed.

Flat out? He liked her company. He loved her as a human being. Then and now. She didn't see race, creed, orientation, or class. To her, everyone was equal and worthy of her time. She'd shown that in high school and she'd done it since they'd started dating. From the way she'd spoken to his staff, reporters, and a teenager who'd just lost her mother, Peyton led with her heart first. There was, quite simply, no one else like her.

Then there was her beautiful mind and sense of humor. He could spend days inside her head and never grow weary. Quick with a joke or quip, she thought fast on her feet. Whether the topic was sports or politics, she could keep up. She spoke four different languages, had a photographic mind, and read *The Grapes of Wrath* for fun. Hell, he hadn't been able to get through half the book when it had been assigned in college.

And, mercy. The physical end of their relationship? No matter how many times they'd come together, things hadn't cooled. Not an iota. He wanted her as much as he had the first time he'd kissed her. She not only understood his needs, she accepted his quirks. Gave as good as she got. Was as selfless in bed as she was out of it. Taking all that out of the equation, she made him a better lover. He'd rather spend hours watching her while aroused, worshiping her body, almost more than doing the actual deed itself. Because it made the connection stronger.

Ergo...no. Grateful didn't take up so much as a megabyte of space in his reasons for falling in love with her.

What Kate had said about Mark and Peyton's relationship kept jabbing the inside of his skull. Her guilt, the way Mark's family blamed her, the remoteness of it all...it was very different than Xavier's experiences with her. The Peyton he knew would bend over backward to help anyone in need. She was warm and welcoming to his folks. He hadn't been there, but he doubted she'd stood idly by without attempting everything she could to help Mark. Add in the fact that the guy represented her hope of ever having a family, and Xavier's gut knotted.

He'd seen her with kids at the company parties, at the Fallen Veterans' picnics, and she was a natural. Someday, he hoped to put that light in her eyes with their own children. A daughter with those amazing baby blues or a son with that encompassing grin. Just the thought of her belly swollen with their child had his heart clenching.

And the truth was, she'd been a part of his family for going on three years. His parents had welcomed her into the fold before she'd said so much as hello. They were invested in her, cared about her life, and trusted her with him.

An obligation? No damn way.

Sighing, he flopped on his stomach and buried his face in the pillow. Christ, he fucking missed her. He wondered what she was doing right now. Skiing in the Alps? Floating on a gondola in Venice? Pissing off a bull in Madrid?

His cell rang, and he nearly fell off the bed scrambling to reach for it on the nightstand. Except he died more than a little at Kate's name on the display. "Hey. Is she okay?"

"I'm fine, thanks." Kate laughed, but it sounded forced. "Peyton texted and said she was alive. Her plane lands at ten on Saturday morning."

Rolling to his back, he rubbed his eyes. "Thanks for calling."

She paused. "Are *you* okay?"

"No." And he wouldn't be until Saturday. What if she'd taken this supposed distance and changed her mind about being with him?

"She won't," Kate said quietly. "I think she'll miss you like crazy and come back with a clear head."

He hadn't realized he'd asked the question aloud. "I feel weird talking to you about this."

A sound of agreement, and she expelled a quiet breath. "Maybe we should use the time she's away to get to know each other better. Would you like to come over for dinner tomorrow night?" Before he could ask if it was a trick, she said, "No coconut, I promise. Bygones, right?"

What the hell? Why not? Life couldn't get any shittier, and Kate was right. They needed to call more than just a truce. They were both a part of Peyton's life.

"Sure. I'll bring wine."

Chapter Twenty-Four

Peyton had a ten-and-a-half hour flight to France, five lonely nights in the city of love, and another ten-plus hour flight back to the States to think about nothing but Xavier Gaines.

She'd broken her own rule and had read the magazine article while drinking an espresso at a café table. Daniel had quoted both of them about various topics from their discussion. But his own take and summary was what had thrown her for a loop.

I fully expected to walk into my interview with this corporate giant and be met with crisp, concise answers and clipped disregard. Instead, I got a glimpse of a man who doesn't solely see opportunities to make money, but ways to enhance the compassion inside us all and force others to take a stand for what's right. It's apparent in the way his staff look and speak to him that there is respect and, perhaps, a little fear motivating them. One can't run an enterprise such as his without those elements. But under the spit and polish, I found something completely lacking in today's market and something I think we often take for granted. Heart. Quite a few might argue emotion has no bearing in business. I disagree. It's fundamental, and those at Gaines Industries, starting with the man at the top, are invested. They care. The best example of this is Mr. Gaines' relationship with his Media Relations Director, Peyton Smoke. I, like everyone else, suspected an affair, but I wasn't prepared to type this piece with a smile on my face after witnessing genuine adoration. To succinctly put it, I went into this interview as a reporter, and was reminded I was a human being.

From a job perspective, Peyton couldn't have asked for better press than that. Daniel had put a face and a personality to Xavier instead of just a name. But his reaction? Wow.

She'd caught a clip of Xavier's brief press conference online and, aside from looking tired and worn out, nerves hadn't played a part. He'd had both hands on the podium. Meaning, he hadn't needed to grip the coin she'd given him he always kept in his pocket. And that automatic email reply? Gah. Brilliant and…sweet.

He'd even changed his Facebook status to "In a relationship" and his profile picture to one of the two of them taken in Napa.

From the passenger seat in Kate's car, Peyton rested her head on the window as trees and cars zipped by. Rain beat on the glass, but it was beginning to lesson.

Weary and exhausted as she was, she was really glad she'd taken the trip. She'd needed the time away from him to get a clearer view, and left all her doubts on the runway in Paris. Though she was itching to talk to Xavier, a nap might be in order first.

Kate bypassed their ramp on Highway 101 and kept right on going.

Peyton shook her head. "You missed our exit."

"We're not going to the apartment."

"What? Why?" She straightened in her seat.

Kate strummed her fingers on the wheel. "Xavier and I hung out while you were away."

Not sure what to say, Peyton chewed her lip. "You didn't maim him, did you? Is he in the hospital?"

"Nope." Kate's grin wasn't helping Peyton's nervous stomach.

"Jail? Is he in jail?"

"Lord, he's not locked up, either." Kate laughed. "I've been instructed by your boyfriend not to take you home."

What the heck was going on? "Is everything okay?"

"We'll be at his place in ten minutes." Kate shrugged. "You can ask him yourself. I'm just following orders."

Peyton studied her friend's profile as the rain stopped, wondering if exhaustion was causing her to hallucinate. "Since when do you follow anyone's orders, especially Xavier's?"

Kate glanced at her and back to the road. "White flags were waved. He and I had a couple of good conversations."

"Really? And there was no bloodshed?"

"We both care about you. We thought it was time to get to know each other better." Kate paused. "He told me about his social anxiety and a lot of things make sense now." She sighed, the sound both frustrated and helpless. "I don't know what conclusion you reached on your isolated adventure, but listen to him when we get there. He was a damn wreck, Peyton."

He'd seemed to handle himself well, best she could tell. But part of the reason she'd wanted the distance was for him to really investigate his feelings. If he was upset, then perhaps he hadn't listened. Or listened too well?

Guilt clawed at her stomach, and she closed her eyes as Kate got off on the next exit. By the time they made a few turns and drove past his security gate, Peyton was regretting the second cup of coffee she'd had on the plane. Kate stopped in the circular drive at the front of the house and cut the engine.

Xavier stood on his front steps with his arms crossed, his gaze on the car. Wind whipped his chestnut strands and he had a day's worth of scruff on his jaw. His expression gave nothing away, but he looked sexy in gray corduroy and a fitted black Henley that clung to his lean, muscled frame.

Such a sight for sore eyes.

Kate turned to face her. "No matter what happens, I love you. Truce or not, I'll kill him dead. Just say the word."

With a nervous laugh, Peyton grabbed her friend's arm, grateful to have her. "Thank you."

To her surprise, Kate exited and walked up to Xavier. Peyton followed and paused on the walkway as the two of them exchanged a look at the top of the stairs she couldn't decipher. He nodded, and Kate went in the front door, shutting it behind her.

Rain from the brief shower moments before scented the humid air and wind brought the call of birds while he stared at his feet.

Confused, Peyton pointed to where her friend had disappeared. "She's not just dropping me off?"

He walked down the steps, meeting her at the bottom, leaving a decent berth between them. "I asked her to stay." His gaze swept over her, taking in her skinny jeans and t-shirt with an Eiffel Tower that said *Ooh, la la*. "Is that where you went? Paris?"

His low, hoarse tone was like a beacon, familiar and reassuring. But it held an edge she wasn't used to. Not quite irritation, but darn near close. Tension radiated off him like he was restraining himself from acting on impulse. She worried what that impulse might be at the moment.

"Yes." She wanted to say more, but kept her mouth shut, not knowing what to expect. The man before her was reminiscent of the person he used to be until he'd learned to let go of his insecurity. Like he didn't know how to behave in front of her.

A slow nod, and he glanced away. "Was it everything you expected? Hoped it would be?"

"Yes. And no." His gaze met hers, and longing hit her so hard, tears burned her eyes. A week away from him had seemed like an eternity. She missed him so much, her insides were hollow. "It was beautiful, of course. I hit all the tourist spots, sampled the cuisine. I needed to go, to prove to myself I could." Her voice cracked. "But all I could think was how I wished I was there with you."

The rigidity left his frame and his nostrils flared. Brows pinched, he looked back at her with relief, doubt, and hope. "Did..." He closed his eyes and rubbed his chest. He cleared his throat twice before looking at her again. "Did you find what you were looking for?"

"No." At the growing fear in his eyes, she hastily continued. "What I was looking for was right here. I had to go across an ocean to be sure, but I am. I know you're mad at me, but hear me out."

She pressed a hand to her forehead and tried to explain as best she could without sounding like an idiot. It was hard to put to words what had been going through her head, and she hadn't done a very good job phrasing it for him before.

"Loving you scares me, X. What we have is so much stronger than anything I've ever known. I started to doubt myself, doubt you, because I wasn't sure if what we feel is a result of circumstance or if it's real. The problem is, love for me is an abstract term. It's taken away everything, and with us, it only gave back. Does that make sense?"

"Yes." Yet he didn't close the few feet of distance between them or hold her like he always would have before. He remained where he was, stance wide and arms crossed like he needed to shield himself from her. "And what conclusion did you draw?"

"I love you. That's it. I love you." She wiped the tears from her cheeks. "I know because when Mark was away on deployment, I rarely missed him. Not like I do with you. When he kissed me, I didn't get lost. When he held me, I wasn't found." She pressed her hand to her heart. "I can't breathe unless you're around. I can't eat or think or sleep."

"You're done protecting me, then?" He stepped right up in front of her and looked in her eyes. "That's what all this has been about, honey. You think being with you, loving you, is a death sentence.

Life hasn't taught you otherwise. So, you instilled safety measures until faced with the real thing and then all your focus shifted to shielding me from making the mistake of loving you back." He sighed. "Epic fail, by the way. I'll breach any security firewall you put in place."

Choking on a sob, she pressed her lips tightly together. Always, always, he understood her better than anyone. He'd just pinpointed the kaleidoscope of insanity she'd been dealing with for months in a few brief sentences. "I'm sorry I hurt you."

"Peyton..."

Finally, he hauled her against him and shoved a hand in her hair to hold her there. His other arm wrapped around her back, squeezing her closer and dragging her to her tiptoes. And, just like that, the past seven days of torment were erased. She breathed in his light cologne, drew from his warmth, and burrowed in the safety of his embrace.

"You didn't hurt me, honey. You're genetically incapable of doing such a thing. Not on purpose, anyway. Once I calmed down, I understood your actions. You did scare me to death, though." He rested his chin on the top of her head. "I missed you."

"I missed you, too."

He pulled away and swiped the wetness from under her eyes with his thumbs. "I find it incredibly annoying that you're always right. It wasn't a bad idea to give us a little breathing room." He studied her, contemplation twisting his mouth. "Come inside. I want to show you the conclusion I drew in your absence."

Taking her hand, he led her up the stairs and opened the door for her, then gestured for her to go first. She stepped through the foyer into the living room and stopped short.

The entire room was empty. Everything was gone. Furniture, lamps, rugs, paintings. Gone. The only things present were Kate, Joseph, and Xavier's parents standing by the fireplace. Kate leaned her back against Joseph's chest, his arms loosely around her waist, and Edward had Elaine tucked to his side.

In shock, Peyton glanced around the massive room, wondering what the heck was going on. Then, her gaze landed on the fireplace and her heart pounded. Above the mantle was a blown up picture of her, Xavier, and his parents, taken outside their Napa Valley home last year.

Xavier stepped beside her. "Family portrait."

The breath whooshed from her lungs. Trembling, she looked at him.

He smiled. "You wanted me to think about some things, and I have."

"X, you don't—"

"Yes, I do. If only to assuage any doubts you have left." He pulled a deep breath and faced her. "Standing right over there is your family. Blood doesn't always play a part. They love you as much as you love them, and not out of obligation. You have never been an obligation to me, either."

His throat worked a swallow. "I want to extend our family someday with our own kids. Yes, part of that is to give back what was taken from you, but the majority of the reason is because you deserve to get everything you want and someone like you, who has so much to offer, should be surrounded by as much family as possible. There is no better way for me to show you how much I love you than to have children."

Oh God, this man. More tears pooled in her eyes, and she was going to dehydrate if he continued at this rate. Shaking, all she could do was stare at him and hope he understood her lack of response was due to the hot ball of emotion in her throat.

"I love you." Gaze tender, he brushed a knuckle over her damp cheek. "For a multitude of reasons, I love you. You challenge me, never let me get away with anything, take my crap, smile at my dry jokes, and tease me when most would be scared shitless to do so." His endearing grin stole her breath. "You not only hear me, you listen. Your clever intuition saw through me and all my insecurities, and instead of running away, you planted your feet."

Determination in his eyes, in the set of his jaw, he cupped her cheeks. "You make me laugh and burn and think outside the box. You, Peyton, are my best friend, and that's why I love you."

She opened her mouth, but all that escaped was a whimper. Chest full to capacity, she thought she might die from the outpouring of all this man gave her. And the fact he'd done this in front of his parents and their friends only proved how far he'd come, how much he loved her. No matter who was in his comfort zone, declarations like the one he'd just given left a person vulnerable. Yet, here he was, slicing a vein on her behalf.

He rested his forehead against hers. "This is our blank slate. An empty room. Move in with me. Fill it with furniture and memories. Please?"

"Yes." Jeez, yes. Letting out a ragged breath, she pressed her lips to his. "Yes."

On a sigh, he closed his eyes. "I'm really glad you said that because," he dropped to his knees, "there's one more thing."

"Oh my God," she breathed, staring at his outstretched hand. In a little blue box was a…

Ring.

A square-shaped diamond in a princess-cut gold setting. The thing was the size of Mount Rushmore and the center stone was complemented by a smaller sapphire on one side and topaz on the other. Their birthstones. Tiny diamonds inlaid the band and caught the sunlight streaming through the window.

Air backed up in her lungs and dizzy happiness made the room spin. She glanced from the ring, to him, and back again.

"Marry me, Peyton."

Her gaze jerked to his and held. Forget the perfect ring—which he had to have specially designed—because the perfect man was right here before her. Soul in his golden eyes, he looked at her like she was his everything. On his knees, his chest barely moving oxygen, he was hers.

"Marry me, have my kids, and start a family with—"

"Yes." She slapped a hand over her pounding heart. "Yes."

He let out a gale force wind and dropped his head. "Thank Christ."

Launching to his feet, he wrapped his arms around her waist, lifted her clean off the floor, and kissed her so hard, he stumbled forward two steps. Mouths still fused, he offered a slight shake of his head as if in disbelief. "I love you."

His whispered plea against her lips was her undoing. The sheen of tears in his eyes created more of her own.

She held his face and smiled. "I love you, too."

Cheers from the direction of the fireplace echoed through the room and he grinned. "I almost forgot they were there." He gave her another quick kiss. "I'm really, really glad I didn't have to fire you."

She reared. "What?"

"If you hadn't believed me when I said why I loved you, I was going to fire you to prove it wasn't gratitude."

Throwing her head back, she laughed.

Kate snorted. "Go ahead and try. I would've had unlawful termination papers drawn up before—"

"Damn, Kate." Xavier growled in warning and looked from her to Peyton. "She and I are still a work in progress. Joseph? A little help, please."

"Sure thing, man." Joseph swung Kate around and planted a kiss on her in an obvious attempt to shut up anything she might've said to counter.

But then she grabbed the back of his bald head and he wrapped a fistful of her red curls around his hand, and Peyton didn't know which one was being played as the kiss deepened.

Xavier rolled his eyes. "Our wedding party right there. Should make things entertaining." He smiled at her. "Now that I know how to keep her quiet, I insist we have Joseph nearby at all times."

Joseph gave a thumb's up, mouth still busy with Kate's.

"I don't think that'll be a problem." Elaine stepped closer. "Put your girl down so I can hug my daughter-in-law."

The second Xavier complied, he grunted as he got swallowed in fierce embrace with his father.

"Grats, son."

Elaine grinned at Peyton and reached a hand up to smooth her hair. The gesture was so maternal, Peyton's throat grew tight. "Welcome officially to the family."

"Thank you." Peyton accepted a hug. "That means a lot to me."

"Well, you mean a lot to us." Elaine pulled away. "Now, let's talk weddings."

Edward chuckled and hugged the breath from Peyton's lungs. "He just proposed. Give them a few seconds before interrogating them, my love."

With a wave of her hand, Elaine brushed him off. "I have summer in mind. Knowing my son, he'll want a private venue. How about here?"

Xavier coughed and glared at Peyton. Wide-eyed, he shook his head in a clear don't-you-dare behind his mother's back.

Peyton rolled her lips over her teeth to avoid grinning. Distraction, her middle name. "I thought you had the whole thing planned already."

"Well, not the whole thing." Elaine pursed her lips. Blinked in an attempt at innocence. "Okay, I'm excited. So what?"

"Aw." Peyton grinned. "You go right ahead and work your magic. My only request is that we do it in Napa. Perhaps outside by the lavender field?"

Xavier mouthed, *Thank you*, and she winked at him.

"I love that idea." His mother nodded slowly, eyes narrowed. "We could use the barn for a backdrop and—"

"And go home now." Edward wrapped his arm around her shoulders and steered her to the door. "Let's give them some privacy. You can call her tomorrow."

"Love you both," Elaine called on their way out.

"I'm going to rock this maid of honor thing." Kate kissed both Peyton's cheeks. "I will not wear pink, though."

After hugs and back slaps from Joseph, he and Kate left, too.

The door had no sooner closed behind them, and Xavier pinned Peyton to it, hands planted by either side of her head. "I thought they'd never go away." He brushed his nose with hers. "You didn't put the ring on. Can I?"

Smiling, she held up her hand.

He dug in his pocket, removed the ring from the box, and tossed it aside. Gaze focused on the task, he slipped the ring on her finger and rubbed his thumb across her knuckles. "It fits." Peeking at her, he kissed her hand. "You're beautiful. It looks good on you. Do you like it?"

"I love it." She grazed her fingertips across the rough growth on his jaw. "I love you more." As he leaned in to kiss her, she asked, "Would you really have fired me?"

Affection in his eyes, he smiled. "Yes. For a day maybe, to prove a point." He sucked in a rapid breath, a wrinkle between his brows. "I missed you so damn much, honey."

"I missed you, too."

He skimmed his lips down her throat. "It was agony, you know." He licked his way to her ear, earning a sharp tremble from deep inside her. He pressed against her, every hard, yummy inch, and kissed her until her eyeballs thunked the back of her skull. "I'm going to make up for this past week by taking you to bed, and I'm not stopping until the neighbors know my name."

Gah. Yes, please. "You say the sweetest things," she breathed, panting.

"Get used to it." His hands drifted from her hips to her thighs. He lifted her, and she wrapped her legs around his waist. He paused with her pinned to the door as they shared air. "I love you, Peyton."

"I love you, too."

He nipped her lower lip, hot bourbon gaze on hers. "Good. Now, hold onto me." He shoved off the door and spun, heading for the stairs. "Forever."

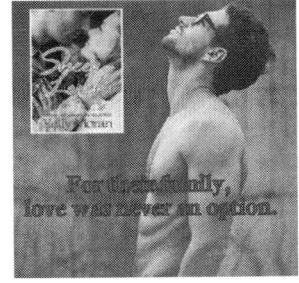

ABOUT THE AUTHOR:

Kelly Moran is a best-selling & award-winning romance author of enchanting ever-afters. She is a Catherine Award-Winner, Readers' Choice Finalist, Holt Medallion Finalist, and a 2014 Award of Excellence Finalist through RWA. She's also landed on the 10 Best Reads and Must Read lists from USA TODAY's HEA. Kelly's been known to say she gets her ideas from everyone and everything around her and there's always a book playing out in her head. No one who knows her bats an eyelash when she talks to herself. Her interests include: sappy movies, MLB, NFL, driving others insane, and sleeping when she can. She is a closet caffeine junkie and chocoholic, but don't tell anyone. She resides in Wisconsin with her husband, three sons, and her two dogs. Most of her family lives in the Carolinas, so she spends a lot of time there as well. She loves connecting with her readers.

www.AuthorKellyMoran.com

Made in the USA
Columbia, SC
15 May 2017